Jessica Greyson has cr[...] living in a place so deftly de[...] have its own personality. Ale[...] [...] understand the truth behind the web of lies that surrounds her will catch both your imagination and your heart, and hold them long after you finish reading.

Torture and true love, laughter and tears, sword fights and sacrifice: all are woven beautifully together into the unforgettable story of *The Captive of Raven Castle*.

-Elizabeth Ender, author of *Ransomed*

Jessica Greyson's work is gripping and satisfying to read both as a reader and a writer. *Captive of Raven Castle* is one of those books that immerses you in another world without beating you about the head with description. A very satisfying read.

-Anneliese Blakeney, author of *Princess and the Sage*

A wonderful story that transports you to the days of medieval castles and kings. *Captive of Raven Castle* is full of delightful twists and turns and kept me guessing as I turned each page. You will want to read it over and over!

-Melody M. writer

Captive of Raven Castle is a thrilling adventure with plenty of exciting and unexpected twists. The characters are amazing— perfectly developed, it is impossible not to fall in love with them. *Captive of Raven Castle* is yet another superb story by Jessica Greyson. Definitely five out of five stars for this book!

-Kayla, writer

Loyalty, bravery, and self-sacrifice are strong themes in *Captive of Raven Castle*. Personable characters, growth and change, gripping danger, heart-stopping plot twists, a conflict of kingdoms, and deep relationships of trust pervade its pages. Adults and young people who enjoy a thrilling, involved tale will love this page-turner. Above all, the strong faith that the characters exemplify will challenge and inspire the reader. *Captive of Raven Castle* is indeed a keepsake to be read, reread, and long treasured.

-Erika W.

Captive OF RAVEN CASTLE

By
JESSICA GREYSON

Captive of Raven Castle
First Edition
Copyright © 2013 by Jessica Greyson

Published by: Ready Writer Press

Cover Design by Louie Roybal III
www.louieroybal.com

Map of Chambria by Pepper Darcy
www.pepperjdarcy.deviantart.com

ISBN-10: 0988461420
ISBN-13: 978-0-9884614-2-0

DEDICATION

This book is lovingly dedicated to the One who took my place and set me free.

My loving family, who makes my writing possible.

Lily, my heart twin, who always gives me courage.

SPECIAL THANKS TO

Davin K. for being such an inspiration.

Mama, for all that you have done to help make this dream come true.

Auntie L. for all of your love and support.

Aunt C. for sharing your time and skills.

Louie Roybal, for sharing your incredible talent with the world through book covers.

My beta reading and blog friends. You are such encouragements! Thanks for being so wonderful

Erika W. For reading it so much.

CHAPTER INDEX

Captive of Raven Castle

Pronunciation Guide

Chambria	Cham-brēē-ă
Cassandra	Cu-sănd-ra
Taleon	Tālĭan or Tāl-yĭn
Aric	Āre-ĭc

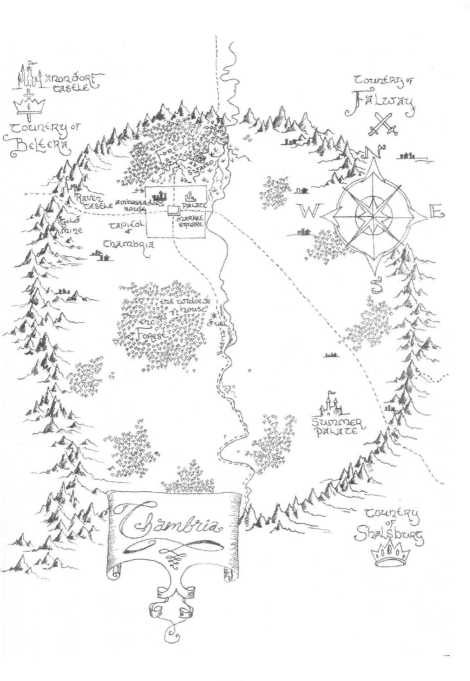

Chapter 1

"Alexandra! Alexandra, are you ready yet?" echoed a thundering voice from below.

The dark-haired girl looked self-consciously into the mirror. A worried expression crossed her face and shone in her blue eyes. "Judith, are you sure I will be all right?"

The middle-aged nurse laid her hands gently on her charge's rich black wavy hair, smoothing it as she placed a delicate crown on Alexandra's head. "You will be fine. Your father just wants to show you off to the people and the ambassador. See how pretty you are, my darling?" she said, bestowing a kiss on the pale wan cheek. "They need hope. The drought has been too long, and the people need something to forget their sorrows. Besides the ambassador has a gift from the prince to present to you, and he wants to ensure that you and the prince will be happy together. Seeing you will be the perfect cure for all of them. You will give them hope. They will adore you. I promise."

"But Judith, I…."

"Your father wants you. You know how he gets when you make him wait."

Alexandra looked once more in the mirror at her purple dress, white pearl necklace with an amethyst pendent, and pearls in her dark locks.

"I am just scared to go, Judith…the ambassador is so strange and the people so restless. I am afraid of what might happen; we are so near Raven Castle. What if they should storm the city?"

"Your father has too strong a force with him to be in danger of those men coming."

The voice hollered again, louder this time.

"Oh, wish me luck." And Alexandra hurried away as fast as she dared, stopping at the head of the stair to look at her father waiting impatiently below.

He was standing in a richly decorated hallway of the castle, waiting for her—tapping his foot, always a bad sign. A man of noble stature, his silver chainmail glistened with readiness beneath his short-sleeved tunic with the royal coat of arms boldly woven thereon. A jewel encrusted crown sat on his head, his black hair was already graying at the temples.

Alexandra took a deep breath and began her lady-like descent down the staircase.

He turned to bellow once more, then caught sight of his daughter. A smile burst out on his countenance upon catching sight of her.

Alexandra wondered how, even when he smiled, he didn't seem handsome. His features were so stern and the set jaw showed even behind his well-trimmed beard.

"Hello, Father," she said, stepping down beside him and glancing timidly upward.

"Turn around for me, won't you?"

She turned slowly.

"You look quite lovely, my dear; however, do you think you will be warm enough? We can't be too careful of your delicate health."

"I am quite warm as it is right now. Are you sure it won't rain?"

"We will have a servant carry your furs just in case there is a cold breeze, we can't have you catching ill."

"Do we have to go to see the ambassador? Why can't he come here like he usually does?"

"The full-length likeness of your future husband has just arrived at the Shalsburg Embassy, and there is to be a tournament this afternoon. We shall kill two birds with one stone. We will see the ambassador, decide if we like the portrait enough to show it to the people. If so, it will be brought to the tournament to show the people their future king, your noble husband-to-be who will take all the cares of this country off your slight shoulders that are barely able to carry a crown."

"Yes, Father," she murmured submissively, with a hidden shiver. There was not much for her future. She wondered if she would ever live past bearing her first child. Hopefully, it would be a male heir to inherit the throne that she as the queen would leave him.

Alexandra looked down at her reflection in the white marble polished to a perfect shine.

She had always been a weak thing. Her father had been extremely careful of her frail health. Alexandra was never allowed to embroider, play music, or draw more than half an hour at a time lest it weaken her. Reading was forbidden lest her eyes become damaged by strain over the mysterious black and white pages. She was read to often by her ladies-in-waiting and her affectionate nursemaid Judith, who had been dedicated to her since she was five years of age.

In a minute King Archibald had helped Alexandra into the carriage, after she glanced fearfully at the spirited horses that pawed readily at the ground. The king sat beside her. Guards on horses surrounded them as they rode out of the castle gates and through the streets.

Alexandra peeped timidly at the people who stopped to gawk at them.

"Smile, Alexandra," whispered her father through clenched teeth that were bearing a grin.

"They don't look happy," she said, turning to her father and king.

"I know. If we smile it will bring them hope of a better future."

Alexandra tried to smile as she looked at the people, but they only stared at her blankly.

"I wish I hadn't come," she said, nearing tears.

"Nonsense, Alexandra," he murmured, his voice bordering on stern.

There was a resounding thump as something landed against the carriage. Alexandra jumped.

A second thump made her scream involuntarily.

"Pick up the pace!" her father shouted, and the horses burst into a gallop.

Alexandra clung to her father as the carriage jostled and jolted and tossed her about—too afraid to cry. Objects were hurled at the carriage, making loud frightening noises. Some splattered, some thudded, a few bounced boldly in the window, and one barely missed hitting her in the head.

Soon they were in the safety of the Embassy's closed courtyard. She was scooped up in her father's arms and carried safely indoors.

Pale and shivering but tearless, he laid Alexandra down on a lounge. In a few moments the ambassador appeared.

"I am so glad you are here safely," said the ambassador in his funny accent.

"As am I," replied her father.

Unexpectedly the ambassador came over and kissed Alexandra's hand. "It is an especial pleasure to see you, my dear. You are looking quite lovely despite that dreadful scene. How does one managed to look so beautiful while being frightened. I must say you have handled it rather well. But come; I have something most delightful to show you. You have been waiting for it for such a long time," he said, pulling her unwillingly to her feet.

She shuffled beside him as he took her arm under his own.

In a few minutes she stood before a veiled frame taller than herself.

"Please take a seat, your highness," he said, offering her a chair.

"I have for you a masterpiece of fine artwork. Prepare to be most pleasantly surprised with the most handsome Prince of Shalsburg." He motioned two attendants to reveal the image. The silk fabric fluttered and shimmered to the ground, revealing a young man with dark hair and eyes, most royally dressed in red. Holding a dead bird by its feet, blood streaming off its body, a large hawk resting on his other arm.

Alexandra's jaw dropped unexpectedly from sheer horror of the man who stood in front of her.

"Ah, I knew her highness would be most pleased."

"Is he fond of dead birds?" she managed to utter at last.

"He is a most avid sportsman in any sport that you can name. An excellent hunter, he can bring down anything, from birds to wild boar and wolves. That hawk there is his favorite. Its name is Kashir; lovely bird it is. You should see it fly through the air. Ah, yes—his highness is most well suited for a beautiful princess such as yourself."

Alexandra looked up at her father, seeking his thoughts on the matter. He was smiling. There was no hope. Her destiny was sealed: she would wed the second prince of Shalsburg.

"Ah, but I have forgotten his gift to you." The ambassador pulled out a box inlaid with mother-of-pearl and placed it before her.

Alexandra's hands were still trembling from the carriage ride, and the portrait was just too much. What new horror lay in wait for her here? Had he sent her a necklace made of bear teeth?

With a trembling hand she pushed back the lid of the box. A shimmering necklace lay before her. A solid mass of diamonds dazzled her eyes.

There was the sound of shattering glass. Her father ran to the window, hand on his sword. The dull roar that had gathered had become nigh deafening.

"We need to get out of here now. The people don't understand I am doing what is good for them."

"What shall we do?" asked the ambassador, dumbfounded.

"They aren't after you. They are after us. I need you to conduct my daughter safely into the countryside while I take care of this mob. Take your carriage out the back entrance and I shall distract them with mine. Once she is married, there won't be any more difficulties like this. I promise. Now, go."

"Father! What is going on?"

"I said go!"

The ambassador slammed the inlayed box into her hands. Before she knew exactly what was going on, she was being pushed into a carriage with the shades drawn, the horses hitched, and they were riding out of the back gates.

Alexandra shivered as she sat next to the ambassador. The carriage tossed them about at a dreadful rate. Suddenly, Alexandra wanted to laugh as she wondered whether her future husband would have the same funny accent as the ambassador. She glanced at the man, a slight smile on her lips.

"I hope you do not find this amusing, my dear?"

"I do not, sir. I was just wondering…" She never had a chance to finish that sentence as the carriage came to a sudden halt, flinging them forward into the opposite seat.

There was the sound of a struggle going on without.

"I am going to see what this is all about," he said, pulling back the curtain.

Instinctively Alexandra ducked below the curtain's view.

"This is ridiculous; they are your father's guards. I am going to clear this all up," he fumed as he stepped out of the carriage.

She heard voices rise in anger as they talked. A wild cry was raised and the carriage bolted into a full gallop, tossing Alexandra back into her seat. Hesitantly she peeked out between the curtain. There was a lone rider urging the horses on.

A rider in plain clothes.

Not one of her father's men.

Nor one of the ambassador's men.

Alexandra's heart pounded like a drum in her ears, throbbing in her dry throat. Voices cried very faintly behind her. Glancing back, she could not see her father's men pursuing her. Quietly she began to pray out of pure fear.

"God help me. God help me. Oh, God help me."

As the carriage entered the forest, the ride became more bumpy and furious than ever before. It came to a slow stop. Alexandra held her breath listening, wondering what would come next. There was the sound of him dismounting and coming towards the carriage.

I have to do something. Where are my father's men? Somebody help me!

A voice spoke. "Your highness? Cassandra!"

Cassandra? Who does he think I am?

The boots were coming closer and rapidly. Alexandra surprised herself by bursting out of the opposite door and running through the woods, making loud noises as she went. There was a loud slap and she glanced behind her. The carriage had resumed its breakneck run along the road. A man was chasing after her, close in her wake.

Alexandra had run very little in her short life but, began to do so now. In a few short strides, she was panting for breath but strove forward. A force from behind pulled her to the ground and they went tumbling through the underbrush.

"Stay down; they'll see us," whispered the man who had been chasing her, pinning her shoulders to the forest floor.

Alexandra listened. Horses went thundering by. Her father's guards! She tried to cry out, but his hand nearly suffocated her and she hadn't any breath left to fight him.

When they had thundered past, he stood up and whistled. A black horse came charging from the woods nearby. Before she could think of how to get away. He swung her up and pulling her in front of him. He kicked the horse into a gallop.

Alexandra clung to him for dear life. She had never ridden a horse and now to be taken in such a manner—to be flying at such a frantic rate over the ground through forest—took her breath away. Fear clutched in her chest so hard she thought she might faint.

When they at last came into a clearing, Alexandra glanced behind them, searching for help—for hope—for a rescue. This man who carried her away was not one of her people.

He was from Raven Castle.

Chapter 2

At last they appeared on the horizon—a torrent of men wearing black and silver and racing towards her. So far away, she wondered how they could rescue her. Still they steadily approached and her heart beat with hope.

They grew closer as the black steed fought its way up a steep hill. Her father's men disappeared as the steed charged over the crest and down the steep embankment head on. Her captor leaned backwards, his arm wrapping around her waist.

She wanted to scream, but sound wouldn't come as he charged them headlong into what she felt was certain death. The horse splashed into the river without injury, to her great shock, starting up the steep mountainside that would lead to Raven Castle; weaving in and out of boulders and trees as they made their ascent.

Alexandra watched as her father's men came up to the crest of the hill and stopped.

"I am over here!" she cried out desperately.

His hand sealed her mouth firmly.

The men stood there. Not one dared to attempt the steep incline. They watched for several minutes as she was being stolen away, slowly climbing further and further out of their sight.

An arrow was drawn and sent flying after them, but it didn't even make it halfway up the hill.

The commander gave a signal with a wave of his hand and they turned, disappearing as they descended the hill.

Alexandra could not believe her eyes. Her father's men *left* her.

She, the princess of Chambria, was left alone with a rebel who was no doubt, bound and determined to destroy her and her kingdom. The rebels were constantly tearing it apart into little pieces, causing uprisings and discontent with the people and wrongly creating reasons for them to rebel against their rightful king.

Yes, times were hard. They are hard for all of us. Last month we had nearly run out of mead at the castle. If they would only work harder, we could all live better, the lazy people.

But to be abandoned like this! To be left with the people who killed my mother, who shielded me with her own body! They didn't even look back! What kind of betrayal is this?

Alexandra burst into tears.

For a long time the man didn't speak, but as her crying continued, he spoke.

"It's all right, your highness; you are safe now."

"Safe with you?" she challenged him.

"Of course; you are going home, Cassandra."

"I am not Cassandra. I am Alexandra Elizabeth Serena Dauphine Rembolt of Chambria."

He pulled his horse to a stop and looked into her tearful blue eyes, his own puzzled. He frowned and shook his head. "You have no idea, do you? Well, they'll soon set you straight." He urged his horse back into a trot and they climbed up the slope.

Reaching a small mountain stream, he stopped and dismounted. Dropping the reins around the horse's neck, he let the creature drink.

"Care for some water, your highness?" he asked, nodding towards the stream.

"Yes please," she answered hesitantly.

He helped her down. She wobbled a little, trying to get feeling back into her legs. He knelt down and buried his face in the stream. It came up dripping wet and he smiled at her.

"No better way to take a drink."

"You don't use a cup?" she asked, disgust lining her voice.

"Nothing like that out here."

She looked at him, shocked.

He bent down for another drink. An idea struck her: to push him headlong into the stream just as he came up for a breath.

Alexandra revolted; it was such an unladylike idea…but maybe it would give her a chance to escape. She glanced at the horse. He was too big to ride but maybe…

Before she had really thought anything through, Alexandra shoved the man with her foot headlong into the stream and slapped the horse, sending it on an unexpected crossing that nearly trampled the man. With a quick spin, she fled into the forest.

There was a roar of sputtering anger coming up behind her and she sped faster into the forest, trying to find a hiding place.

In too short a time he had her again, grabbing her from behind. He ran his arm through the crook of her elbows and held them tight against himself. Alexandra kicked furiously, but he spread apart his feet, so her kicks found nothing but air to abuse.

He whistled, and the black steed came prancing into view, rather damp from his river crossing.

With a wrench, he held only one of her wrists in a painful position. She cried out at his brute force.

"Ow…let me go."

He did not relent, but dug into his saddle bag, pulling out a thin leather cord.

"I didn't think I would need this, but I guess I do—if the princess of Chambria doesn't even know who she really is."

He tied the wrist in his grasp first, it cut off her circulation. She whimpered, and he took her second wrist and began to pull the leather cord tightly.

She gasped as it burned across her wrist. He paused and tied it more gently on her second wrist, then loosened the first, but not so much that she could slip her hands through the bonds.

Biting her lower lip, she looked up at him. His dark hair hung in front of his eyes dripping with water. His brown-green eyes snapped with frustration. He was soaked from head to toe. Alexandra had no doubt that there was water in his boots. His drenched clothes had transferred dampness onto her. This was going to be a long uncomfortable ride.

"There. That's better. Now don't try anything else."

Submissively she nodded her head. In a moment, he had mounted and pulled her up once again in front of him.

"I would let you ride behind, but I have a feeling I have to keep my eye on you, and I don't want you falling off for no reason. Hya!"

In a moment they had burst into a gallop and were pressing up the steep mountain, seeming to follow no particular path but her captor's sweet will.

The trees slowly thinned until they were riding in almost all open space. Here he found a trail and began to weave his way up, as stars climbed into the sky from the east. Mist rose from the valley towards the summit of Raven Castle, perched on a perilous cliff with a commanding view of the valley and surrounding mountains.

Alexandra struggled against her bonds—she must escape. Her resentment grew against her father's men. *How dare they leave me?* Raven Castle was a place haunted by ghosts, legends, and something much worse: the rebel army. It was only a daring man or a resolved rebel who would dare set his foot on this mountain. At this moment, her captor was speeding the way towards the summit and an unknown fate.

Every step placed her in more danger. With a cry of fear and rage, Alexandra turned and pummeled her captor with her bound hands.

"I say stop that!"

"Let me go!"

He only shook his head. Threading his arm between her bound hands, he cinched his arm tight to her waist, preventing another attack.

"Only a little further," he murmured to himself.

The path was now windy and steep. He slowed the horse to a walk. Its black coat was white with foam. Alexandra felt sorry for the beast, yet held a little resentment for him. He had been driven hard. However, his mountain spirit had outwitted and outrun all of her father's grain-fed purebred steeds that were supposed to help keep her safe.

Her fearful eyes looked up and beheld Raven Castle in its twilight glory. The dark stone was barely etched against the ever-deepening sky. The stars, unafraid to witness such a monstrosity of turrets and spires, shone their pure light upon it. With a shudder, Alexandra looked away.

"Don't worry; you will be home soon, your highness, and they will have a fire ready to warm you."

A fire to roast me over more likely, she muttered in her heart. Could she withstand the flame without screams? Alexandra had never been one for pain. Her mother had died defending her from the rebels.

What will they do to me? How soon will Father be able to ransom me? What will happen if he can't?

The last thought made her gasp in pain as her heart twinged. They were crossing into Raven Castle. The large metal gate clanged shut behind them, and Alexandra felt her fate sealed with death written upon its closure.

Chapter 3

"Hello, Williamson!" shouted a stable boy coming towards them. "We are all glad to see you have her," he said, taking the horse's bridle.

"I hope it's worth it. Is James back?"

"Hour ago. Not much worse for the wear even though he parried with the Imposter himself." Unexpectedly the stable boy offered Alexandra a shy smile from the side of his mouth. "Hello, your highness."

Alexandra looked at him baffled. None of the stable boys would have dared to speak in her presence back at *her* castle. If they had, they might have had their tongues cut out for impertinent boldness. Why, he didn't even take off his cap.

"Doesn't talk much, does she?" he asked the man she now knew as Williamson.

"Not much," he said, dismounting. Williamson's boots made an unusual squishing noise as his feet landed on the cobblestones.

"What happened to you?"

"Ask her," he said, pulling Alexandra down from the saddle.

The boy smuggled a laugh behind his hand and Williamson pushed the lad's hat down over his eyes. "Do your job," he said, annoyed. "Come on, this way. They'll be waiting for you. Your father will be delighted to hear of your safe arrival."

"My father?" she said, halting dead in her tracks. "He had me kidnapped? Why would he do such a thing?"

"To keep you safe from the Imposter."

"But this is Raven Castle. I don't understand. You are the enemy of my father; why would he send me here?"

"Your father King Aric. He has been endeavoring to keep you safe from his brother Archibald for years."

"My father is Archibald, King of Chambria. Aric is the imposter."

"Your father and Archibald are brothers."

"My father has no brothers or sisters."

"We'll see about that. Now, come on. They are waiting for you," he said, pulling her bonds. They walked into the castle, up several flights of stairs, and into a large room with regal chairs set in a semicircle around a fire.

Men were talking in low voices. The chatter died as they came into the room. All of the men stood.

"So this is our princess," said one of the men with a smile and a bow.

Alexandra pulled back.

"Come, both of you, warm yourselves by the fire. It must have been a long ride," offered one of the men with a sweeping gesture.

Williamson stepped forward, but she dug her heels in. He pushed her from behind with an unexpected force that sent her stumbling forward. She tripped on her long damp skirt and fell to the floor, rolling onto the tiger skin rug.

Alexandra raised herself partway up, but her bound hands made it almost impossible to push herself into a seated position. Her loose hair tumbled about her face and she hid behind it as much as possible.

"Are you all right, your highness?" said a voice she hadn't heard before, drawing close. "Williamson, you have her hands bound. What a way to show her hospitality!" he scolded.

He was kneeling before her. Unsheathing a dagger, he raised her hands and slashed her bonds. Pulling ropes from around her wrists, he tossed them in the fire.

"Better?"

She nodded and glanced up into his face. It was smiling down into hers. Hesitantly she found herself liking him and his blond hair that was neither wild nor ruly but tumbled about in some well-kept fashion that suited him. His blue-green eyes were kind and friendly.

He slipped the dagger back into its sheath.

"Why did you tie up her hands?" he said, turning to her captor.

Williamson stepped forward, the squish, squish of his soggy boots making part of the reason apparent.

"She pushed me into the river."

The young man beside her let out a low chuckle, amused by the fact.

"That and the fact that she believes that we are a band of rebels and her father is Archibald."

There was a silence in the room that could be felt after that last statement, and Alexandra wanted to hide as all eyes seemed to fall on her with dismay. Turning her face to the side, her black wavy hair hid most of her face.

"Is this true, your highness?" he asked, breaking the torturous silence.

"Archibald *is* my father."

The room grew more serious and displeased.

"Cassandra must be tired," spoke up one of the men from the throne-like chairs.

"My name is Alexandra. Not Cassandra. Why do you all keep saying that?"

"Because that is your name," he said calmly.

"It is not!" she protested, tears rising into her eyes.

"My lords, may I take the princess to the room we have prepared for her? I think she needs some rest."

"Yes, please do, Taleon."

Taleon stood up and offered her his hand to assist her up. For a moment she hesitated, then placed her hands in his.

"Follow me, if you please," he said, leading the way.

Alexandra hovered as close to his shadow as she possibly could, wanting to hide from all of the men who seemed to be staring at her with such unfriendly eyes.

He seemed to lead her through a maze of hallways, rooms, and staircases, but at last they arrived at her room.

He opened the door for her to enter. She stopped on the threshold.

"It's not much of a room," she murmured.

"I am sure it is nothing like your room in the valley, but it is the best we could do under the circumstances."

"I am sure. This is the best I could expect from the people that murdered my mother."

"What did you just say?"

Alexandra stepped back and away from him into her room, trying not to be fearful. The words had come out before she had really thought.

"Nothing," she said shyly, glancing at the ground for a moment.

"You blame us for the death of your mother?"

"Yes. I do."

"The person who killed your mother was Archibald. The reason the people are so unhappy is they are barely able so scrape together a living and your uncle is forcing them into slavery. If they cannot pay their taxes, they are forced to work with no wage, save what they eat until their debt is paid. Do you know how long that usually takes?"

"A few months?" Alexandra risked hesitantly.

"A few years."

"That's not true. The people are lazy; they do not work like they should. With the drought, everyone must work harder and they have done nothing to help. Why, last month we nearly ran out of mead at the castle because they were not doing their work."

"Was it that or the fact that your father threw a two-week celebration for his birthday?"

Alexandra stepped back baffled. "We had enough mead for that."

"Of course you did. It took him almost two weeks to run the cellar dry. He wants to destroy this country because he wants to destroy your father. Don't blame us for your mother's death. Archibald was the one who killed her. It's amazing he hasn't killed you. The Imposter is a beast out to destroy anything that has hope. Your kingdom he will leave in tatters."

Alexandra's jaw dropped, and she stepped back in horror. "You have to understand that my father would never do such a thing. The king loves the people; they just don't understand him. He isn't that kind of man. My father loves me and the people and my mother. He would never have murdered her or anyone else without due cause."

"We didn't kill your mother."

"You and your wretched army of rebels killed my mother. She was protecting me from all of you and someone thrust her through with a sword. My father was barely able to rescue me from certain death."

"So that is the story he has been telling you for the last thirteen years?"

"It isn't a story. It is the truth and to hear it talked about distresses me, so I would appreciate it if you would stop."

"It distresses you?"

"Yes," she said calmly. "It does."

"You don't look distressed to me."

"I am violently distressed about it. No one is allowed to speak of my mother's death on the penalty of..."

"Death. Doesn't that give you a clue how desperately he is trying to hide the truth from you?"

"No, it tells me that he is kind and considerate and thoughtful. He loves me. Now stop speaking this nonsense."

"And to the subjects who suffer death because they speak of the rebel king as a good man?"

"He isn't. Your king oppresses the people. That is why you, a rebel army are up here shouting justice for all—when you really mean oppression for all. Now go away."

"You aren't distressed. Just confused."

"Go away!"

"Very well, your highness," he said with a cold bow. As he reached the door he turned to face her once again. "We aren't your father's enemies. We fight for his cause. It is your uncle that we oppose."

The door closed firmly behind him. There was no anger in it. Just a tiny click.

Alexandra rushed to the door and tried to make it open. He had locked it. She rattled the door, pushing and pulling.

"It is no use, your highness. It is locked."

Alexandra kicked the door and immediately regretted it as her foot throbbed. She retreated, hopped across the room, buried her head under the pillows, and burst into tears.

Raven Castle was filled with liars and thieves. How would she survive?

Chapter 4

Alexandra lay in bed long after her tears stopped. She stared blankly at the ceiling, sorting through her tumbled mixed-up feelings. Just this morning the worst thing that seemed possible was being betrothed to the second prince of Shalsburg. Now her fate was so much worse.

Her whole body ached from her carriage and horse rides, her breathless running; and her wrist still burned from the leather cord he had pulled so tightly across it. Alexandra tried to sleep, but her eyes refused to close. Her stomach rumbled. She hadn't eaten since just before she had dressed to meet the ambassador, and her stomach had been in such butterflies that she hadn't eaten much then.

Alexandra decided to explore her room in the light of the enchanting moon. A small dressing table was arranged with pretty things, not as fine as hers' in the valley, but there was something about them that exuded charm instead of lavish wealth. Taking up the brush, she ran it through her tangled hair, pulling out the few interwoven pearls that had survived her raucous adventure.

Still brushing her hair, Alexandra crossed the room to the window. The air that came through the arched window hole was cool and refreshing to her troubled mind. Resting one shoulder against the window, she gazed out on the valley covered in mist below her.

The mist looked friendly in the moonlight, shining and soft as freshly washed lamb's wool. Alexandra ran her fingers through her combed hair and smiled at the feeling of silk.

Twisting a lock around one finger, the smile disappeared. Her father had always said she got her hair from her mother—black and shining as a raven's wing.

Raven.

She shivered and turned away from the window. She walked the floor and opened the large pine chest for clothing. It was hard to heave up the heavy lid and more discouraging to find nothing in there for her to wear. Alexandra pulled back her hair, wishing she knew how to braid, and slipped into bed, forcing her eyes shut.

Alexandra woke with a start. The dream had been so real. It was the one she always had when her mother was talked about. She had told the whole dream to Judith when she was nearly ten and had been told it was a foolish dream.

But was it?

Alexandra walked to the window and gazed down. It was a sheer cliff that dropped down to a glistening thread of a river that wove its way through the base of the mountains around them: tall, majestic, rocky, and green. She stared at them hard, trying to forget the dream and the queer feeling it always left with her.

She was little, maybe three years of age—riding on a man's shoulders, laughing. Her childish hands gripped in his brown curly hair. He was galloping around the garden. The woman that she knew was her mother by the portrait that hung in the gallery was laughing too. They came to a halt when a messenger came running through the door in a strange coat of arms.

The man with brown curly hair pulled her feet closer together so he could hold them both in one big hand. She tried to wiggle her feet. Sitting still was boring. She bounced a little on his shoulders. He read the message, and, handing it back to the lad, he had gone over to her mother.

Her face was always so sad. He bent and kissed her mother. Alexandra leaned forward and kissed the man's head; she loved him. In a minute he was pulling her down from his shoulders and she let out a squeal of dismay, kicking her little feet, but when she saw his eyes, she stopped and clung to his doublet. Something was wrong.

She was caught in an embrace in which she could barely breathe between her mother and the man with the brown curly hair. He always whispered in her ear.

"Goodbye, my Cassie," he said, pressed a kiss to her cheek, and left.

What did it all mean? The words she had exchanged with the young man Taleon whirled through her mind.

"Your highness, your highness? Are you all right?" asked a female voice from behind her.

Alexandra whirled around.

"Oh, hello?"

"Are you all right? You seem far away."

"I am quite well, thank you. Just thinking."

"Here is a dress for you. The king hopes you will like it. It is nothing like what you wear at the castle, but it is the best the people have to offer."

"Thank you," she said, approaching the woman.

She laid the dress down on the bed.

It was royal blue with white trim.

"I'll be making others for you, but this should last for a few days. Do you need help?"

"I am afraid I do. I know so little about these things."

The woman's hands were quick and skillful while Alexandra stood perfectly still.

"There now, don't you look like a pretty picture. The blue matches your eyes. Your father said it would. He picked it out before he left for the valley."

"How long have you been here?" asked Alexandra, her interest alerted.

"Six months, ever since my husband died," she said, her eyes dropping sorrowfully.

"Did the rebels kill your husband?"

The woman looked at her curiously. "Rebels? If you mean King Archibald's ruthless men, yes. They are quite reckless. Their king gives them rein to do whatever they wish to the people and they delight in doing it."

"What killed your husband?"

"His tongue was loosened by strong drink. We were having a hard time. Our taxes were due the next day, we didn't have enough money, and he went to drown his sorrows with a useless cup. While he was there, he got in a fight and spoke against the Imposter. He was slain instantly by Archibald's soldiers. A neighbor was good enough to alert me as to what had happened. I escaped with my life and a few valuables before the soldiers came to burn our house and crops to the ground."

"My father would never allow such a thing."

"Yes, King Aric, if he ever graces the throne again, will set everything to rights."

"I meant King Archibald would never allow such a thing if he knew what was going on."

The woman looked at her with wrinkled brow. "Taleon said you had some queer ideas, but that is the queerest I have ever heard."

"I am not queer. If you had been able to pay your taxes and your husband had kept a civil tongue in his head, I am sure that everything would have been fine."

"We couldn't pay our taxes."

"I am sure if you hadn't been so lazy you could have."

"Lazy—you are calling my husband and I lazy?" The woman's voice grew indignant. "We worked ourselves to the bone to make ends meet. We nearly starved trying to keep our farm, and you dare to call us lazy?"

Alexandra looked at her, confused. The woman obviously expected an answer. But what was the question?

The woman shook with emotion. "You call us lazy?"

"I—I don't know."

"That is not an answer," the woman glowered.

"I am sure if King Archibald had known of your situation he would…"

She got no further as the woman attacked her with a cry of rage.

Alexandra was lying on the floor curled into a ball, protecting herself from the woman's blows.

"Enid, Enid...get a hold of yourself," said a familiar voice as Alexandra found herself free from the woman's pounding fists.

Alexandra dared to peek over her shoulder to see Taleon pulling a woman crying and spewing with rage from the room.

The door closed behind them and she listened to the cries slowly die down. In a few minutes he returned.

"It's okay to get off the floor now. She isn't coming back."

"Are you quite sure?"

"Yes."

Alexandra sat upright and found Taleon's hand offered to her. Reluctantly she took it and he pulled her to her feet.

"What made her so mad at you?"

"She told me that her husband was killed by my father, King Archibald's army. I said that she and her husband were lazy because they couldn't pay their taxes," admitted Alexandra, with slight hesitation as to his reaction.

"So you didn't learn anything from what I said last night."

"What is there to learn? It's all lies."

Taleon's eyes narrowed and Alexandra felt guilty, though for what reason she wasn't quite sure.

"The man whom you claim as your father is a robber and a thief."

"My father is nothing of the sort."

"Your father isn't, but the man whom you claim to be is."

"You are speaking in circles. Stop it. I don't want to hear any more," she said, turning away.

"You are going to hear it whether you like it or not," he said, turning her around to face him.

Their eyes met, challenging one another. Alexandra conceded by looking to the side. It wasn't ladylike to look so boldly into a fellow's eyes even if you didn't agree with him.

"Let's begin with what you know," he said, dropping his hold.

"What I know?"

"What has," Taleon cleared his throat, "King Archibald told you?" It was hard to refrain from adding "the impostor," but apparently that wouldn't break through to her.

"Everything I need to know about you."

"And that would be?"

"You are rebels that cause trouble, splitting my nation in half, causing my people to be discontent with what they have. There is a drought going on and more people are abandoning their fields to join your cause. They need to be in the fields and here you have them screaming for justice when we are doing all we can for them."

"You really think you are doing all you can for your people?

"I am willing to marry a man I don't love for them."

"And that's a sacrifice for them?"

"Yes, it is. If I don't have an heir and I die, the country will go to ruin."

"You are dying?"

"Not yet, but I will. There is no doubt about it. I have never been strong."

"Well, marrying a foreigner will do your country no good."

"Why not? It will bring a good alliance."

"The prince of Shalsburg knows nothing about you or Chambria and couldn't care less about your people. He would be nothing but a puppet in your...the...king's hands just like you are. He wouldn't care a bit but carry on the same way *he* does."

"I am not a puppet!"

"Really? Then tell me one original thought that you have had—one that hasn't been influenced by your *father's* teaching. Tell me, what have you thought about Raven Castle that hasn't been told to you by him? What observation have you made that doesn't even have a hint of his thoughts in yours?"

Alexandra's brow wrinkled. Everything she had thought had a hint of something he had said. The people were lazy because he said so.

Raven Castle was full of rebels because that was all she had ever been told; her mother had been slain by the rebels. Up here...things were so different. He was daring to challenge so many of the things she had always believed.

"You can't think of anything, can you?" said Taleon after a long silence.

"I am not a puppet," she reiterated weakly.

"Puppets only do what their masters think, say, and do. So far that is all you have done up here. What are some of your own ideas?"

Alexandra stood there puzzled, trying to think of something to say, but her thoughts only...there were no thoughts. Her mind went blank—utterly and wholly empty.

"I don't know if I have any," Alexandra said, dropping the defensive tone she had been using.

Taleon smiled. "Do you have any original thoughts?"

Alexandra smiled as a thought crossed her mind.

"What is it?"

"Yesterday, I was wondering if the second Prince of Shalsburg would have the same funny accent as the ambassador."

"You consider that an original thought?" he asked, eyebrows raised.

"Original as they come," she said with a sheepish smile.

"I see. Well, Willamsen didn't tell us you hadn't had anything to eat until after you were asleep. I am guessing you are hungry."

"Yes, I am."

"I'll be bringing up a tray of food in a few minutes."

When Taleon returned, Alexandra had combed out her hair and was attempting to style it in some fashion with no success.

"Do you know how to braid?"

"No."

"Well, if you promise to keep quiet so everyone won't hate and attack you on sight, I will have a little girl come and show you how it's done. All of the women are already working."

"You make the people work?"

"No, they choose to help. When they are able, they are assigned a specific task. Now here is your breakfast."

"That isn't fit for swine. I am a princess; I don't eat gruel!"

"You said you weren't strong, so I brought what we feed those who aren't well. It's easier on them and gives them strength."

"I am not bedridden. I refuse to eat it."

"It is sweetened with honey."

"I won't eat it! It's pauper food."

"I'll be back in a half an hour," he said, closing the door.

"You can't just walk away. Don't close that door; I am not done speaking with you yet. Come back here!"

The door shut and the lock clicked.

"No!" she cried out, but Taleon's feet were already retreating down the hallway. Alexandra tried the door. It wouldn't budge.

Reluctantly she went back to her dressing table and stared at the gruel with crossed arms. The smell was surprisingly tempting. Delicately she took the spoon and stirred the "swine food." It wasn't lumpy or thick. Her stomach growled, pleading with her to just try it.

It can't hurt me just to take a bite, I suppose.

It was surprisingly sweet and tasty. Alexandra had eaten half the bowl before she knew it, but could eat no more; it was too filling.

Raven Castle is certainly a strange place.

Chapter 5

Within a half an hour, Taleon returned with a shy little girl who, upon his opening of the door and stepping in, attached herself to his belt, burying her face in his back. He walked forward without seeming to notice.

He smiled at the nearly empty bowl but said nothing.

"I would like you to meet..." he looked on either side of himself then turned around. "Hmm...I wonder where she went. I could have sworn Amy was with me."

There was a muffled laugh from behind him and he whirled around again.

"Amy? Amy...where are you? I heard you."

She giggled again.

"You must be hiding somewhere in here already," and he walked further into the room.

As they passed Alexandra, the little girl looked at her shyly, putting a finger in front of her mouth asking her to be silent.

Alexandra giggled, and then her face became grave. *When is the last time I laughed like that?* Her mind searched for an event, a time, a place, but could think of none in her recent past.

"Have you see Amy?"

"Have I seen Amy?"

A small face peeped out behind his back, shaking her head and mouthing, "Don't tell him."

"Well, I have seen her, but I am not telling you where."

"You and Amy have a secret?" he sounded incredulously offended but, his eyes were teasing. "Now I am jealous."

There was another giggle from Amy.

"Amy, Amy, where is Amy?"

"Here I am," she said, bursting from behind his back.

"There you are," he said with a smile, then, sitting on his heels, he turned her to face Alexandra. "I would like you to meet Princess Cassandra."

A wave of shyness overcame the girl and she buried her head in his shoulder. He only smiled and put his arm around the girl, drawing her close.

"Do you like being shy?" he whispered in her ear.

Amy shook her head, then after a moment nodded it in contradiction.

The smile grew, but he didn't say anything.

Alexandra never knew what came over her, but in a moment she was kneeling on the floor across from Taleon. There was something about the girl that appealed to her heart.

"How old are you, Amy?"

"Eight," was the muffled reply from Taleon's shoulder.

"Eight. When I was eight I was dreadfully afraid of having to meet new people. My..." she halted just as she was about to say *father*. A reference to him had gotten a bad reception earlier, so she had better hold her tongue on that subject. "The king in the valley was going to hold a grand banquet and I would have to come walking in all by myself in front of all these strange people. I was so scared; I told my nursemaid that I couldn't walk in all by myself, in fact, I wouldn't. I didn't care what my...the king said; I would not. So you know what she told me?"

Amy barely peeked up from Taleon's shoulder but shook her head.

"Judith told me that she would put a special pearl in my hair that would make me unafraid of anything I ever had to face. So that night when I went down to dinner, just before the doors opened, I touched my hair and I felt several in my hair. I wondered which pearl was the special one. But the doors were opening and I had to be ready and hope it worked. And you know what?"

"What?" said the face, peeking up from the shoulder.

"That night I wasn't scared at all and I talked to all kinds of people and did everything I was supposed to. Which is a miracle because the last time I went to a party, I had forgotten everything I was supposed to know and I made a huge mess."

"But you had the pearl."

"You are right. But do you know what? That night when I told Judith what that pearl had done for me, she pulled it out of her pocket and told me she had forgotten to put it in my hair."

Amy looked at her with horror. "No."

"Yes, she had forgotten to put in the pearl and that is when I realized I didn't have to be afraid or shy as long as I thought I could."

"Are you still shy?"

Alexandra blushed. She was still shamefully shy when it came to one-on-one conversations, or small groups of people; but in front of ambassadors and important people, never.

"Not as much as I used to be, but I still like to wear pearls in my hair." She reached over onto her dressing table and picked up one of the pearls she had combed from her hair the night before.

"See? Isn't it pretty?"

Amy nodded.

"Would you like it?"

Her eyes grew large.

"Would you?"

"I might lose it."

"Well, what if we put it on a string to wear around your neck? That way you couldn't lose it too easily."

"I'd like that."

"Someone left a thread basket in my room," she said, rising and going to the small work table. "What is your favorite color?"

"Red."

"Oh, there are lots of reds. You better come show me which is your favorite."

Hesitantly Amy left Taleon's shoulder and crossed the room. Alexandra placed the basket on the ground and sat beside it. Amy knelt down a little distance away, but in a few minutes was rummaging through the basket without a care.

31

When Amy had picked out the thread, Alexandra threaded it through the pearl's small hole. Then, tying a firm knot, put it around Amy's neck.

"There."

"It's so pretty," she murmured softly.

"Amy," it was Taleon calling her attention.

She turned her head to look at him.

"I have some things I have to do. I'll be back in a half hour."

"Okay."

"Teach her how to braid, all right?"

Amy looked curiously up at Alexandra, wrinkling her little nose. "You don't know how to braid?"

"No, I don't. I can sew, draw, sing, and play the lute, but I can't braid."

"I can't do any of those—well, I can sew a little, but Mama says my stitches aren't very fine."

"You will learn eventually how to make them fine and straight."

Amy muffled a laugh behind her hands. "How do you know they aren't straight?"

"'Cause mine weren't straight and fine either when I was your age."

Amy giggled.

The time passed swiftly, and before either knew it, Taleon had entered once again.

"Back so soon?" whined Amy.

"Yes, you have been here more than a half hour and your mother wants you, so it's time for you to go."

Amy skipped across the floor to Taleon's side.

"Bye, Cassandra," she said with a wave of her hand as she disappeared through the door.

"Bye, Amy."

Taleon closed the door and Alexandra heard it lock. It was lonely to be all by herself. Her hair was braided and tied with a ribbon that matched her dress. She was pretty as a picture with no one to admire it, and staring in the mirror wasn't much of a comfort. It only reminded her how alone she was.

Going to the work table, she searched for something to amuse her hands. There was no fancy work or embroidery. Just the lonely thread basket, and she couldn't do anything with that.

She walked around and around the room, wishing for something to pass the time. There was nothing to do but stare out the window and think—think of everything she had been told.

Taleon's words ran through her head over and over again. *"Puppets only do what their masters think, say, and do. So far that is all you have done up here. What are some of your own ideas?"*

What are my ideas? What do I think? Someone is trying to control me. But who? The rebels, my father, or both?

Chapter 6

Later that day Taleon appeared with another tray of food, much more substantial and palatable than the last tray he had brought her.

"The council men and I have been talking. After what happened with Enid this morning, the council thinks it best for you to stay here until your father returns, and he will decide what should be done with you."

"Are you are afraid I will turn the people against him?"

Taleon smiled. "No, more afraid that you will be black and blue."

"Is Enid all right?"

Taleon sighed. "You caused quite a problem for yourself. Thankfully she isn't much of a gossip. The council has heard her grievance against you and has—well, she will be talking to your father when he gets back. Enid has promised to hold her peace until then."

"And when will that be?"

"What?"

"When will he come?" she asked, unsure exactly how to address *him*.

"Your father?"

"Yes, *him*."

"He'll be here within the week."

"Why isn't he here now?"

"*He* is taking care of people in the valley. We can get grain from over the mountains, and he takes it to the people below so they don't starve from your uncle's treatment."

"I wish you wouldn't call him my uncle."

"Then what would you have me call him? The tyrant, impostor…"

"Stop that!"

Taleon shook his head. "Have a good night, your highness."

"That's it; you are just going to leave me in here?"

"That is the general idea."

35

"It's quite maddening that there is nothing to do."

"Well, I am sure once your view about us changes, your view on that will change as well."

"Very clever of you, but I am not amused."

"I am." And without another word he walked out the door and shut it behind him.

"I have never met a more vexing person in ALL MY LIFE!" fumed Alexandra.

"Don't forget your dinner is getting cold."

Alexandra let out a cry of frustration. She could just imagine Taleon laughing on the other side of the door as she heard him walking away. *If I could get my hands on him I'd...I'd. Oh, I don't know what I would do. Too bad the river isn't closer.*

Chapter 7

The hours passed. Night came and Alexandra wasn't tired. She listened to the castle slowly grow quiet. Being alone was driving her mad. Taking a long needle from the sewing basket, she went to the door.

"I don't know if this will work, but it might be worth a try if I can only get out of here for a little bit."

Alexandra knelt near the door and fiddled with the needle in the key hole. Several minutes went by.

"Nothing, nothing at all," she said, resting her hand on the doorknob. To her surprise, it twisted. With an eager pull, she opened it.

There was Taleon, elbows resting on either side of the door frame, his head leaning on his fist. The other hand hung loosely downward. His feet, crossed, resting in one corner of the doorway.

Alexandra's jaw dropped in dismay. She let out a cry of surprise.

"I was wondering when you would figure out I had forgotten to lock it."

"How long have you been standing there?"

"Just long enough to know you were fiddling with the lock, too bad it didn't work. If it had, you would have saved me having to lock you in."

Alexandra slammed the door.

Taleon opened it.

She shoved her feet against it, holding it shut.

He pushed hard.

Alexandra found herself losing ground as she slid across the stone floor.

Propping himself in the doorway he held the door open with one foot.

"I was actually wondering, since it is dark and almost everyone is sleeping, if you would want to go for a walk?"

Alexandra looked at him skeptically.

"I am not teasing you. Do you want to go or no?"

"It would be better than sitting here all night."

"Very good. Come, I'll take you to the top of the castle."

Alexandra rose to her feet without waiting for his assistance. He motioned her to pass through the doorway he was standing in.

"You aren't going to tie my hands?"

"No," he said with a smile, "I am pretty sure I could outrun you if you took to that fancy."

She shot him a brief glare as she passed him. He closed her door and nodded to the right. "This way."

In a few minutes Alexandra found herself panting as they climbed the stairs. Taleon stopped at a window to look out. She took that moment to sag against the wall and catch her breath.

"Can't see it from here; we'll have to wait till we reach the top." He sighed and kept going.

By the time they had reached the top, Alexandra was panting but Taleon took it all in stride.

Turning to look at Alexandra he smiled. "It's the mountain air; you'll get used to it eventually."

"I can hardly breathe."

Taleon shrugged and looked around as if trying to gauge his bearings, even though he had been up there hundreds of times. Unexpectedly he took her hand.

"Come on; I want to show you something."

They soon stood at the far edge of the castle, facing the valley that shone in the light of the moon. The wind was strong and cold, sweeping Alexandra's skirt and hair about her.

"Do you see the lights down there?"

Alexandra searched the landscape but could see nothing.

"No."

"It's very faint, but if you look just to the right of that tree…" he said, pointing with one eye shut.

Alexandra gasped. "It's…"

"The heart of Chambria, its capital of the same name. Creative people, our ancestors."

"It's so small," she murmured with a shiver as the wind blew with a chill over her.

Taleon nodded. "It is a whole new perspective. It's almost an entirely different world. Being up here gives you an idea how small everything really is."

Alexandra realized the wind had stopped blowing with such force. She glanced to her right where Taleon was standing. He was blocking the wind with his back and was facing her. The moon fell and shone brightly on half of his face.

"We see things differently up here. I hope you'll see that in time. Everything here will be contrary to anything you have learned down in the valley. We don't fit in down there. Not until things change and until it changes…"

"And if it doesn't change?"

"We'll have died trying."

A chill ran up her spine. "Take me inside. I am cold."

Taleon didn't speak another word as she followed him. As they came around the corner, the wind struck her with its full force. She stopped. It felt as if it was trying to take away her breath.

Why is it so fierce up here? Who will protect me when I am so alone?

Taleon stopped, waiting for her to catch up. In a moment she moved on. When they were inside the castle she was grateful that she was no longer in the grasp of the cold wind. Taleon could not get her to her room fast enough.

Alexandra was surprised to find herself happy that the door was locked behind her. The world that wanted to change her was outside it. Everything seemed to happen so quickly, yet she did not alter. What was there to change about her? Everything, yet nothing.

Going over to the door, she pushed it to reassure herself that it was locked. Yes, it was. The world that threatened hers' was sealed out, but it still held the key.

The next few days passed quietly for Alexandra.

Taleon was surprised to find her less eager for anything. She did not complain about the food that he brought her. Oftentimes she refused to even acknowledge his presence as he opened the door. She would go to the window and look out until he was gone.

After the third day, Taleon had had enough. The first day it had annoyed him, the second he had tolerated it, but the third day was the last straw.

"What is it, Cassandra?"

She turned her head away from him.

"Was it something I said?"

Alexandra glared at him over her shoulder.

"So I said something and you won't tell me what it is. This should be an interesting conversation since it will be one sided."

Alexandra rolled her eyes and turned back to the window.

"If you want me to be sorry for what I said on top of the castle, I can't. I am sorry that it offended you. But I won't be sorry for what I said. We want you on our side. Your country needs you."

"My country needs me where I belong and that is down in the valley—a proper princess—not captive of a pack of rebels."

"And engaged to that insipid second prince of Shalsburg, I suppose?"

"He's not insipid!"

"How do you know? Have you ever met him?"

"No."

"How can you defend a man you have never met yet turn your back on the people of your country who have stood in this very room? They need your help. Open your eyes." Taleon turned to leave.

"They are open. You know what I see?"

"What do you see?" Taleon asked, turning around.

"I see people who have abandoned their country for a reckless cause that will never win. You will never ever get the power to attack us below. Your numbers are too few. So you sit on the mountain and crow your useless cause hoping that some miracle will happen. You don't help; you only tear *my* country in half."

Taleon's demeanor was frighteningly calm. "We are ready. We've been waiting for you. Your father wouldn't attack until he knew *you* were safe because the last time he attacked, you weren't. Your mother died; *you* were the only thing that stood in the way of our attack. Chambria needs an heir. There is only one. You. When your father is done with his fight, I hope you are ready. He's been waiting for years."

"Your king is not my father. He never has been and never will be."

"Just the same, the throne will be yours. Whether you deserve it or not."

"I—I!"

Alexandra looked into Taleon's face, but words wouldn't come. She was so confused.

"I don't believe you."

"You don't have to. Your father will be here in a few days and he will explain it all to you whether you want to believe it or not. It is the truth."

"And how do you know he isn't lying to you?"

"It happened when I was a boy of seven. I am older than you, you know. Even if you don't remember, I do."

Alexandra's hand moved to strike him. Taleon stepped out of reach and shook his head.

Alexandra burst into tears. *Why does this place have to be so, so horrid and confusing?*

Turning, he walked away, closed the door, and locked it firmly.

Chapter 8

Alexandra stood at her window trying to dream of something else—anything to get where she was out of her head—but they always returned: questions, asking like a disease in the back of her mind, eating away at her.

The door opened and shut quietly. It was unlike Taleon. He had a decided sound all his own when opening the door. *If it's not Taleon, who is it?* Her heart quickened with hope and fear. She turned around.

For a moment, she couldn't breathe. The man from her dream stood before her.

Curly brown hair slightly silvered at the temples. His striking blue eyes were tender instead of worried as she remembered. He was tall and wearing that strange...but familiar...coat of arms on his tunic: red and gold checkered with a white lion.

Had her mind become so crazed with questions that she could see her dreams? Panic tried to surge through her being, but it could not move from her mind and stir her into action. She was numb head to foot.

He was walking towards her, such a tender expression on his face. The man with the brown curly hair was before her, taking her face in his hands, lifting it to gaze into his own.

This is frighteningly real. I can feel him. Wake up, it's only a dream Alexandra. Only a dream. A dream. I tell you, a dream!

"Oh Cassie," he was saying, and he bent and kissed her forehead. She was folded into his arms. She heard the beat of his heart through his tunic and chainmail.

How can this feel so real? I must be insane.

"My Cassie, you are safe at last."

Why does he call me Cassie?

She was aware of tears running down her cheeks that were not her own. Something in her caved, and she began to cry though she didn't know why.

"You remember me. I hoped you would. Taleon said you didn't."

She broke free from the embrace. "Taleon saw you?"

"Of course he did. He is the one who let me in."

"So you are real?"

He laughed.

The same laugh from her dream. But was it a dream? Was her whole life a dream or was Raven Castle one horrid nightmare that she would just wake up from safely in her own bed? Or worse, was it all real—so real that she didn't even know it was true.

"Of course I am real." Then he looked at her, scrutinizing, his countenance becoming grave and grieved.

The countenance change somehow broke her heart, making it ache. Her tears came harder.

"Don't you know me, Cassie?"

"I don't know."

"I know you were little, only three years old. But don't you remember anything? Just the slightest bit about me?"

"No. I don't." She looked into his blue eyes, her heart aching but so afraid. "I really don't," she reiterated, trying to make it true—to let herself believe that this was all just a dream—a crazy dream that would just go away when she woke up. If she could only wake up.

"Do you know who I am, Cassie?"

"No!"

There was a long silence as he looked into her eyes as if trying to rekindle the memories that lived in his heart, in hers. "I am your father. I am King Aric."

A chill ran up Alexandra's spine. Her legs folded beneath her. Darkness sheltered her.

"Cassandra, Cassandra?" the voice was faint but familiar, unpleasantly so. She fought the light that was coming back to her, but it was no use. She opened her eyes.

"Are you all right?" It was Taleon kneeling beside her.

"Oh Taleon, I had the queerest dream about your king."

"Cassandra," he murmured very softly, "It wasn't a dream."

"What?" she said, sitting up.

Then that voice that was so familiar, yet so strange, spoke. "Cassandra."

Turning her head, she saw the man with the brown curly hair. A thousand emotions rushed over her. A scream of terror rushed over her. Turning, Alexandra spun into Taleon's tunic and clung to him.

"Make him go away," she sobbed.

"Cassandra, it's all right. He wants to talk to you," he whispered in her ear.

"I don't want to hear it. I don't want to hear anyone. I want to go home!"

"It's all right, Taleon."

Alexandra listened as the man with the brown curly hair left. His footsteps sounded dejected and heavy. Suddenly she wanted to take back the words she had said and go rushing to his side to tell him....

What would she tell him? That she had a dream about him every few months—it was always the same dream as real as ever, day or night. It just burst upon her at unexpected moments, especially when she thought about her mother. But that seemed insane, more absurd than him being a dream and walking in her room. Or was that more ridiculous? Alexandra didn't know any more. She just wanted to cry and have Judith gather her up in her arms, talk about pleasant things, and make it all go away. Judith always did. Why couldn't she do it now? Why did she have to be here? Why wasn't her mother still alive to explain all of this to her? Why in the world did she have two fathers?

"Cassandra. Are you all right?"

Alexandra pulled away from Taleon. She had forgotten that he was there, that she was holding onto him for dear life. "I am fine."

"Are you sure? You fainted."

Alexandrea blushed. She didn't need to be reminded about that embarrassing fact just at the moment. "I'll be okay."

"You don't remember him at all?"

Alexandra pushed herself to her feet and walked to the window.

"Do you remember him?"

She didn't answer.

He stepped closer.

Taleon was infringing on her personal space. He was attacking her with this horrid question. Her fate lay in the way she answered it.

Turning to him, Alexandra swallowed the dry lump swelling in her throat; it made it almost impossible to breathe.

"No. I don't, Taleon." Tears rose in her eyes as she admitted it. Fear held her tongue from saying more.

He nodded. Silently he left and closed the door. It locked with a click.

Alexandra gasped, holding back tears that wanted to tear her apart. Spinning, she put her face in her hands and hid in the corner, trying to conceal herself from the light gently streaming in the window.

Chapter 9

Taleon locked the door. His hopes had been crushed. The girl was more stupid...no, that wasn't the word. Clueless? Yes, that was it. She was more clueless than he had calculated. That, and maybe just afraid.

He looked over his left shoulder; there stood king Aric at the window looking down into the courtyard. Quietly he approached.

"You tried to warn me. I should have listened. My hopes were so high I couldn't hear you. She is so much like her mother."

"Her eyes are blue like yours."

"That is the only trait she inherited from me—that and the slight twist to her hair," he said running his hand through his.

"Sire, I am sorry."

"Don't be," he said, turning and placing his hand on Taleon's shoulder.

"I tried to break through to her, but she wouldn't listen."

"I am not disappointed in you, Taleon. I know you did everything possible," he smiled as he looked into the young man's honest blue-green eyes. "How are the preparations coming?"

"Quite well. We are nearly ready."

"How is the mine?"

"It'll hold, as long as the war doesn't go on for years and years."

"I hope not. Archibald still in the capitol?"

Taleon nodded. "We set up a rabble rousing in the streets. That is how we rescued her."

"I never thought I would have to kidnap my own daughter."

"It is an unusual predicament."

"Isn't it," King Aric said with a brief laugh. "I can't believe she is terrified of me. After all these years I thought I would get my little girl back—the one who sat on my shoulders and laughed at nothings, and gave me butterfly kisses before she went to bed. But no. She is all grown up."

"Not quite grown up, sire."

"Archibald has seen to that. I would have moved the army on him long ago, if I knew that he wouldn't destroy her. I never thought my brother was capable of harming, much less killing anyone. After he slew Serena, I couldn't risk Cassandra too."

"Not even for your country?" Taleon asked probingly.

"The reason we failed in our first attempt, Taleon, is that my forces weren't strong enough. We should have stormed the capitol and taken it, but we were returning from a war and surprised to find ourselves over taken and the world of Chambria turned upside down. My little brother was sitting on the throne, he claimed for his own. He took many of my men's wives and children captive. Some he killed; some he set free. I was shocked. I never thought that was a part of him, but I was blind—blinded by my own good fortune that I assumed he was happy to share.

"We were all so stunned by his actions that we came up here to Raven Castle—the only place that remained safe from his reach. He hadn't made it his own. We were being overwhelmed between his two forces. He thought we would be crushed into accepting his terms of surrender, but they were beyond unacceptable and we retreated here under the cover of darkness."

"Why didn't you ever marry Fiona?"

The king shot him a glare.

Taleon bowed his head. "I am sorry, sire; I was out of place."

"Funny that you should ask that now. It's been years. How did you remember?

A smile tugged at the corner of Taleon's mouth. "One of those questions that I asked when I was little that no one would ever explain to me, I guess, and by the time I was old enough to know about it, it was unimportant."

King Aric's lips smiled as distant sadness lurked in his eyes.

"Everyone thought it would be best, but I couldn't. I tried to give the people hope, but in my heart there will only be one person I love. I was blessed beyond compare, Taleon. My wife, my queen, she was the other half of my soul. I couldn't love another woman, and I knew that it would be unfair to Fiona to be in a marriage where she would love me and I would fight to love her with the memory of Serena always between us. I couldn't do it. As much as I needed a new heir with the risk of Archibald brainwashing Cassandra against me, I couldn't bear the thought of raising my children as enemies."

"What are you going to do about Cassandra?"

"I don't know. Has she fainted like that before?"

Reluctantly Taleon shook his head.

"She was really terrified of me. I don't understand her behavior. It was all so strange—like she knew me, but yet I was a foreigner to her."

"Do you think she knows more than she is letting on?"

"If Archibald has brainwashed her completely, no. If she has kept her wits about her despite him, I say yes. I don't know. I am too much in the midst of it to be able to tell. Were I to spend more time with her, I might be able to discern, but the way she is terrified of me..." he turned back to the courtyard below.

The troubled look on King Aric's face twisted Taleon's gut. He wanted to shake Cassandra for what she had done. *How can she be so blind? So willfully blind.*

The king had one weakness: his daughter, and to make him so troubled at such a time.... Taleon's hand curled, wishing he could make her understand.

King Aric cleared his throat, interrupting Taleon's thoughts.

"The trip into the valley went well, but I have to return soon. There is a fever going about and they are in dire need of help. If we attack and Archibald takes it out on the people, we'll all be in a strait. We need them strong and ready if this campaign is to be successful."

"How is the drought?"

"It's lasted too long; three years and hardly a decent rain. It's a good thing we can get grain over the mountains; we'll need to stockpile it. Once a war starts, our money will be near worthless. People will be afraid to accept coin that will be of no value if we lose."

"They could always remold it."

"And mess up their countries currency? Risky. Only a few merchants would take the chance, and those willing aren't usually worth doing business with."

"True. What do you want done with—?" and he nodded towards Cassandra's door.

"I wish I knew. If I had more time, I would talk with her. That is, if she would talk with me, but I should be back in the valley. I'll have to take time to think it over."

"How soon do you think you will go down?"

"Three days. It will be enough to get supplies ready and hear from the scouts and decide who needs the most help. Well, Taleon, I need to go talk to the council and an upset woman named Enid," he said with a smile.

"Of course, Sire."

"Want to come along?"

"Yes, Sire."

Chapter 10

Three days later, Taleon watched as King Aric mounted his horse, wearing peasant clothes.

"Taleon, I can't think of anything else. Leaving her locked up in that room isn't doing her any good. Her thoughts are eating her. She needs to see as well as hear about the way we live. Telling her how we live isn't going to change her," he sighed.

"Maybe she will wake up?"

"One can only hope. Protect her for me until I return."

"Yes sire."

King Aric's hand was laid on his shoulder. "Thank you, Taleon."

Glancing behind him, King Aric noticed that the men accompanying him were ready. "Move out," he shouted, with a fleeting look behind him at the upper balcony.

Taleon's gaze followed. Alexandra stood exactly where she had been told to stay, her head lifted high with a touch of arrogance gracing her features. Taleon turned to watch his king ride out of the gate.

Then he glared back at her. "She has no idea what she is doing to him." Striding through the courtyard and taking the stairs two steps at a time, he soon stood close to her.

"How long will he be gone?" Alexandra asked, not turning around.

"Two weeks, a month, maybe more; depends on how much the people in the valley need his help."

Alexandra bit her lower lip and nodded. Unexpectedly she turned to him. "So what exactly is going to happen?"

"He told you."

"I know, but I don't think it makes any sense."

"You are to shadow me around the castle. Most things that need to be done you can help with; some things you will just have to watch."

"And if I don't want to help?"

"You can just watch, but your father thinks that being closed up in that room is bad for you."

"I won't change."

Taleon looked at her silently.

"I won't," she reiterated as his silence annoyed her.

"Come on; there are things to get done."

"Like what?"

"Refugees."

"Refugees?"

"People that come up from the valley looking for help. A few came in this morning, just before your father left. They need tending to and I need to oversee what is being done."

Walking down the steps, he took her into a corridor where people lined the wall in various attitudes of rest. A few were well-kept, but most were looking worn and tired. Their clothes had seen better days, and there were just a few that looked, to Alexandra, terrifying. Covered in dirt or blood, they lay on the floor, weak from their climb to safety.

Immediately Taleon was among them, helping the few women and men already there assisting those in need.

Stunned, Alexandra stood on the steps, one hand gripping her elbow. Clutching her arm to her side, she watched with wide eyes. No one seemed to see her or mind her wide eyes or surprised gawking gaze. In fact, to them she didn't seem to exist at all. Hesitantly she started to follow Taleon. Standing there on the steps was frightening and discomforting. At least with him, he might try to make some sense out of the situation for her. But he was almost impossible to follow as he darted here and there. Then he would spend a long time feeding a sickly child or weak, elderly adult.

He didn't seem to really notice her until a woman carrying a jar of wound ointment nearly spilled it as she ran into her.

"Cassandra, go, sit there in the corner. You can still see and you won't be in the way."

Quietly she shuffled to where he pointed, feeling ashamed and awkward. Nearly an hour passed and Taleon was still busy. Alexandra felt as if she had fallen off the face of the earth. No one paid attention to her; she was stranded in a corner with nothing to do but sit and stare.

And he thought that this would be better for me than sitting in my room all day. Why, I am invisible! No one knows who I am and even if they do, they don't seem to care. She sent a glare in Taleon's direction, but he failed to receive it and Alexandra was left to search the room for anything that would catch her fancy. There was nothing.

A woman was standing in front of her, pushing a small noisy child onto her lap. "Hold this baby. Here is his bottle. I'd do it, but I have too much to get done."

"But I—I've never held a..."

The woman was already walking away and she looked down at the thing in her lap. A pair of large blue eyes were staring pitifully up into her own, tears streaming down his little rosy cheeks. He had long black eyelashes and a crop of dark ringlets. He took a few small gasping breaths. Then started to cry very softly. Slowly it grew louder. Alexandra was clueless about what to do with him. He was such a sad little thing. Then she looked at the bottle the woman had forced into her hand.

Gently she put it to his mouth. The small being closed his mouth around it and sucked with joy. Relaxing his tears and crying, he lay back in her arms. Alexandra was surprised to find herself admiring the babe in her arms, as awkward as she felt with him. He was really very cute. When his bottle was finished, he pushed it away. Alexandra looked around helplessly.

What am I supposed to do with it now?

They stared at one another, his small chubby hands exploring her face with soft chatter that seemed to ask questions by the bright expression in his eyes and the lifting of his eyebrows.

"If you are talking to me, I have no idea what you are saying."

A garble of coos mixed with what might have been words warbled back at her.

Alexandra found herself smiling at the little fellow, and he smiled back showing his small rows of tiny white teeth. His babyish charm enchanted her.

"What am I supposed to do with you, little man?" she asked him.

He didn't seem interested in answering and warbled babyish things, pointed at various objects in the room, exclaimed, "En gat!" looked at her with one curious eyebrow raised, and cooed to himself before letting his eyes wander again.

After a while he grew fussy. Alexandra swung him back and forth on her knees, holding him at a distance. Still he did not quiet down.

Anxiously, she swung him back and forth a little faster, hoping he would quiet down but to no avail. He grew louder.

Desperately she looked around for anyone who could help her. No one was even looking in her direction.

Where is Taleon? He should be done by now. We have been in here all morning!

Almost frantic, she tried to distract him. But he only raised his little head and wailed all the louder.

Unexpectedly a larger set of hands enclosed around hers. "Let me take him," it was Taleon.

"You won't get him quiet either."

"Just let me have him for a minute," he said softly.

Alexandra pulled her hands away, frustrated.

Taleon took the baby, wrapped the blanket closely about him, and, swaying very softly as he walked. Hummed a little tune beneath his breath.

In a minute the baby had stopped his crying and pillowed his head on Taleon's shoulder with a last feeble cry.

She was infuriated!

I could have done that. You big show-off, I have never held a baby; how was I to know he was tired! YOU! I could just hate you! The next moment she was wondering why she didn't hate him.

The little fellow's eyelids had drooped shut under Taleon's supervision, and in a few minutes Taleon was laying the infant beside a thin peasant woman who looked worn out in body and soul. She smiled as the baby was laid by her side. Alexandra watched as her transparent hands pulled the sleeping bundle close, and she kissed the top of his curly head. A sudden longing for her own mother came over her and thoughts of the curly brown haired man flooded her mind. Should she call the man in her memory King Aric? He looked so exactly like him. Mentally she compared the man in her memory with her father. They were so different, yet there were similarities that she couldn't deny even if she wouldn't admit them.

It's not King Aric in my memory; it is my father. It has to be.

Alexandra shoved her father into the memory, making it him whose shoulders she rode on, him whom she laughed at. It was he who kissed her mother and whispered "Alexandra" in her ear. The dream crumbled into a failure. Her father had never done any of those things with her; ever. She realized Taleon was standing in front of her and saying something. He looked at her expecting an answer.

"I am sorry; what did you say?"

Taleon smiled.

She could almost glare at him for that.

"We missed the midday meal, we were so busy. Are you hungry?"

"Yes, I am."

"Then let's head to the kitchen. They should have something for us to eat."

"The kitchen?" She had *never* gone in the kitchen before. That was the place for servants.

"Follow me," he said with a nod of his head.

It seemed another labyrinth of various hallways before they reached the kitchen. Taleon entered without ceremony.

"Hello, Cook!"

"Greetings Taleon, my friend. I thought I would see you."

Taleon chuckled, "Well, you were right. But I am going to need two bowls today. We have a guest."

"Two bowls of stew coming right away."

In a few minutes, Taleon and Alexandra were seated side by side with carved wooden bowls of stew in front of them.

Curiously she prodded her victuals with a spoon. It seemed riddled with unfamiliar food—strange blocks of white and orange and squares of something thin and transparent floated about in it.

"What are these?" she asked in a delicate whisper, pointing at the orange and white objects.

"Potatoes and carrots," he said casually.

"Root vegetables?"

"Yes," he answered carelessly.

"Root vegetables are for peasants!" she uttered harshly under her breath.

"You ate gruel and that is only fit for swine," he said all too casually.

Alexandra's face flamed red. Her ears hurt from the burning. She wanted to kick Taleon, but that was unladylike. Even if he couldn't be a gentleman, at least she could be a princess. How low was she brought? What would her father say if he could see her now? His precious daughter was sitting in a kitchen with the servants eating a stew with peasant vegetables! He would fume at the thought. Taleon would be dead for treating her so. At that thought she smiled.

With the thoughts of her father, the earlier dilemma returned: the haunting memory of the brown-haired man. The soft words, "Goodbye, my Cassie," rang in her mind, refusing to be Alexandra. She tried to imagine her father saying those words, but with no success at all. It was always the brown-haired man who looked like King Aric.

Why am I calling him King Aric? He isn't a king he is an impostor who claims he is my father. How much time will they waste before they realize I won't buy it?

Finding her own thoughts disconcerting, she pushed them aside to find out what was going on in this busy kitchen.

"What is going on down in the valley?" asked the man who had served them the two bowls of stew.

"According to the scouts, it's pretty hard. The drought is harming everyone," sighed Taleon.

"How soon will we be ready to fight?"

"Soon, maybe as soon as King Aric comes back."

"That can't come soon enough. I'll never forget what it was like in the valley. I can only imagine it's gotten worse with that tyrant Archibald the impostor sittin' pretty on the throne. The sooner he is off it and King Aric back where he belongs I'll be happy. The world will be right again."

Taleon glanced uneasily at Alexandra, but she seemed too weary and preoccupied to cause trouble or take offence.

"I know. I just hope we are as ready as we think we are."

"Oh we are," replied the cook confidently, stirring something mysterious in a pot. "Taleon, would you like some bread with that?"

"Yes, thank you."

To Alexandra's surprise, a small loaf of brown bread came flying from the cook's hand towards her and Taleon. He caught it with his left hand, pulled his dagger out with his right, and sliced the bread easily in half. Taleon pushed the second half toward her, sopping his half in the stew.

Alexandra looked at him, puzzled. He smiled as he took a bite of the soggy bread. She let a shiver climb up her back with a good shake at the end.

It's bad enough to be eating in the kitchen, but to sop your bread like that! I shall never stoop that low. I hope. These peasant vegetables aren't bad, but if I die suddenly I'll know who is to blame: Taleon and this whole pack of thieves at Raven Castle. Well, that baby is an exception; he was so cute. But I can't imagine talking important matters with kitchen servants. It just isn't dignified.

Chapter 11

"Cassandra. Cassandra? Are you all right?"

Alexandra picked up her head from her crossed arms with a start. She really didn't remember pushing her bowl away and laying her head down. All of this kitchen chatter had put her to sleep.

"Did you fall asleep?"

"No," she said with a little shake of her head and blushed as the kitchen people—for they certainly weren't servants—stared at her.

"I think you have had enough for one day. Come, I'll show you more later," said Taleon, getting up from his seat.

Wearily Alexandra followed him as they went through what seemed eternal labyrinths of hallways back to her room.

"Thank you, Taleon."

"Rest up; tomorrow will be a long day and I might not let you off as easily as I did today."

Alexandra ignored him and closed her door, only waiting long enough to hear it lock before jumping gleefully into her bed. Yes, sleep sounded so welcoming.

A few hours later she woke up. That same horrid dream awakened her.

Why on earth must it haunt me! He is NOT MY FATHER! I WON'T LET HIM BE. I won't; I won't! If I believe he is my father, that means everything I believe in was a lie. I am not wrong; I am princess of the noblest blood. Archibald is my father and always will be. Those people I saw today were their own abused victims. They are just trying to make me believe their exaggerated claims. Once I believe them I will become a victim of their conniving schemes. I will find myself stabbed in the heart by their wicked treachery.

Turning over onto her stomach, she buried her face in the pillow, clenching her eyes shut. She tried to erase the dream. It would not go away.

Frustrated, she screamed into her pillow and beat it with her fists. Sitting up, she hit and hissed defiantly at it.

"I will not believe it. He is *not my father*. You hear me. Do you hear me? I refuse to believe you. All of it. He can't be my father. The people are misled. You are not wrong, Alexandra. You aren't. But they are so helpless, to see them..." With a cry of rage, she struck her pillow sending it from the bed onto the floor watching it tumble with mixed delight, anger, and humiliation at her own actions.

There was a sudden click at her door. Startled she turned around. It was Taleon opening the door with a food tray.

"Are you all right?"

Alexandra flushed bright red. "I thought I saw a mouse," she said, feigning fear in her voice.

"I see," he said, his lips trembling as if trying to keep back a smile. "We have a few cats about the place. I'll see one is placed in your room."

Alexandra slipped out on the far side of her bed and retrieved the tumbled pillow. With an air of penance, she squeezed it apologetically for her mistreatment of it.

"Thank you," she murmured under her breath. Wondering if she should protest about having a cat in her room since it would do no good, since there were no mice.

Taleon watched her curiously. It was apparent that she was unaware that this was his second entry into her room. He had heard the full confession to the pillow and witnessed its mistreatment before retreating silently and reopening the door.

Mouse indeed, he thought. *Just the same I will make sure she has a cat to keep her company and, if nothing else, remind her why he is in her room.*

"Did you enjoy yourself today?" he asked casually, setting down her tray.

"A little, I guess. That baby was sweet, except he fussed awfully."

"You'll get to know how to care for children by and by."

"Did you have any brothers and sisters?"

Taleon shrugged off the question. "Know any songs? There might be one that puts him to sleep."

"My nurse Rita used to sing one to me. I liked it. Judith never sung to me."

"Rita?"

"Yes, she was my nursemaid for a while. Then, I had Judith. Rita left for some strange reason. One night she sang me to sleep. The next morning she was gone. Father said she had run away or something like that. It was Judith who watched me after that, so everything was all right. I mean, people don't stick around forever."

"What do you mean by that?"

"Well, my mother died; Rita left me; I have never had a friend my own age for more than a month. They were always too rambunctious for my state of health and were sent away. The only people who have stayed in my life are my father and Judith, but even they are gone now that you have trapped me up here."

Taleon raised one eyebrow and sighed. *That certainly is a glum outlook to have on life.*

"Well, you better eat and rest up. You might not get off so easily tomorrow. There is a lot to get done."

"You already said that."

"Just saying I warned you."

"But my health might not permit it. I am not strong, you know."

Taleon shrugged and closed the door.

Alexandra had just finished braiding her hair the next morning when there was a knock on the door.

"Come in?" she answered.

There was a rattle of keys and Taleon popped his head in. "Time for breakfast. I think it's time you took breakfast like civilized folk."

"I do take it like civilized folk. I am not at all like the rest of you."

Taleon laughed. "Just the same, you are going to come take it with the rest of us for once."

"I don't want to."

"All right, then, you don't have to have breakfast if you don't want to."

"I didn't say that."

"I know. You have two options: come with me down for breakfast or stay here and skip it. I'll be back for you in a little while because you can't stay in your room all day."

"Who says I can't?"

Taleon tipped his head to one side. "Do I have to remind you already?"

"I outrank you and you must obey my orders."

"The king outranks you and I am obeying his orders so I have a higher ranking."

"You do not."

"I am not going to argue with you. Are you coming to breakfast or not?"

"I am not hungry; in fact, I am feeling rather ill from yesterday. I think I might have caught some sort of illness from being with the refugees."

"Are you sure?" he asked, stepping closer.

She felt uncomfortable. "You shouldn't come close. You might catch it from me."

"Really?"

"Yes."

"What are you feeling?" he asked concern clouding his face.

Alexander panicked, searching for symptoms she could easily fake.

"I have a headache, and my stomach feels awful." Unexpectedly her stomach rumbled.

"For that kind of illness I prescribe breakfast. You are probably lightheaded from not eating and your stomach is obviously suffering from the same deficiency," he said.

"I suppose you are right. I didn't think of that."

"I am sure you didn't," he said with a smile.

In a short while Alexandra found herself in a hall full of talking people and tables lined with food.

"There is a group of girls your age; why don't you go join them?"

"But I…"

Taleon was already gone. The story she had told Amy ran through her mind. She could do this. Really she could. Quietly she went and slipped onto the end of a bench where there was an empty plate.

None of the girls seemed to really notice her; they were so deeply involved in their conversation. She listened in. They were talking about her!

"Did you see that pearl she gave to Amy?"

"Wasn't it beautiful?"

"Oh I know! I want one, but I doubt that that will ever happen. Can you imagine not being able to braid your own hair?"

"No; I have been doing my hair since I can remember."

"Me too."

"Do you think we will ever get to see her?"

"I doubt it. She is always locked up in that room of hers."

"Do you know why?"

"I hear she is sickly."

"I hope that is not true. King Aric is so good. To be cursed with an heir who is ill would be so bad. He has waited so long to get her here."

"What will he do if she dies? Her mother has already died, the poor thing."

"I don't know. They say that his wife's death broke his heart. What would it do to him to lose his daughter too?"

"I can't imagine. Who would he name as heir to the kingdom?"

"I don't know."

"The council pressed him to name a second heir just in case something should happen. He wouldn't name anyone. He didn't want to put Princess Cassandra's life in more danger than it already was. Can you imagine what it must be like living in the same castle with King Archibald?"

"No, I would be deathly ill just from that thought."

"I feel sorry for her. Can you imagine growing up with no mother and with him for a father? King Aric and he are so different."

"I feel sorry for her. If we thought his treatment down in the valley was bad, what must it be like for her?"

"I wouldn't want to know. I wonder if she is allowed to bring up her mother without the threat of death looming over her head."

"Probably not."

"I am just glad we don't have to go through any of those horrid exercises anymore."

"Weren't those awful! I was always afraid I would fail. The soldiers always looked so stern when they gave the test."

"Your brother Ronny—is he getting any better?"

"Yes, he was a spitfire of a lad; still is. When the soldier asked him who is king, he answered all too boldly, 'King Aric the mighty protector of the realm, sir.' That soldier got so angry. I thought he was going to kill him. Instead they gave him a lashing that went on forever. They almost branded him, but decided he was so young they would make an example out of him instead. They left him on the stocks for two whole days then rode out of town with him. I thought I was never going to see him again. The next day he barely stumbled into town all by himself. They let him go after he swore allegiance to Archibald. Father couldn't stay another day. We left for Raven Castle that evening as soon as night had fallen. It took us almost a month to get here, hiding from the soldiers and everything."

"Your brother is amazing."

"I know. He is my hero. I didn't have the guts to say it. I gave the answers they wanted to hear; he answered from his heart. Except for his allegiance to King Archibald—that was not from his heart. He says he has no greater joy than looking forward to breaking his word, and he usually keeps it with such honor, I am rather shocked."

"Why did he give his allegiance then?"

"He says he figured he was worth more alive than dead to King Aric."

"That is true."

"What about you?" said a girl, turning to Alexandra. "What made you come to Raven Castle?"

She found herself tongue tied. "I—I—I didn't really have a...a choice," she stuttered out, her mouth feeling dry and hopeless. Her palms began to sweat.

"We all feel that way. What did Archibald do to your family?"

Glancing down at her plate, Alexandra whispered, "I'd rather not talk about it."

"I am so sorry; I didn't mean to pry. It must be awful. Of course you don't want to talk about it. When I first came, I didn't want to talk about it either. I should have been more thoughtful," she said, wrapping her arm kindly about Alexandra's shoulder.

Shock reverberated through her at the familiarity.

"Please excuse me," she said, standing.

"Oh please stay; we shan't ask any more questions of you."

"Really I must be going. Thank you very much."

"You are welcome back any time."

"Thank you," she whispered and slipped out of the hall into a lonely corridor. Pressing her palms against the wall, she leaned with her back against it. Her hands were sweaty and clammy; strangely, her pulse was racing and her mind was swimming in circles.

Taleon must have told them to talk like that. They must know who I am; they are all out to get me. That or they are speaking the truth, and if they are speaking the truth, then there has been some horrible mistake on my part. It cannot be. I refuse to be wrong. There is no way I can be. Everything my father has told me is so contrary to what they are saying. How can this be?

"You all right, Cassandra?"

Taleon's voice made her jump in surprise. "You scared me, Taleon."

"I am sorry. I didn't mean to. How was your breakfast?"

"Interesting to say the least. Yours?"

"Delicious."

Alexandra giggled, "I meant the company."

"Oh, that was very good as well, but not to be categorized with food. So what did you girls talk about?"

"Everyone up here talks politics and badmouths my father. I wonder how they would feel if I talked about their father in that way."

"They all admire your father and hate your uncle. When will you ever get that straight?"

"When you finally realize the truth."

"And the truth would be?"

"King Archibald is suffering from a dreadful misunderstanding by the people."

"And you understand him? You spend hours every day talking with him. Everything in the country is known by you and him."

"Not really. He doesn't spend much time with me."

"So you really don't know him, do you?"

"I am tired of this conversation."

"Have you seen that mouse in your room again?"

Alexandra held back a glare. "What torture do you have planned for me today?"

"I am in charge of the refugees for now. So come with me," he said with a smile.

Oh great, muttered Alexandra under her breath. *I get to be invisible again.*

Chapter 12

Upon entering the wide hall where the refugees were staying, Alexandra retreated to her corner to wait out the long morning.

Taleon will ignore me. I will get in people's way and my whole morning will be wasted. Though how it will be wasted I am not quite sure, since I don't have anything planned.

Alexandra tried to keep her mind anywhere than in the little hallway glowing with the soft light of the morning, filled with people hurting and needing hope.

Alexandra found her skirt being tugged on by tiny hands. The baby she had held the day before was pulling himself to his feet by clinging to her dress. Soon he was standing, his little fists filled with her dress. His legs bounced, nearly giving way beneath him. He compensated and straightened himself with a delighted coo.

"You did so well," Alexandra complimented him softly.

He gave her a toothy grin.

"He likes you," murmured a voice quite near to them.

Alexandra looked up. It was the woman with the transparent hands that had spoken, his mother. She had been moved into better lighting.

"He doesn't usually take to people," she said with a wan smile.

Alexandra noted the lines of care about her face; a few strands of white were betrayed by her nut brown hair; sadness seemed to pour from her grey eyes. Her heart ached for the woman.

"His name is Brendan," she offered.

"I am Alexandra."

"And I am Edith."

Brendan looked up into Alexandra's face and babbled a full length sentence of gibberish.

"Is that so?" Alexandra said with a laugh.

Edith smiled faintly. "How old are you?"

"Sixteen. I'll be seventeen in the fall."

"Oh, what I wouldn't give to be sixteen again," she said with a sigh. "It is hard to believe I was that just six years ago."

Cassandra looked at her with shock. The woman in front of her could not be that young. She had to be at least middle-aged, not just six years her senior.

Edith looked at Alexandra's face and laughed—a laugh that ended with a racking cough that left her breathless and tired.

"Can I get you anything?"

"No, I am fine." There was a long pause as Alexandra felt her mind go blank and Edith recovered her strength.

"You think it is strange that I am only twenty-two? I know I look a lot older. My life has been full of worry and trouble." A tear glistened in her eye.

"I am so sorry," whispered Alexandra, not really sure what else to say. "What happened?" she asked, her curiosity overcoming her delicacy.

The woman smiled her wan smile. "Maybe someday I'll tell you, but I am too tired just now." She closed her eyes.

Alexandra turned her attention back to Brendan who was "talking" in his own babyish language that only he could understand, but thought the rest of the world could. He sat down and lifted his blanket over his head and left it there.

Alexandra laughed and he pulled it off with a smile.

Putting it over his head once again, he waited for her to laugh. Alexandra bent forward and swept it off his face. He let out a delighted squeal of laughter.

A mischievous thought overcame her and she put the blanket over her own head. Instantly a small pair of hands leeched onto her dress and proceeded to pull themselves up. A babyish hand grabbed the blanket and pulled it off onto the floor with a gurgle of delight.

They both laughed. Gently she pried the blanket from his hand and covered both of their heads with it. Brendan laughed and batted it off. In a little while, though, not even blanket games could keep him happy and he fussed loudly.

Edith's eye opened. "He's hungry," she sighed.

"Ma'am," Alexandra asked a woman who was working nearby, "Can I get a bottle for him?"

"Of course you can; go to the kitchen and ask Cook for a bottle; he'll give you one."

The kitchen? That is one place I don't want to go again. She looked at Brendan. He was so little. His face was distressed with hunger. Her own pangs of hunger had been few and far between, but the expression on his face was unbearable.

"Come on, Brendan; let's get you something to eat," she said, gathering him into her arms and wrapping his blanket about him.

Now if I can only find the kitchen. The way Taleon goes around here I never know where I am going. I think he tries to confuse me. Summoning her best recollection and prompted by Brendan's need, she found the kitchen.

Standing at the door, she took a deep breath. *I am a princess about to enter a kitchen and ask for a baby's bottle.* Not in her wildest dreams had she ever imagined such an occurrence.

Brendan didn't give her much time to think how odd the situation felt as he let out a soft whimper.

Hesitantly she entered. There was no need for her to summon Cook's attention; Brendan did that for her with a hungry cry.

"Well, hello," he said, turning around. "I didn't expect to see you back so soon. What can I do for you? Did Taleon send you for something?"

"He needs a bottle."

"Ah, I see. You'll have to give me a few minutes, poor little fellow."

Brendan let out another wail and Cook came over to see him.

"Hello there, little man. What is your name?"

Brendan shied away and looked up hesitantly with his blue eyes.

"His name is Brendan."

"Brendan, Brendan, my dear boy, you look hungry." He looked at Alexandra. "He has his teeth. Do you know if he can eat solid food? It will be a little while before his bottle is ready."

"I don't know."

"Well, let's give it a try. I have some bread and fruit fresh from the garden. Sit over there and I'll bring you something in a moment."

Hesitantly Alexandra went and sat where she and Taleon had sat the day before. Setting Brendan carefully on the table; for he was too small and far too short for a chair.

In a moment Cook set a bowl in front of Alexandra with bread spread with butter and then placed an apricot with a knife next to her.

"Make sure you take off the skin and cut it into bite sized pieces for him."

Alexandra looked at the knife. *I have never peeled fruit in my life, much less used that sharp a knife.*

She broke off a piece of bread and offered it to Brendan. He devoured it, then took the slice of bread into his own hands, and began to chew on it.

"Brendan!" she said, taking the bread from him. He let out a squawk until she put another piece in his mouth. Quickly she broke the bread up into Brendan bite sized pieces, and put it in the bowl. He couldn't eat it fast enough. Taking the apricot, she peeled it. The juice oozed all over her fingers, making the fruit slide about in her hand as she peeled it.

"Brendan, I am making a mess of this," she confessed in a low tone.

He babbled back a baby reply.

She tried to slice it in half, but it wouldn't go all the way through. Alexandra cut around the whole thing and at last made it split open. Taking pieces, she drew the knife towards herself, cutting it into small pieces. He was still eating his bread and completely ignoring the juicy yellow-orange-red fruit.

He let out a loud squeal, Alexandra jumped in surprise, looking up to make sure that he was all right. Pain raced through her hand. His little heels pounded on the tabletop in delight. He had discovered the apricot.

At the sound of his squeal, Alexandra had jerked the knife toward herself. Pain had been instant, but not important. Now that Brendan was fine, she turned her attention to her thumb. Blood was flowing off her thumb and down her hand, and drops were dripping onto her dress. She had cut deep.

She gave a little gasping cry of pain, unsure what to do. This had never happened to her before.

Just at that moment Taleon came through the door.

"Cassandra, I thought it was clear…" His words stopped dead at sight of her hand.

Quickly he moved into action. Taking a clean cloth from a pile that sat near the door, he tore a strip from it and wrapped it around her thumb. It quickly grew red and he wrapped more cloths and tighter.

"What is the matter, Taleon?"

"She slit her thumb," he said.

In a moment he was standing by them. "I am sorry. I shouldn't have given you such a sharp knife."

Alexandra held her tongue. The pain was consuming her thoughts. Tears were blinding her. She blinked and they spilled down her cheek. Glancing up, she saw Brendan. His little lip was quivering and his own eyes were filling with tears.

"It's okay, Brendan," she said, putting her hand onto his little foot. He had ceased to eat, his blue eyes watching her with concern.

"Here, let me take him," said Cook. "His bottle is ready anyway."

"How does it feel?" Taleon asked Alexandra.

"It hurts," she murmured, biting her lower lip.

"Hold it tightly and see if that helps stop the bleeding."

She did so, her thumb pulsating painfully in rhythm with her heartbeat.

He stood by her for several minutes, annoyingly doing nothing.

"Let me see it now," he said.

She released her hand from the bandage. Her hand was moist with blood.

Taleon shook his head. "Stay here. I will be right back. Cook, is he done yet?"

Cook nodded.

"I'll take him back to his mother," he said, going over to Cook.

"How bad is it?"

Taleon answered in a whisper as he took a contented Brendan from Cook's arms.

Anxiously, Alexandra watched Taleon leave and pensively waited for him to return. Being the center of attention in a kitchen was not ideal.

Time was taking forever. Cook was talking to her. She turned to him.

"I don't give this out too often except for special occasions, but I think this should relieve the pain just a little," he said, holding out a dark stick of something.

"It's bad, isn't it?" she asked him.

"He said they'll have to amputate," said a voice from the background.

Alexandra turned dangerously white.

"Be quiet, Sully!" shouted Cook over his shoulder, then, turning back to Alexandra, he said, "It's nothing of the sort. Taleon's gone to get the doctor for a second opinion to see if you just need bandages."

"Are you sure?"

"Risk my life on it. Now here take this and eat it. I promise it will make you feel better and if it doesn't, I'll—" he paused, unsure what he would do, "stand on my head."

Alexandra laughed, despite the tense feeling in her chest. Reaching out, she took the dark stick from his hand and hesitantly took a bite. A soft rich creamy sweet taste melted in her mouth. Her eyes lit up.

Cook smiled. "Everybody likes a little bit of chocolate."

"Thank you," she paused hesitantly, "What is your name?"

"Cook."

"I know that is what everyone calls you, Cook, but what is your name?"

He threw back his head and laughed. "My name is Cook. That is how I got stuck in the kitchen in the first place: a misunderstanding, but by the time they straightened it out I found I liked it pretty well."

Alexandra blushed. "Oh, I see. I am sorry."

"I was given my mother's maiden name for a first. It's not your fault."

The chocolate stick disappeared very quickly and Alexandra went back to clutching her throbbing thumb.

In a few more minutes, Taleon appeared with the doctor on his heels.

"So you slit your thumb," he said in a rather dry voice that seemed on the verge of ill humor. "Taleon said that it was a serious cut and that I was required instantly even though I am needed terribly elsewhere. Let's see it," he said, holding out his hand.

Slowly Alexandra released her hand from the bandage. The doctor's mouth twitched at the sight of so much blood. With experienced gentle hands, he unwrapped the bandage and looked at her thumb. Alexandra looked too, held by the horror of it.

"You were right, Taleon. It needs stitches, and badly."

"Stitches?" asked Alexandra, slightly panicked.

"You'll hardly feel them, my dear. Now to make sure you're in the best light; yes, you are. Now, Taleon, my bag."

He spent a moment searching for what he would need, then pulled out a needle and thread specific for the job. With terror slowly sweeping over her, Alexandra watched as he prepared everything. Then he took her hand in his and began.

Alexandra looked away and shut her eyes. She couldn't bear the thought of watching.

Unexpectedly she found Taleon whispering in her ear. "If you need something, you can squeeze my hand." He slipped his hand under her free one.

Alexandra pulled her hand away and tucked it beneath her leg. *I do not need his help. It's his fault I am in this mess in the first place! If he hadn't made me stay with him, I would be safely in my room.*

There was a breathless voice at the door. "Doctor, he has gotten worse; he needs you."

The needle dropped from the doctor's hand. "Taleon, take over," he shouted as he rushed from the room.

Alexandra watched him go with shock. She was a princess! Her needs were always first and foremost in the castle. What horror was this? Her wound was to be left in Taleon's care! Why he was just a—a what? Alexandra glanced at him, horrified, as he took up the needle that the doctor had left so quickly.

"Have you done this before?" she asked.

"Yes, I have, but I wanted the doctor to do it because it was you and I didn't think you would have any confidence in me. Hold still now."

Alexandra looked away and shut her eyes tighter than before. Eternity seemed to pass twice, while her eyes were closed. Finally Taleon announced that it was done.

Alexandra glanced at her thumb; she couldn't tell where the doctor's stitches left off and Taleon's began. Then she looked away. It wasn't something she really wanted to see.

"I'll tie a bandage around it so you don't have to look at it. There, all done. At least we know you don't faint at the sight of blood," said Taleon, trying to lighten the mood.

Alexandra kicked his shin before thinking twice.

"Ow, what was that for?" Taleon asked in an offended voice.

Unexpectedly Alexandra burst into tears. The day had just been too much to take at once. She hid her face in her hands, wishing the tears would stop but knowing they wouldn't. Sliding off the chair, she ran from the room. She had wanted to get out of there for so long and she wasn't about to take anymore of Taleon's words—not in front of all those people.

After a short while she realized she didn't know where she was going. Finding a dark corner of a hallway, she sank into it and curled up into a ball to cry. How infinitely more she would have loved to hide in her room, but no, she didn't know where that was. Her head was aching, her thumb was throbbing so hard if felt like it would burst, and Taleon had been unnecessarily cruel.

In a few minutes she heard Taleon with his back against the wall sliding slowly, lowering himself to sit beside her.

Chapter 13

Taleon sat down on the cold stone floor of the castle hallway. He looked at Cassandra—a bundle of sadness and pain: pain he had caused.

Sensitivity wasn't always his strong suit and now he had just shown it off brilliantly. He had sort of known it before he said it; but to be frank, he had been rather offended by her refusal to accept the comfort he had offered. *Sure it's not delicate to take a lady's—a princess'— hand but in such situations you can't always afford to be delicate. I was offering my hand as a friend and she turned her royal nose up at me. That is what you get for being a snob, offended feelings.* He wondered if that was how people became snobs: by having constantly offended feelings. Well, that was too much of a question for now. The real question was how he should go about convincing Cassandra to not hate him.

I should apologize and I will. I really shouldn't have said that to her. It would be nice if she would apologize every once in a while for the ways she acts. I wonder if King Aric knew she would be such a pain when he assigned me to look after her? Well, he trusts me. He would not have given it to me if he had thought I couldn't handle it. Can I really handle it? Don't question yourself, Taleon. You just fell flat on your face. You failed. Now it is time to pick yourself back up again and start over.

Taleon looked at Cassandra again. She was still crying, except now it had escalated almost into hysterics.

"Cassandra," he whispered softly.

"Go. Away," she sobbed between gasps for breath.

"You know I can't do that."

"Why not!"

He could bring up the point that she couldn't even find her own room, but that would hurt too much and he needed to build a bridge, not tear it down. "Your father asked me to look after you."

"King Aric is not my father!"

When will she ever believe us? It is so vexing. She is afraid of something. But what? "Cassandra, whether he is your father or not, he told me to look after you. He is king here, if nowhere else, and we are all bound to obey him as are you, because you are under his authority and protection."

"Just leave me alone. Please," she begged.

"I will leave you alone, but let's get you to your room first. All right?"

"Fine."

"Let me help you," he said, getting to his feet, taking her forearms, and gently pulling her up.

"Thank you," she muttered under her breath.

"Come, we aren't too terribly far from your room."

Cassandra kept her head down and walked, letting a few loose hairs fall in front of her face. It was obvious she didn't want anyone to see her. Carefully Taleon guided her through less crowded hallways to her room.

"Try to get some rest, all right."

She nodded.

He started to close the door, then opened it again. "Are you in a lot of pain?"

She nodded.

"I'll be back in a few minutes with something to help," he said, closing the door and not bothering to lock it. *She doesn't want to be seen by anyone. There is no way she is going to go walking out in the hallway on her own.*

Going to the physician's quarters, he found the assistant who was grinding up herbs.

"Do you have anything made up to lessen pain?"

"How bad is it?"

"Stitches in a badly cut thumb."

"Ouch."

"It's her first time for something like this."

"How is she handling it?"

"Not well, but not badly either."

"I have just the thing for her then," he said, taking down a jar. In a few minutes, he handed Taleon a mug filled with a steaming tea sweetened with honey. "Tell her to take this. It should help."

"Thank you."

Taleon knocked on Cassandra's door.

"Come in," was the quiet reply.

She was sitting at her dressing table, her hair brushed, pulled loosely back, and tied at the nape of her neck. Unconsciously she was rocking back and forth slightly to comfort herself as she squeezed her thumb; trying to stop the throbbing pain that was now racing up her arm and into her shoulder.

It struck him how young and helpless she was. Here was the princess in a strange place with no friends, at least no one she wanted to claim as her ally. Confronted with so many new things and thoughts; no wonder she was exhausted, especially with all the extra trauma of that morning.

"Here is some tea. It should help the pain in a little while."

Carefully she took a sip.

"When you have finished, you should lie down and get some rest."

"I am not a baby that needs to be told what to do," she fired at him, the temptation of hate lurking in her eyes.

"No, you are not," he said. "I'll be back this evening, your highness. Rest well," he said, retreating and locking the door.

Taleon returned that evening with a tray in hand. He knocked to see if she was awake.

"Come in," she answered.

He unlocked the door and entered.

She was sitting at the far corner of her room looking over the mountains and valleys that surrounded her. Twilight was just creeping into the sky and the rosy hue of day was fading on the far horizon behind a mountain.

"How did you rest, your highness?"

"Well," she answered briefly, not deigning to turn around.

"Cook sent up stew for you. Figured it would be easier if you didn't have to cut anything up."

"Would you tell him thank you for me," she said, speaking over her shoulder.

"He also said you'd like this dark stick of something. Why, I can't imagine," he said trying to tease a reaction from her, other than bland hate.

"You don't have to imagine it if you don't want to. But I shall," she said, rising from her chair.

"How is the pain?"

"Not too bad. It's not throbbing anymore, at least—though it still hurts. How long will it be like this?"

"Give it a few days."

"Days?" she whined.

"A week. Then we'll see how well it is healing. It is your left thumb and your thumb gets used a lot. We want to makes sure it is fully healed before we take out the stitches."

"I don't think I will ever understand: why you put more holes in people to make them all better."

Taleon couldn't help his laugh. "I am not sure why either, but it works. Can I look at it to see how it is coming along?"

"I guess," she said with a shrug.

He took her hand and unwrapped the bandage. "It looks good. I don't think we run the risk of anything, but we want to make sure it heals well so it won't leave much of a scar."

"A scar?"

"Sorry; it happens with things like this."

A pout grew on her lips.

"There is no need to cry. Almost everyone has scars and just because you are a princess doesn't mean you get to escape it. It'll be so thin no one will notice and eventually you'll forget that it is even there, I promise. Sometimes they completely disappear, too," he said with a hopeful nod.

"Do you think mine will?"

"Only time will tell."

Unexpectedly Cassandra looked up into his face and asked, "When do you think King Aric will return?"

"I don't know. Why?"

"I had a question I wanted to ask him."

"What is it?"

"It's a question for him, not you."

"Of course. How is your pain?"

"It's coming back again."

"I'll bring some tea when I come to pick up your tray, your highness," he said, opening the door to take his leave.

"Thank you, Taleon."

He smiled. *She is learning her manners and it makes her almost charming.*

As he left, Taleon locked the door.

Chapter 14

The next morning Alexandra braided her hair, barricading herself at the far window waiting for Taleon to make his appearance. She wasn't going down to breakfast this morning even if that meant she had to go without it.

There was a knock. She knew it was Taleon, but hesitated a moment before answering.

"Come in."

"Good morning, your highness. Are you ready for breakfast?"

"I don't wish to go down to breakfast this morning."

"Because...?" said Taleon with raised eyebrows, tilting his head to one side.

Not finding the right words for her explanation, she held up her thumb. "I don't want to answer questions and eating with it might be rather awkward."

"That is understandable. I'll bring breakfast up to you. Anything in particular that you would like?"

"Nothing I can think of," she said, holding back a smile.

With a nod, he left.

That was easy. Maybe he is finally coming around to seeing things my way. He is even calling me your highness. It feels good to have him know who I am. A princess the daughter of Serena Francis Anne Delenamore, but who is my father? Aric or Archibald, kings of Chambria—to whom am I the rightful heir? Oh, I don't know anymore.

She laughed. That wasn't the problem. She was the rightful heir to both. But to whom did she owe her allegiance and love? Alexandra mulled over the question she had in her mind that she wanted to ask King Aric. *What was my mother like?*

Yes, she wanted to know. *I want to compare stories of my mother with the few that Archi...father has told me. I must remain strong. They are just telling you stories, Alexandra, stories of—of horror and misery so that you will feel sympathetic and believe them. You can't believe them. You can't; they are just stories. Could the stories be true, and, if they are, am I being dull and stupid not to believe them? Oh, Alexandra, you are not wrong. You are not. If you are...?*

Oh, if you are, you are nothing but a lie. Thirteen years of your life will have been worthless, taken away and destroyed right before your very eyes and you let it happen. You stood by and let your people be destroyed—their livelihoods, their homes, their very existence. And you did nothing about it. That is, if they are right, which they are not. Oh, I hope to God they are not.

Alexandra was still mulling over this quandary when Taleon reentered.

"Will I have to help you today?" she asked rising.

"No, a few days' rest might do you some good."

"I would like that."

"Good, then we need say no more, your highness. Good day."

"Good day, Taleon."

With a delighted sigh, she ate her breakfast. A whole day to herself. What should she do with it? Then again, what was there to do with it? At least there would be no one asking her to sit in a corner in an out-of-the-way place or do errands that weren't fit for a princess. She would run no risk of slitting her finger on something sharp or comforting a crying baby or witnessing things she didn't want to see. Best of all, it would be a day without Taleon.

Alexandra waited for the morning to speed by to the noon meal, but it seemed to take forever. She toyed with the threads in the work basket, arranging them, then, dissatisfied with that, she rearranged it again. Disgusted, she played with it on the edge of the table until it tipped and the thread fell on the floor. The spools went spinning, dancing, and rolling in every direction. She scrambled to catch all of them before they disappeared. Next, a good deal of time was spent rewinding the spools, untying tiny knots, and arranging them. Finally, it was done to her satisfaction.

Taleon should come any time now. But no, the morning dragged perceptibly on for hours. Every sound of feet that went by made her heart leap with hope and expectation, but no. It was not Taleon coming to visit her in her prison. Well, it wasn't really a prison, but it was beginning to feel like one.

Time ticked by terribly slowly, and she was happy to hear Taleon's knock.

"Come in."

Taleon entered. "How was your morning?"

"Nice and quiet."

"I suppose you won't want to come with me this afternoon then, will you?"

"Not really; why?"

"Brendan was crying this morning. I had to quiet him. No one else could do it. I think he was crying for you."

"Don't tease me, Taleon. Why would he cry for me?"

"I don't know. Maybe because you played with him yesterday."

"That doesn't make sense. He is just a baby."

Taleon gave her a cryptic look that could have said about a thousand different things but probably only meant one and that one she couldn't figure out.

"How is your thumb?"

"I don't know. It still hurts, but it isn't throbbing like it was yesterday."

"Can I see it?"

"If you must," she said, holding out her hand.

With a quick hand, he unwrapped her thumb and turned it to see it in better lighting. He took his time and Alexandra found the question coming to her lips even though she had forbidden it.

"Do you really think Brendan was crying for me?"

"Hmm?" asked Taleon, looking up at her. "What did you say?"

Alexandra bit her lip, annoyed that she had to repeat the question.

"I am pretty sure he was."

"How is Edith?"

"Her cough hasn't seemed to get any worse, but she doesn't seem to be getting any better. We are thinking of moving her to a small quiet room just for herself and Brendan. She could use the privacy and the rest it would give her. With a life as difficult as hers, I know she could use it."

"Do you know her story?"

"No, but I know enough of what goes on in the valley to guess."

"What do you guess her life was like?"

"That isn't for me to tell you. Besides, you wouldn't want to hear it from me, and I doubt that you would actually believe me if I told you."

"I would."

"You haven't believed anything I have said about the valley or King Aric. Why would you believe me now?"

Alexandra blushed. It was true, but he didn't need to say it that way. She pulled her hand from his and walked away.

"Walking away won't make it any less true, you know. The truth is the truth."

"The truth is whatever you want it to be," she fired back.

"Is that what you believe?" asked Taleon, his eyes narrowing with questions.

"I—I don't know."

"So the truth is whatever you want it to be. So I can say the sky is pink, but it doesn't make it pink."

"It is at sunset," she answered almost coyly, knowing she was tempting Taleon's patience while grabbing at straws to save herself.

Taleon's jaw was fighting between laughter and outright anger at her pointless and futile but also true answer. *The sky at times is pink at sunset.* He let out a sigh. "True, but if I said the sky was pink all of the time that wouldn't make it true."

"Maybe you are looking at it through a pane of glass that is pink and that is all you see."

"But does it make it true?"

"It's true to them."

Taleon's mouth twitched. "But is it really true? What color is the sky?"

"Blue."

"Do you know that for yourself or just because that is what everyone has told you?"

"I know it is a fact."

"Well then, maybe it is time you take off your rose-colored glasses and saw the rest of the world the way you see the sky: the way it really is."

"I do see the way it is. Everything is quite clear to me, Taleon."

"I think it is quite clouded by King Archibald's view."

"It isn't. Now go away."

"Why?" he asked, stepping closer.

"Because I say so."

"Would you care to give some clarity to that?"

"No. I am a princess. I don't need to give you clarity on anything."

"Is that the way it was in the valley? Your Uncle Archibald never had to give you clarity for his actions?"

"I never doubted his wisdom."

"You followed him blindly and he took advantage of that."

"He did nothing of the sort. My father loves and cares for me. That is more than anyone up here on this forsaken mountain does."

"You are greatly mistaken. There is a man who has dedicated his whole life to loving and protecting you and you wouldn't even speak to him, much less own that he was something to you once. He was, wasn't he? Somewhere deep inside you know something—something you aren't telling me or anyone else, maybe not even yourself. If you don't listen to it, it will eat your body and soul. Live in torment if you wish. Just don't be blind to the fact that some people have risked their lives trying to save you."

"Go away!"

Taleon looked at her challengingly, his eyes piercing and intense.

She was a princess. She would not back down. She wouldn't. Alexandra couldn't help it. Turning with a sob, she broke into tears and sank into a chair.

The door closed, a few seconds later it opened again. "I almost forgot—for your mouse." Taleon set down a small crate and closed the door.

This was too much to take in one day. Running across her room Alexandra flung herself onto her bed. Her thumb throbbed as she landed on her hands—just one more good reason to cry. Overwhelmed, she buried herself beneath the pillows.

Why did he have to be so cruel? Why did he have to pierce so closely to her burning, throbbing, breaking heart? Why? Alexandra kicked her feet against the bed in rage, wishing she could be kicking Taleon instead. Exhausted from her vexed tears and thoughts she drifted off into deep sleep.

It was dusk when she awoke and emerged from her pillow haven. She glanced around. A fire was lit in the grate, a fresh tray of food had been brought up, and her midday meal was gone.

Getting out of bed she felt something brush against her leg. Alexandra screamed and jumped back onto her bed. A moment later something jumped up beside her and, purring it rubbed itself against her.

"Oh, it is just the cat. The cat I don't need. You must be hungry, and you won't find anything to eat here in my room. There are no mice. Should we see what Taleon left me?"

Picking tidbits from the tray, she fed the cat who sat patiently at her feet waving its tail back and forth with an elegant swish that curled at the tip.

Chapter 15

The next three days passed slowly and icily between her and Taleon. He would not speak to her and Alexandra was dying for something, no someone, to speak to. She had tried to talk with the cat, but it seemed more interested in stalking the room for non-existent mice than listening to her. It was the morning of the fourth day when Taleon brought her tray in that she dared to speak.

"Taleon. Won't you let me come with you today?"

Taleon looked at her blankly. "You want to come?"

"It is getting very dull in my room and I think I could take off the bandage so people wouldn't ask me questions."

"Edith has asked for you. She has been moved to a different room. I suppose after breakfast I could take you to see her if you wish."

"Oh I would," she said, jumping at the opportunity to escape her room, her thoughts, and the things that haunted her existence in it—one of which being the all too amiable and elusive cat.

"Be ready after breakfast, and leave the bandage on. We don't want to expose it to anything."

Alexandra nodded obediently, too excited about escaping to really care what she had to do to get out.

In a little while Taleon knocked on her door.

"Come in," she answered.

"Ready?" asked Taleon shortly.

"Yes," she said, rising to her feet.

He nodded with his head for her to come out the door and she followed his instruction. They walked silently—the kind of silence that is irritating. It had been eating at Alexandra every day that he didn't really bothered to speak to her but silently went through all the tasks required without a word.

She stopped in the hallway. "Why won't you speak to me, Taleon? You have hardly said ten words to me in the last three days."

Taleon turned and looked at her with his blue-green eyes searching her face, his brow drawn together. "Maybe it is because I don't know what to say to you anymore," he said in a voice just above a whisper.

The words struck her. "Why not?"

His eyes were still searching her face. "You just don't get it, do you?"

"Get what?"

Taleon shook his head and kept walking. In a few minutes they reached a small room and Taleon opened the door.

"Edith is in here," he said. After she entered, he closed the door.

Looking around the small room, she noticed the care that had been taken to make it lovely. Brendan squealed and crawled his way to Alexandra's side. Pulling himself up on her skirt, he held one hand out, asking to be picked up.

Gathering Brendan up, she gently kissed his cheek and buried her face beside his tiny shoulder.

"At least you like me no matter what I believe."

"Alexandra, so you have come to see me. Come here; sit by me." sighed Edith happily.

Alexandra did so, swinging Brendan back and forth on her knees.

For a long time they were silent. Then Edith broke the quiet.

"I don't know why. Ever since I met you I have felt I was to tell you my story. It's not something I ever wanted to tell anyone, but...I want to tell you." Alexandra felt the thin transparent hand slip into her own.

"In the valley, there is a secret trail that leads to the safety of Raven Castle. Did you use it to come here?"

"No."

"Have you heard of it?"

Alexandra shook her head.

"Even though Chambria is surrounded on all sides by other nations, there is one way to reach them all safely. It is through Raven Castle. Only a few make it through. King Archibald has so many of the secret trails under his control now that it is hard to come here. Once you are here, you may go anywhere you wish. My father was a guide for the trail. He made many successful trips, then one day one of King Archibald's men posed as an abused citizen and asked for guidance to Raven Castle. They suspected my father was a guide, but they had never been able to catch him. It was to be my father's last time. He knew that we were being watched and he wanted to take us all to safety. We were all on the trail with him. The man betrayed us and my family was ambushed. They killed my father, mother, and brothers, but kept me alive."

"Why?" she whispered, as a shiver ran through her.

"You certainly are a sheltered thing, aren't you?"

Alexandra squirmed slightly.

"King Archibald wants to change the people's minds. So he has single girls, marry his soldiers—staunch believers in his cause, men who carry out his plans. He believes this will change their minds, if not we will suffer the consequences. Once a woman has a child she will do anything to keep them safe, even stay in hell. I was one of the rare and blessed girls. The soldier who married me was beginning to doubt. When he found out that we were going to have a child of our own, he decided it was time to leave Chambria. He knew that his superiors were doubting his loyalty. They were testing him, and though he hadn't failed, he didn't want to wait until he had do something he couldn't live with. We decided to run while we still had a chance.

"We didn't want to leave each other, but we both knew our chances would be better if we split our ways. Our meeting place was set halfway to Raven Castle. I arrived safely and waited for him on the ridge. He arrived at the appointed place. I was getting ready to scramble down to greet him, when soldiers poured from the forest. I don't know where they came from. I watched helplessly as they took him. They slew him before my very eyes. I know he saw me. We both were silent, for Brendan's sake."

Edith's eyes were closed and tears slid from beneath her eyelashes down her cheeks, soaking her pillow.

"I was too ill to move from where I was hiding. I don't know how long I stayed there. Everything became a vague blur. When I was well enough to remember anything, I discovered myself in a forester's cottage with his wife and family. He had found me and brought me home. By the time I was well enough to be on my own with Brendan, bad weather was coming, so we stayed the winter with them. Soldiers found the cottage. Brendan and I had gone out for a walk and we saw it all happen before our very eyes. They had tracked a fleeing family to the forester's cottage. It wasn't our fault, but Brendan and I had to flee for our lives and hide among the woods for several weeks before we finally reached Raven Castle.

"I know they took the forester's daughter. She is probably wed to a soldier by now, and I pray her fortune is better than mine. How I long for this war to be over. There is no battle, but we all fight its cause. King Archibald will torture the people's lives, if only to torture King Aric's heart and the people into submission. We won't give up, will we, Alexandra?" she said with that wan smile, tears still falling from her sad grey eyes.

"No," whispered Alexandra under her breath, too choked to say anything else. She lowered her head to hide the thoughts whizzing through her brain with lightning quick stabs at everything she had ever known. Brendan had curled up in her lap and now was sleeping. She kissed his temple and gathered him close in her arms. She glanced at Edith who was watching her gently.

"Thank you for telling me your story."

"I don't know why, I just knew I had to tell you. It feels good to have someone else know."

Alexandra nodded. She wondered what it would be like to tell someone her own horrible dream about King Aric and have them understand and tell her what it all meant. She wanted her mother desperately—oh so desperately.

"I don't mean to be rude, but I need my rest now. If you would give me Brendan..."

Gently she laid him beside Edith, watching how tenderly she cared for him. It was too much. Rising, she controlled her steps, making them quiet, and softly closed the door behind her. There was so much going on in her heart.

Walking, she tried to sort through her thoughts. She heard the girls she had eaten breakfast with a few days before, sitting in a large group sewing and talking.

"Have you heard of the new law King Archibald has made? Every farmer is to give half his crops to him. Half. Can you imagine! What will they live on this winter?"

"I don't know."

"King Aric won't let them starve."

"I know, but even with everything that comes from the mine, he can't possibly buy enough food. With the drought, half of their crops will hardly leave the people with anything at all."

"I can't believe that King Archibald would make such a decree," spoke up Alexandra.

"It's hard to believe he is so cruel, isn't it? What on earth is that man made of to make up such laws?" replied one girl.

"How do you know that he made up the law? How do you know it's not just his soldiers?"

"Because it goes out by royal decree. Royal decree means it comes from the king."

"Do you really think he is as bad as you all say he is?"

The girls looked at each other, baffled by this girl they thought to be one of their own. "Why? Don't you?"

"Not really. I just think you might all be wrong about him. Maybe it is because his wife was killed. Wouldn't you be angry with the people that sided with the rebels responsible for killing your wife? Don't you think he would have the right to be just a little angry with them and if they didn't respond, perhaps a little harsh?"

The girls looked around at one another, disturbed and unsure of what to say or do.

"Are you all right?" asked one girl, rising and inching very slowly towards her.

"I just think that you are all wrong about him. Wrong. You hear me, wrong."

There was a vice-like grip on her shoulder.

"Come with me, please, *Alexandra*," Taleon whispered between his teeth. Then he turned to the girls. "Sorry about this. I am afraid she hit her head pretty hard. It will pass, though." Then he uttered under his breath, "I hope." He smiled. "Excuse us please," he said.

Taleon moved his grip to her arm and propelled her before him down a long maze of corridors to the far side of the castle that seemed empty. Alexandra found herself turned to face Taleon, her back against the wall, his hands resting on either side of her shoulders.

His steady blue-green eyes frightened her. There was no anger in them, only a steady gaze that made her heart jump. The lump in her throat rose and her mouth went completely dry. Nervously she licked her lips, then began to giggle.

It wasn't really funny, but she couldn't help it.

Taleon's face became graver and she giggled harder.

His eyes became sad. "Is this funny to you, Cassandra?"

"No." She barely managed not to giggle.

"Is that all you think we are? A game you can play—something to laugh at. Is that what we are?"

The pain that showed in his eyes caused her heart to twinge as she answered. "No. I don't."

"Then prove it to me?"

For a long moment she paused, "I can't, Taleon."

"Just who do you think you are? Don't you think that these people have been through enough without you stirring up their anger; claiming that Archibald the impostor is king? Do you know what they would do to you? Do you have the slightest clue what you just did? The slightest clue!"

Alexandra burst into tears. "I—I just wanted to talk to them. They all have the wrong idea about my father."

"You have the wrong idea about your father. He has been kind and thoughtful and loving to you and you go and try to stab him behind his back. I am tired of getting you out of situations. You need to sit down and think about what you have said and what is really going on here. Stop thinking about yourself! Think about the people who need your help!"

"How dare you speak to me like that! I am a princess."

"You aren't a princess. You are a pain and until you start acting like a princess, I will not give you the honor of that address. You will have to earn it from me."

Alexandra's jaw dropped. *No one has ever dared speak to me like that before.*

"Stop talking to them and start listening. Maybe you will learn something."

"I just think if my father knew what was going on, he wouldn't be so harsh. I am sure he wouldn't."

"You really think so?" said Taleon, stepping closer.

"I—I don't know." The world seemed to swirl around her, all shouting different things. What should she really believe? She almost didn't care anymore.

"I want you to meet someone," he said, taking her hand.

After a rather long jaunt to the other side of the castle, they entered a small room where a woman sat pounding wheat into flour.

A shock reverberated through Alexandra. The woman who sat before her was familiar—a face she had never dreamed in her life that she would see again: her old dear beloved nurse. "Rita! What are you doing here?" exclaimed Alexandra, rushing forward. Then she stopped as the woman turned her head. "Why are your eyes closed?"

"Taleon. Did you have to bring the child here?" the woman asked, her face becoming drawn with displeasure.

"I have been trying to tell her, but I don't know what else to say."

"Come here, Cassandra."

Alexandra took a step back, startled. "Why does everyone call me Cassandra? You used to call me Alexandra and now everyone here calls me Cassandra; why?"

"Child, come here," she said, patting her knee. Slowly Alexandra approached and knelt beside the woman whom she had known so many, many years ago. Rita laid her hand on Alexandra's head. A small smile softened her features.

"You are very much like your mother. I can feel it." She took a long breath before continuing. "Your name is Cassandra, child. It has been since the day you were born and you were laid in my arms only a few minutes old. Princess Cassandra. Your uncle Archibald ordered everyone to call you Alexandra under severe penalty."

"Are you quite sure about that?"

"As sure as I know the sun rises and sets even though I can't see it. I was your mother's nursemaid and yours until Archibald had Judith take over."

"Why did you leave me? You were there one day and gone the next. Father said you were taken ill and then later he told me you had died."

"Still calling him father?"

"What else am I supposed to call him?"

"He is not your father, Cassandra."

"Stop it! Everyone keeps saying that and I don't want to believe it!" she said, fighting back tears.

"It doesn't matter if you want to believe it, Cassie; it is the truth. You remember the stories I used to tell you?"

Alexandra nodded, then, realizing the woman had not yet opened her eyes, said, "Yes, I loved those stories about my mother."

"Your uncle came in one night while I was telling one. I didn't see him. When you were quite asleep, I called you Cassandra. I never wanted you to forget who you really were. I lamented quietly, but aloud, that your parents weren't there. Next thing I knew, there was a dagger in my back and he was telling me to leave silently or be murdered right then and there. I didn't wish to wake you and scar your young mind with such a memory, so I left quietly."

"Why didn't you come back? Why won't you look at me?"

"Cassandra, I could not come back. He blinded me."

"No! He did not," gasped Alexandra, refusing to believe it. It could not be true; it was not true.

"Yes, Cassandra, your uncle took me out into the courtyard and made me blind, then turned me out into the streets as a warning."

"No. He did not; he couldn't have."

"Cassandra, I saw him do it with my own eyes. He took my sight with his own hands. Your uncle Archibald is not the man you want to believe he is. Cassandra." Rita's hands slipped to Alexandra's shoulders. "You have grown tall. But you must also grow in so many other ways. Let go of those childish fears that you are holding onto and accept the truth. You know it is true; I can hear it in your voice. Let go."

Alexandra bolted. Losing herself in the maze of corridors and stairways, she by chance found her room. She slammed the door shut, wishing she had the keys to keep everyone out. All of this was too much to take. Going to the furthest corner of her room, she slid down against the wall. She buried her face in her knees, gasping for air in an attempt to hold back the tears.

In a few minutes her door creaked open. It was Taleon's soft steps coming toward her. She wanted to scream.

"Go away," she murmured.

Taleon sighed. "You say that an awful lot, you know."

"Well it's true. I want you to go away. Please leave me be."

"I will leave you alone if you let me show you this one thing.."

Alexandra peered out from behind her folded arms. "One thing?"

"I promise you, and then we will leave it alone. Please, Cassandra," he said, offering her his hand.

Alexandra took his hand reluctantly and he pulled her to her feet. Taking her elbow, he led her to the table where he had placed a large book.

The front showed signs of unusual wear. Most of the page edges were dark brown, scars, a testament of survival.

"This book was saved from a fire that your...King Archibald had ordered in the valley."

Opening the book, he flipped through to a marked page. "There," he said, pointing to a certain passage. "Start reading here."

"What is it?" she asked, not really looking at the page.

"Read it for yourself. There it is right in front of you—proof of who we are. It was written by the court historian."

Alexandra looked at the page. It made no sense to her.

"Read it," urged Taleon.

Alexandra lowered her eyes to the floor and they filled with tears. "I can't read. My father wouldn't allow it."

Taleon spun her to face himself, lifting her chin so her eyes met his.

"You can't read? A woman like you, of your rank, can't read?"

"No," she answered, shame filling her as she looked away.

"Can you see how desperately he wanted to keep you in the dark? I can read it to you, but you may never know if it was the truth. I could easily be making it up as well as reading it. Do you even know your letters?"

"I know them and a few small words, but not many, not enough to read anything."

Taleon took her hand beneath his. Extending her pointer finger, he placed it on the page.

"You still won't know if I am making it up, but it is worth a try." Taking a deep breath, he started.

While King Aric was away at war, he was overthrown by his younger brother Prince Archibald. Retuning to Chambria he was surprised to find that Prince Archibald sat on the throne, and had declared war against him. King Aric's wife, Queen Serena, was slain as she tried to take their daughter Cassandra to safety in King Aric's ranks. Defeated, but not conquered, believing that his wife and child were dead, King Aric moved his forces into the unsecured stronghold of Raven Castle...

Alexandra watched as the words passed before her fingertips. Memories were bursting from the past.

She pulled her hand away. "Stop it, stop reading!"

"What is it, Cassandra?"

She turned away, holding back her tears. "I don't know!" Alexandra cried defiantly, trying to shut out the feelings that were bursting on her, the memories that spoke the truth that she wanted to defy.

He touched her arm.

She curled away from Taleon.

"No! I hate it! I can't! I won't!"

"Cassandra?"

"If I do...If I do. That means everything I have lived, loved, and believed for the last thirteen years of my life has been a lie, Taleon. All of it a lie. I can't be what everyone wants me to be; I don't have it in me. I don't. I can't be what everyone needs me to be. I look into those people's faces, and I know the whole world rests on my shoulders if I accept what you are saying. Down in the valley, they were not the problem..."

There was a long pause as she took a deep breath, tears filling her eyes.

"It was *me*."

"You understand?" he said, trying to keep the excitement out of his voice.

"I have understood for a very long time. I have tried not to. I don't want to understand everything. Everything that my uncle has put my country through—the torture, the agony, the pain of these people is his fault and I have stood by and let it happen. I remember everything. I was an idiot. I am..." She stopped. *What did I just say? Of all people to tell, why did it have to be Taleon? Why!*

He stood there, looking at her half-expectant, half-puzzled. "Did you hear what you just said?"

"I know what I just said. Now go away. I don't want to talk to you." Cassandra turned to run, but he caught her wrist. She was torn. Did she fight him and run away, or stay and listen to what he had to say? She was tired of fighting, tired of trying to make the world seem perfect, but if she didn't, what would happen? What would change?

"Cassandra." He said her name softly.

She closed her eyes, trying to fight. She had already conceded so much to him. To admit more would be torture.

"What is it you remember? Tell me."

"Everything."

There was a long pause. She fought back the words, but they came anyway. They were dying to escape, to help her be set free.

"My mother didn't die shielding me from a rebel sword. I was torn away from her arms by Uncle Archibald. I cried for her; I screamed; I threw a fit in his arms, but he wouldn't let me go. I cried until I didn't have any tears. He wouldn't let me go until I called him father. I remember. I remember! Now you are going to hate me?"

"Why would I do that?" he asked, closing the wide distance she was keeping between them, still wanting him to go away.

"Because I hate myself. I am so, so..." She burst into uncontrollable tears.

Taleon pulled her close. Cassandra was too confused and frustrated to fight him.

"It's all right, Cassandra."

"No it's not. I have been so stupid."

"Just think how happy your father will be when he returns."

"He'll hate me for it."

"Why would he do a thing like that?"

"Because he'll be ashamed."

"I don't think so."

"I have been a fool. An unforgivable fool."

Taleon lifted her chin to look into his gently smiling face. "I think you will be the only person who can't forgive yourself. Your father is dying to love you. I don't think he'll care a bit as long as you know the truth and accept it."

"But Taleon…I've made a huge mistake of everything."

He laid a finger over her mouth. "Shh. There is nothing that can't be fixed."

"How can you be so forgiving?"

Taleon's face softened. The smile disappeared. "If you could see the tortured look in your eyes, even you could forgive yourself."

She pulled away. "Will he forgive me?"

"He is your father, Cassandra."

"Taleon," she said, turning to him, her arms wrapped tightly around herself. "That means nothing to me. Uncle Archibald is the only father I have really ever known and had I done something like this to him, I would be close to dead."

"He will love you, Cassandra. He loves you now more than anything in the world. He has waited thirteen years for you to come home."

Cassandra burst into tears. "I don't deserve it. I don't."

"Someone who has lived in the house of a tyrant for most of their life deserves all the love they can find."

"Oh, Taleon, how can you?"

Taleon smiled at her. "You finally get it."

Chapter 16

Cassandra looked up at Taleon. Her whole world was changed in an instant and she wasn't sure how she felt about it.

"What is going to happen now?"

"Well, I don't need this anymore," he said, producing the key from his pocket. "So now it is yours."

"Are you sure you can trust me?"

He narrowed his eyes and looked her over. "I'll risk it, because I think I can. If you break it, well, then you'll have worse things than just a locked door to worry about," he said, placing it in her hand.

"Thank you."

"Would you like a tour of the castle? So I can stop taking you in circles."

"You have been taking me in circles?"

Taleon nodded.

"Why on earth?"

"Just in case. It took me a lot longer to do anything, but the castle has to be protected because of the people in it. I couldn't risk you escaping your room and hiding. If I kept you confused, the more likely it was that you wouldn't try anything on your own."

"You really didn't trust me, did you?"

Taleon laughed. "Maybe, maybe not."

"If you don't mind, I would like to take a rest for a while. Everything is so—" she shook her head.

"I understand. Rest well, Cassandra," he said, leaving.

Cassandra smiled. There was no sound of the door locking. She liked her name. Going to the door, she locked it. She wanted to be utterly alone—to let the reality sink in.

Going over to the book that Taleon had left, her finger traced over the words. Doubt rose in her heart. What if he was just lying? Her hand fell over her mother's name. That one she knew. The memory of

Archibald seizing her from her mother washed over her powerfully, sending a shiver up her spine.

Raven Castle is where I belong. King Aric is my Pappa. She started crying. *He is my Pappa; he is my Pappa,* she repeated over and over again, making her heart thump in her chest. Going to the window, she leaned out and breathed deeply. She threw back her head and laughed.

"I am Cassandra, the daughter of King Aric of Chambria," she shouted to the mountains across from her. Then she laughed with bubbling joy. Pulling back into her room she twirled round and round on her toes across the floor. Spreading her arms out, she felt as if she could fly. When she stopped, the cat brushed against her legs with a purr. She scooped it up and held it out before her.

"I am free, kitty. Free." And she whirled back across the room.

To say the least the feline was not fond of this treatment and yowled.

"Well, since I am free, I don't have to keep you any more, do I? Taleon no longer controls what comes in and out of my room."

She unlocked the door and shoed the kitty out, who left with a joyful meow and flaunted its tail in the air. Just as she was about to close the door, a man came around the corner. She faintly recognized him as one of the first faces she had seen upon her arrival. He had been sitting around the fire. His armor and clothing, though not fine, bore the symbol on his left shoulder said that he was a man of rank.

He bowed at the sight of her. "Princess Cassandra."

"My Lord?" she answered with a nod of her head.

"Taleon told me of your choice."

"Oh," she said, with a blush rising on her cheeks. She had been so foolish, she really didn't want anyone else to know, but of course everyone would have to eventually.

"I wanted to say welcome to Raven Castle."

"Thank you," she said, opening the door a little wider. "May I ask who has honored me so?"

"I am Lord Keenan."

"It is a pleasure to meet you, Lord Keenan."

"Likewise your highness," he said with a bow, and turned to leave.

"Lord Keenan."

"Yes, your highness."

"Have you heard from my Pappa lately? Is there any news of where he is or when he may return?"

Keenan shook his head. "We hear very little from your father while he is in the valley. It is for his own safety as well as those whom he helps. The last thing we want is Archibald to get his hands on information that we don't want him to have."

"Of course. I should have thought of that."

"Are you eager to see him?"

Cassandra nodded. She could feel her eyes light up at the thought of him. It excited her.

"Would you care to go for a walk, your highness?"

"I would like that very much, I think."

"Come then." And he offered her his arm.

Finding her arm tucked safely under his, her hand resting on his chainmail, his sword ready at his side, gave her a comfortable feeling she was safe here, protected, and maybe eventually she could be loved. It was so different from her last encounter in the valley, a carriage ride with the Imposter. The thought sent a shiver up her spine. That had been an unpleasant ordeal.

"How long have you known my father?"

"Almost my whole life. He and I were boys together."

"What was he like?"

"Your father was a gentle man and a good sport. He never minded losing as long as everyone did their best. He was an amazing man even then."

Shyly she looked up at him, wanting to ask a question but not daring.

He looked down into her face and laughed. "You want to know what Archibald was as a young man?"

Cassandra laughed and blushed. "Yes, I would like to know what you thought of him."

"Well, when he wasn't winning, he was nowhere to be found. He had to be the best at it or he wasn't around at all."

"Why did he turn on my Pappa?"

"No one really knows. All seemed to be going well, but when your father left for war, everything changed. He amassed a second army "just in case" and when we returned we found ourselves attacked by our own flag. Then he raised his new standard, and we knew we were at war with our own people." He seemed to shiver at the memory.

"Keenan? Keenan! There you are; I have been looking for you everywhere. Your opinion is wanted."

"May I leave you here, your highness?" asked Lord Keenan before releasing her arm.

"Yes, you may. Thank you so much, Lord Keenan."

"It was my pleasure, your highness." And with a slight bow, he left.

Cassandra looked about her. He had taken her to the garden. The flowers were beautiful, and, after the turmoil of the day, it was wonderful to be in a place of beauty. She wandered happily and aimlessly about the garden, until she came into a sunny corner where a woman sat sewing a thing of glory: King Aric's standard, the flag of Chambria.

The woman dropped the needle and let out a sound of frustration.

"What is the matter?" asked Cassandra, coming to the woman's side.

"My eyes aren't what they used to be. I just can't seem to stitch this right. It is King Aric's battle standard, and I can't sew like I used to. My fingers just won't do what I want."

"May I please?"

"Can you sew finely?"

"Yes, I can."

"Well, I guess you can give it a try," said the woman, surrendering to her the needle.

In a moment, Cassandra had undone the tangle and had stitched neatly through the problem and continued on.

"You sew so well. Who taught you?"

"My nurse."

"Nurse?"

Cassandra nodded.

"So you are a noble?"

"You might say that," said Cassandra with a blush, looking down at her clothes. There was nothing about her garments to distinguish her from a person of any level.

"Who is your father?"

Cassandra bit her lip. "His name is Aric."

"King Aric?"

Cassandra nodded, happy to claim such a precious man as her father. *But can I live up to his name? Can I make him proud? Will he truly forgive me for my stubborn, stupid, willful disbelief?*

"Oh, your highness, I should do this; it is…"

"Please," interrupted Cassandra, "Allow me to do this for my Pappa. It would please me very much if you could trust this beneath my hand."

"I can trust it beneath your hands, your highness, but do you mind such work?"

"Not in the least; I am quite used to it. I have missed it since I came up here."

The woman watched as the tiny straight careful stitches flew from Cassandra's fingers. "Well, it is obvious you don't need me to watch you sew this. If you don't mind, I'll sew something else."

"Oh, please do, and don't mind me."

For a while they sewed together mostly in silence, then the woman was called away.

It was strange to find relief in such work, but Cassandra found it eased the pain in her heart and strengthened her belief with every stitch. King Aric was her Pappa and somehow that was all that mattered in the world.

How will I tell him when he returns? Will he understand? Will he forgive me? Her heart fluttered in her chest. Did she dare hope for forgiveness and love all at once. He had been so willing to give it when they met the first time but to shut him out like that so cruelly— Cassandra realized how much her heart craved it.

Time passed quickly with her thoughts, and she felt a steady gaze looking at her. Timidly she glanced up.

It was Taleon leaning comfortably in the archway, a contented and pleased smile on his face.

"Well, isn't this a sight. One I thought I might never see."

Cassandra blushed and her eyes dropped back to her work. He came and sat beside her on the bench, watching her careful stitches intently.

"Stop staring."

"Why?"

"Because it is the way of it. You watch too long and too intently and I will make a mistake."

"Really, who says?"

"I don't know. I think it is some freak of nature."

Taleon threw back his head and laughed.

Cassandra looked at him for a moment. Taleon had never really laughed in her presence. She had been there almost three weeks and now, for the first time, she heard him laugh wholeheartedly. Cassandra decided she liked the sound of it and turned back to her sewing. Taleon continued to watch intently.

"There you made me do it. See?" she pointed to the queer uneven stitch.

Taleon leaned closer, looking over her shoulder at the misbehaving thread. "I don't see what is so bad about it."

"I do. It will have to come out and be done over again," she said, picking up the needle she had put down in her moment of frustration.

Taleon's hand over hers paused her attempt to remove the mistake. "Leave it, please."

"Why?"

"Nobody is perfect."

"This is my Pappa's standard."

Taleon swallowed before speaking. "I know, but when I am following this flag, I would like to know that that stitch was there."

"Why on earth would you want to be thinking of that?"

"Because it was the day King Aric got his daughter back."

Cassandra moved the needle and made a new stitch. "It's a good thing to remember."

Chapter 17

The next month passed quickly. Cassandra found herself slipping into the lifestyle of Raven Castle. For the first few weeks, she helped Taleon with the refugees until they were well enough to take care of themselves; or moved on into safer realms far from Archibald's grip but not too distant to be at the call of King Aric.

In the afternoons, she instructed young girls in fine sewing, from a pile of things to sew and mend. In the evenings, Taleon was helping her learn to read and she was progressing quickly. At last she was able to read books entirely on her own, Cassandra devoured everything she could get her hands on.

One day after Cassandra had just dismissed the little girls from sewing and was curled up reading a book when there was a knock at the door.

"Come in," she answered rather absentmindedly as she turned a page and continued reading the words in front of her.

"Cassandra?" It was Taleon's voice.

She looked up. The book dropped to the floor. Taleon was standing behind her father.

"Pappa!" she said, springing to her feet and running across the room.

He opened his arms to her and she hid her face against his doublet.

"Cassie!" he murmured in her ear and pressed a kiss into her hair.

"Oh Pappa. I—I am so..." she burst into tears. Her heart was full. She could feel his love. It was in his voice, in the tender way he wrapped his arms about her. It shone in his eyes.

"Shh...it's all right, Cassie. All is well now."

"But I have been such a...oh."

He gathered her into his arms and carried her to the seat she had just left by the window.

She wrapped her arms about his neck, her head resting on his chest. His arms were wrapped about her, holding her so close. There was so much to talk about.

Taleon watched her race across the room into her father's arms. King Aric had given her such affection that he…

He quietly walked out the door and closed it firmly. Just at that moment, a little girl came running around the corner.

"Oh hello," she said, pausing and looking up admiringly but slightly fearfully at Taleon.

"Do you need something?" he asked, dropping down to her level.

"I forgot my needle in there," she said shyly.

"Come," he said, offering her his hand. "I will make you another needle. Cassandra can't be disturbed just at this moment; she is talking with King Aric."

The little girl's eyes grew wide with wonderment and she placed her small hand in his. "Will you truly make me another?"

"Cross my heart," he said with a smile and they walked away. When he had made her a needle and she had gone off to finish her sewing with her little mates, Taleon sat whittling a scrap of wood—not really caring what he made out of it as long as it meant he would have to sharpen his blade later. He needed something to distract him.

"Taleon?"

His name being called made him perk up his head. "Yes," he answered blankly.

Keenan smiled and sat beside Taleon. "Making anything in particular?"

Taleon examined the mutilated piece of wood in his hand. "Fancy piece of kindling," he quipped with a smile.

Keenan chuckled under his breath. "How is the king?"

"Happy, and so is Cassandra."

"And you?"

"Quite well."

Keenan hummed an assent.

For a while they sat there in silence while Taleon whittled at his piece of wood. When he was frustrated, he dropped it and rose to his feet.

"Excuse me, my lord," he said with a slight nod of his head.

"She can't replace you, Taleon."

Taleon stopped and turned around.

"What?"

Keenan strode to his side. "She can't replace you. You still mean the world to him."

"But that world has always revolved around her."

"Maybe, but don't let her get in the way of doing your duty."

"She can't get in my way."

Keenan nodded. "I'll see you tonight at the table."

Taleon nodded and watched Keenan walk away, his own heart refusing to speak to him. There were too many more important things to think about just then anyway.

That evening he stood in the shadow of a pillar, his usual half-hidden spot, when his king and Cassandra entered. She was leaning on her father's arm and looking adoringly up at his face.

"Cassandra, this is my council: twelve members in all." He proceeded to introduce each by name and each council member nodded his reverence to her. She bowed her head in return, gracefully. Cassandra took the new challenge on with ease and a smile.

She is a born princess, Taleon thought, his eyes flickering around the room. *The men like her. It is good.*

In a few minutes she was seated in the alcove next to where he was sort of hiding. He was the council's page and often they would ask him questions or request his opinion.

For a long time they discussed the status of the kingdom: who was hurting, who needed help, those who could hold out.

"We need to make our move before the crops are harvested. Or at least what crops there will be to harvest. I don't want a long campaign, and the last thing I want is Archibald stocked for the winter while the people starve. It gives us three months to prepare the valley ready. We will need everything we've have to make it happen. Our forces are nearly the same size, but the terrors they wreak lends fear to their side. Have we heard anything from the sparrows in his court?"

"Not a word, but that is typical. They'll let us know if there is anything urgent. We can't afford to have either of them caught."

"Of course. What do the scouts in the valley have to say?"

Keenan pulled out a map of Chambria. "We know he has forces here, here, and here," he said, placing black pieces on the map.

"He is still holding that town hostage. They need us desperately and yet we can't get to them."

"What if we put our small army to work on them, your Majesty?"

The king's mouth twinged. "Taleon, Cassandra, come over here if you please."

Both came before him.

"I trust both of you. I want to know what you think." He moved the pieces around on the board, showing what was being suggested.

"What do you think?" asked the king, turning to them.

Cassandra looked up to Taleon, deferring to let him answer.

"Ladies first," Taleon admonished.

She sent him a glare before answering her father. "I know little of tactics, Father, but the action suggested seems better than no action at all."

The king smiled and turned to Taleon. "What do you think my lad?"

"I was wondering, sire, if this wouldn't be a better approach?" and he moved around the pieces.

Cassandra watched her father as he smiled at Taleon's ideas, placing a hand on his shoulder, and the other hand leaning on the table. He was listening intently to everything he had to say. She wished that she had been able to say something wise and interesting.

She listened to the conversation, trying to understand why this was all so important.

"We want to pressure them so that they move into one area. One stronghold is easier to take down than several scattered over the country."

"You are right, my lad. It is as you say. What do you think, my lords?" he said, turning to his council. They nodded in agreement. A few made additional suggestions, many of which were applied.

"Very well; we start our war."

There was a grave feeling in the room. Everyone understood the gravity of such a decision. They knew what it meant. It was time to fight for king and country.

Cassandra looked around the room, her heart pounding in her chest. Taleon and her father were looking at one another. A smile twitched at Taleon's mouth and he nodded. Her father patted him on the shoulder. Then his eyes shifted to Cassandra. They were grave and affectionate. This was the beginning of something wonderful and fearful, but which was the greater Cassandra didn't know.

Chapter 18

"Very well, we will move into action tomorrow. Cassandra, I suggest you retire. We have some things to discuss."

Cassandra felt baffled. She glanced at Taleon. He wasn't being asked to leave. She glanced around the room and realized it was her, they were going to discuss. Her jaw tightened.

"Good night Pappa. My lords." She glanced sideways at Taleon. *I don't want to wish him a good night, but if I don't that means he is ranked among the lords.* "Taleon," she added with a slight nod.

Hiding her wounded pride, she slipped out of the room quietly. She walked the hallways, thinking, wondering what Taleon would tell them all and blushing at so many of her rash words and actions.

"Why couldn't I have kept a civil tongue in my head?" She looked at her left thumb. The stitches were gone but a fine line still showed. Taleon and the doctor had sewn it up quite nicely. Cassandra decided to visit Edith and Brendan; they always put her in a good humor—especially Brendan.

She knocked on the door where they were staying.

"Come in," Edith invited.

As she entered, Brendan let out a squeal of joy and Cassandra scooped him up in her arms.

"How are you, my little Brendan?"

He babbled at her and she laughed in delight.

"What, shall you grow up and be someday, a statesman? I think you would make a very fine speaker."

"An honest man. Any living he makes with integrity will make me a happy mother."

Cassandra smiled. "Yes, your mother is quite right, but how are you, Edith?"

"Much better now that we are alone. When we first arrived, I was afraid I was going to die, leaving him behind motherless and fatherless.

117

Thankfully no, I praise God that He didn't see fit to take us both from him," she said, coming over to admire her son.

He flashed her his charming smile and garbled another babyish, almost plain-word, sentence.

"But how are you? Something seems to be on your heart."

"I should be happy since my father came today."

Edith smiled at the girl. "I hear a very large except in there."

"Father brought me to the council tonight and later dismissed me. I am pretty sure they are going to talk about some of the rash things I've said."

Edith laughed. "Is that all you are worried about? Them talking about you?"

"It is far more than that. I was so stupid and foolish when I first came here."

"How much did you talk about your father behind his back?"

Cassandra blushed. "Don't remind me," she groaned, then slowly told Edith the whole story.

"Well, you are a new convert. They will have to make sure it sticks before they trust you with too much information."

Cassandra nodded. *They already have entrusted me with a lot of information.*

"When you are royalty, there has to be something called secrets, and that you know plenty about, as is obvious by your own story."

"I can't believe how blind I was to my uncle's schemes. I should have known. I should have."

Edith took Brendan out of her arms and set him on the floor. She pulled Cassandra to a seat beside her and took her hands.

"You can't undo what your past has done to you, but you can change your future, and you aren't going to make a change until you look past what you have already done and let it go."

"But I…"

"But nothing. Cassandra, no one blames you but yourself, do you hear me?"

Cassandra looked away.

"The people forgive you. They know you were squeezed into his form like we all were. All you have to do is forgive yourself. That is the only thing holding you back. Your father forgives you; the people forgive you; what are you going to do about it?"

Cassandra studied the floor in earnest, her thoughts whirling around in her head. Brendan came and pulled himself up beside her, bouncing happily on his two wobbly legs.

How does one go about forgiving themself? Taleon's words ran through her head: "*If you could see the tortured look in your eyes you would forgive yourself.*" *Is that what it means to let it go? To not torture yourself and relive every moment?* She closed her eyes. *Just let it go. Let it go. It is the only way you will move on. You are needed here. You need to move on. Let it go, Cassandra, Let go.* She found herself smiling. It was another release. Unexpectedly Edith's arm slipped around her shoulder.

"You've got it now, don't you?"

"I hope so."

"Now remember. Sometimes it will come back; just keep forgiving yourself. It is the only way to conquer it."

Brendan let out a crow of delight and Cassandra slid to the floor. Time passed quickly with Edith and Brendan, and in a little while, Brendan's eyes were drooping shut as he tried to play.

"I best put this little fellow to bed. I'll see you soon, Cassandra?"

"Yes, soon," said Cassandra, knowing full well she had stayed her welcome and that Brendan wouldn't sleep as long as she was there.

She slipped into the night air and walked through the empty courtyard. Cassandra stopped and looked up at the moon hanging so brightly in the sky. In some ways it seemed so close that she could touch it; in other ways, it seemed so far away that no one could ever reach it. She walked on, staring at her feet, thinking.

"Your highness?" a voice asked in the dark.

"Yes," she asked, pricking up her head as she recognized the voice that had brought her there: Williamsen.

"How are you doing?" he asked, stepping out of the shadows.

"Well; and yourself?"

"Quite well, your highness. Are you glad to have your father home?"

"Yes."

"Do you know when he is leaving yet?"

"No, he hasn't told me."

"Are you sure? They didn't talk about it in the meeting at all?"

"No, they didn't. But how do you know about the meeting?" she said, getting a strange prickling up her spine

"Common knowledge."

"I see." Somehow it didn't calm her nerves.

"So what did they talk about tonight?"

"The meeting might be common knowledge, but what they discuss isn't, Willamsen."

"Taleon always tells me what they talk about, so you can too."

"I think I will leave Taleon to fill you in then. He is more capable than I."

"Your highness, you aren't going to hold the fact that I am the one who brought you up here against me, are you?"

"No, I am not."

"Then why won't you tell me?"

Willamsen was making her uncomfortable and flustered. "I just don't want to, all right."

"So you are mad at me."

"I am not."

"Then tell me."

"No."

"I'll leave you alone if you do."

"And you won't if I don't?"

"Exactly."

Cassandra never knew exactly how he had done it but he had her cornered with no escape.

"Willamsen. Stop it. I am not interested in discussing this with you any further." She pushed past him, but he caught her by the arm. For a moment they struggled before a voice broke in.

"That's enough."

Willamsen stopped at once, but Cassandra still had momentum and went stumbling forward. A moment later, Taleon caught her in his arms.

"You did well, Cassandra," he whispered.

"Well?"

"It was a test."

"A test?"

Taleon nodded.

"But I —" she glanced around. The upper balcony was filled with men scattered in the shadows—the men from the council. She looked down at the ground, holding her breath as well as her emotions. She had to think thoroughly before she took another breath. Some time passed.

"You can breathe, Cassandra."

"I know. I just don't know what to say."

"You don't have to say anything?"

"Will there be more things like this?" she asked glancing up into his eyes.

They gave no reply.

"Wrong question to ask, I guess," she sighed.

"I am sorry, Cassandra, but we had to know. I am the one who asked for it."

"You?" Cassandra looked up at him, pained. "Maybe you want to take the key back to my room?"

"Cassandra, it's not like that..."

"Good night, Taleon."

Silently she brushed passed him. Not for the world would she let him know by her steps how angry she was with him. After all, hadn't she said enough things to regret as it was? Why do something else she would regret?

Going to her room, she locked the door and went to bed—listening with hope for the sound, a knock. She desperately wanted to talk with her Pappa. After a long time, no knock came and she found she couldn't sleep with Taleon's unfinished sentence running in her head. She gave up on sleep. Pulling on her cloak, she went to walk along the castle walls. There she could think and breathe with ease.

Unexpectedly, she saw Taleon sitting on the castle wall. One leg dangling over the edge and the other wedging him firmly in the crenel of the battlement, he was staring down at the Capitol Chambria, deep in thought.

Carefully she walked past him and sat in the next crenel. For a while neither spoke.

"Taleon, what did you want to say to me that I didn't stay to listen to?"

There was a long pause. Not even the look of recognition crossed his face.

Cassandra wondered if she would have to repeat herself. He seemed fond of making her do that when she didn't particularly feel like it.

"It's not like that because we do trust you, but you need to know that you can't always trust everyone here. Raven Castle is a place of safety, but more than once we have had a spy disguise himself as a refugee and get up here. Just because you like someone or know them doesn't mean they are always on your side."

"I told Edith my story."

"You can trust Edith; she is one of us. It is just meant to keep you on your guard, to train you how to look for things. They won't all be as obvious as Willamsen."

"How will I know who I can trust and who I can't?"

"You'll figure it out."

"Can I trust you?"

Taleon smiled and for the first time looked at her, the answer in his eyes. "You did well tonight; you caught on fast. As Lord Gaveron would say, you have a good gut feeling."

Cassandra blushed and looked modestly down. It wasn't exactly a compliment, but then again it was. Taleon smiled and looked away, down at Chambria. Turning around, she leaned out on the wall, looking down on the city that seemed so small but was so large.

"Miss it?" he asked.

"A little, but I am not sure why. There is really nothing for me to miss down there."

"The people."

She looked down at the mountain spreading out below them, her mind racing over what had happened the last day she was there. The people were so needy. She glanced at Taleon who was lazily swinging his leg back and forth along the outside of the castle wall.

"How on earth can you do that?"

"What?" he asked.

"Sit over the edge."

"It is quite comfortable."

Cassandra shook her head.

"You don't think so?"

Cassandra laughed, the thought of trying such a stunt frightened her.

"You should try it sometime," he said with a chuckle.

"I don't think so."

"Can you see the star that is just hanging above the mountain? It's sort of a reddish color."

Cassandra looked but couldn't see it. "No, why?"

"That's a planet."

"A planet? And how do you know about such things?"

Taleon's smile smirked on one side of his face. "Your father used to teach me about the stars."

Cassandra looked away and tried to see it again. In a moment Taleon was beside her. "Let me see, if I can see it? Sometimes vantage point changes everything."

Cassandra pulled back and Taleon leaned out over the wall. "The turret gets in the way." He moved back to where he had been seated and leaned out. "Come, you should be able to see it from here."

She walked to his side and leaned out over the wall, searching in the place where he directed.

"I still can't see it."

"Probably because you are shorter than me."

"And how in the world does that make a difference?"

"You can't lean as far out. Now, if you were sitting in the gap, you could see it."

She looked at him skeptically, then carefully pulled herself up into the crenel.

"Put your back to the wall and wedge yourself there with your feet. Now you can inch towards the edge and look out."

Taleon was surprised that she dared to do it. He sensed a rivalry burning within her. She wanted to be in on everything her father had taught him. She had been denied all of it—the education, the attention, and the affection of father and mother. He had the education and attention and some of the affection, but she had none until now. For the first time in her life, she was experiencing something more than just a tiny box of expectations; she was living.

Could he not forgive her for taking away King Aric's...everything that he had been to him? She had stolen it in one sweep and he had helped her do it. There was so much she needed to learn; she was the one with a crown hanging over her head; she would have to be responsible for the kingdom; why should he envy her? Why? But still he did, somewhat.

He looked at her as she dared to lean closer to the edge. Her hand shot for the inside edge, clinging to it for dear life. She barely leaned three inches out to see, her hand gripping the rock. Even in the moonlight, he could see her hand turning white from the tight hold.

Taleon put his hand around her wrist. "I've got you."

Unexpectedly her hold relaxed and she leaned further. "Oh, I see it now. It's pretty." She looked down. With a small scream of terror, she turned and flung herself at Taleon, clinging to his doublet and hiding her face against it.

Taleon couldn't help himself. He laughed, but quietly.

"It's not all that bad, is it?"

She nodded.

Looking down at the dark head that hid against his doublet, he couldn't help but feel for her. She was young and afraid and what was to come would be much harsher than looking over the wall of the castle. Cassandra clung to him; she trusted him. He put an arm around her shoulders and another beneath her legs that were holding her fast in the crenel gap lifting her safely off the castle wall.

She seemed to realize what he was doing and pulled away from him as he set her gently down.

"I am sorry I…"

"You don't need to apologize, Cassandra; I am just here to help."

She looked up at him, with a mixture of emotions that he could not quite translate in her eyes. "Thank you, Taleon. Good night."

"Good night, Cassandra."

He watched her leave. He felt as if they were being watched; he turned and scanned the castle walls. It wasn't the sentries; it was someone else. He thought he saw a shadow flicker and then disappear into the safety of a far turret. He could run after it, but it would be too late by the time he got there to trace the elusive shadow, and there was no knowing where it would hide. Turning, he looked up at the stars. What would they witness in the coming years? What did the future hold?

Chapter 19

Cassandra closed the door to her room and locked it; she tossed the key on her dressing table. Taking off her cloak, she slipped into bed. She tried to close her eyes, but what just had happened flashed before her eyes. Blushing, she hid in her pillow.

Why did I have to do that? I didn't have to. I just wanted to see it because father and he saw it together. Maybe I should ask Pappa to show me the stars, but he is so busy. I can't compete with Taleon. He has had my Pappa forever and I just a little while. Taleon is everything he needs and yet my Pappa loves me more than I could hope. But Taleon knows everything and I couldn't let him show me up. I couldn't. Isn't it the mark of a queen to know everything she can and let others help her when she doesn't know? Why does he have to know so much and be my father's right hand? 'Cause you weren't here...

She turned over restlessly and fluffed up her pillow, then buried her face against it, closing her eyes. Taleon's face flashed before her—the way he was looking at her after he had helped her down. Yes, helped her—certainly no more and unfortunately no less. His look puzzled her. It was tender, gentle, concerned, searching, and something else she couldn't put her finger on. The moonlight always boggled her.

No, thinking of that wasn't going to help her sleep either! She turned on her back and stared at the ceiling. Why did she have a sudden urge to scream? Now she wanted to laugh for wanting to scream. She turned over on her side, making imaginary courses between the stones on the wall going nowhere in particular, just wandering. Cassandra wondered about the paths on the mountain, how the refugees had gotten from one point to another, finally reaching Raven Castle. Turning over, she kicked the sheets. Sleep was going to make her fight to find him tonight.

There was a soft knock on her door. Cassandra sat upright in bed.

"Cassandra, are you awake?"

"Coming." In a moment, she leapt out of bed and found the key on her dressing table. She opened the door. "Hello, Pappa."

"Hello, daughter," he said, entering and closing the door behind him. "I am glad you are still awake. I wanted to tell you myself."

Cassandra looked up at him with concern in her eyes. "What is it, Pappa?"

"I am leaving at dawn tomorrow, down to the western valley— where our army has been training. I was planning on leaving tomorrow afternoon, but when everything was pulled together tonight so quickly, I thought immediate action best."

"You are leaving so soon?"

"I'll be gone less than a week."

"But I haven't even had you for a whole day."

"I know, Cassie; that is why I wanted to tell you myself. I'll be back before you know it."

"Promise?"

"Promise," he answered pulling her into a warm embrace.

She buried her head against him. Being with him she felt so safe.

"Taleon will continue to keep an eye on you and make sure everything is all right. How are the two of you getting along anyway?"

"Pretty well for the most part."

"I am glad to hear it," he said, stroking back her hair and looking into her eyes.

"How long have you known Taleon?"

"Since he was eight. You were five when he came up here."

Cassandra nodded. That explained a lot. That is how they knew each other so well. It would take her a long time to get that close to her father. Maybe with Taleon's help it wouldn't take as long as she feared.

"I love you, Cassie," he whispered.

"I love you, Pappa."

"Sleep well now," he said, bending down and kissing her cheek.

Standing on her tiptoes, she returned the caress—and then he was gone. Cassandra locked the door and allowed herself to sink to the floor. Slowly she realized how tired she felt. The world was too big to take on and conquer in one night. For that she needed sleep, and Cassandra crept into bed.

It was dark when she awoke, but she heard the rustling of preparation going on. Dressing quickly, she left her room and went down into the courtyard. The morning air was cold. Several men were readying to mount horses. Among them were her Pappa and a few council members. Taleon was standing beside her father, helping him pack the last things away. It was Taleon who saw her while her father was talking to a council member. When her pappa turned his attention back to Taleon, he nodded his head in her direction. In a moment, her pappa was by her side, pulling her into a warm embrace.

Cassandra could feel his chainmail beneath his thick wool cloak. Wrapping her arms around him, she could feel a dagger at his back, and the sword and dagger by his side. Could it be that this was dangerous?

She looked up into his face, trying to hide the worry that had washed over her. He kissed her forehead and smiled. "They are only precautions, Cassie. Now stay safe. I'll be back in a week."

"I love you."

He smiled and kissed her cheek before turning and mounting his steed which Taleon was holding for him. The gate was opened and the first rays of the morning colored the far sky. Stars still hung in the heavens above them. Without cue or hesitation, the men moved as of one accord out of the gate.

Cassandra watched them go, her heart aching. Taleon came and stood beside her. They watched until the men disappeared, but still they stood. Cassandra stared at the small clouds made by her breath in the morning air. She hugged herself tightly and looked up at Taleon.

"They'll be fine, Cassandra," he said without looking down at her.

"Have they ever had trouble?"

"No, they are just being safe. The Imposter is becoming quite anxious in the valley. Your father is going to bring his army them over the mountains. From there your father will come back and oversee the army from here. You don't need to worry."

Cassandra nodded. "Thank you, Taleon."

He turned and smiled at her. "You are welcome, Cassandra."

She shivered, "Well, I best go back to my room. At least it is warmer there."

"Would you like a fire?"

"I would."

"I'll bring some wood up in a minute."

Cassandra went to her room, curled up in her cloak, and sat beside the faintly glowing hearth waiting for Taleon to appear. He did in a few minutes, carrying a bundle of wood under one arm and a mysterious basket in the other.

"Here we go," he said, setting everything down by the hearth.

Cassandra watched as it took him only a few minutes to get a warm blaze started. Taleon sat down comfortably in front of the fire warming his feet.

"You hungry?"

"A little, I guess."

He uncovered the basket to disclose a loaf of bread, cheese, and a small pot, with two mugs. Taleon placed the kettle over the fire and sliced the bread and cheese. Forking it, he held it close to the fire.

"What are you doing?" asked Cassandra.

"Toasting bread and cheese. Don't tell me you have never had this before."

"Then what should I tell you?"

"The truth."

"But the truth is I have never had it before."

"Well, I hope you like it."

"Can I try toasting it?"

"Sure." And he nodded for her to come sit on the rug by the fire. He handed her the fork and started a second one.

"Did you plan on me asking?"

"It never hurts to be prepared," he said with a smile.

Neither said much and the only thing that broke the silence was the bubbling over of the kettle, which Taleon took away from the heat, pouring the hot liquid into two mugs.

"Yours should be done," he said.

She pulled it back from the fire and tried to slide it onto a plate, but it was too hot. Taleon reached over and did it with ease. She refrained from glaring at him. In a few minutes, they were both eating, still in silence.

It slowly began to aggravate her that Taleon was so silent. Here he had built a fire and brought food, and now they were sitting in utter silence, save for the munching of their toast. But then again, what was there to talk about?

She gazed deeper into the fire and took a sip of the warm cider. She smiled.

"This reminds me of when I would have a tea party with my dolls."

There was a long silence before Taleon spoke dryly. "Do I resemble a doll?"

Cassandra giggled. She tried to restrain it but in a moment it broke into a hearty laugh that even Taleon had to join in. Moments later she gasped for air, barely able to catch her breath.

"It wasn't that funny; you must be really tired," said Taleon, amused.

"I have never laughed so hard in my life; my sides hurt; why is that?"

"Don't know, just is."

The silence returned between them, but was not so strange. In a few minutes, they had both finished and Taleon gathered the dishes into the basket, then he turned to Cassandra.

"Your father wants you to get some rest."

Cassandra nodded. "I will."

Rising, he was nearly to the door when Cassandra's voice halted him.

"You are sure he'll be back?"

"I am sure, Cassandra, but why are you so worried?"

"If he didn't come back, Taleon, I am not sure I would know what to do. It would all be up to me and…" Cassandra turned and looked into the fire. With a shake of her head she turned back to face him. "Thank you Taleon."

He nodded.

Cassandra glanced at her bed. It really wasn't half as inviting as the fire. Curling up on the rug, she closed her eyes and fell asleep. The world wouldn't have to rest on her shoulders quite yet.

Chapter 20

The next few days passed pensively for Taleon and Cassandra. A new group of refugees came up from the valley and most of their spare time was spent with them. Some came ill, with rumors of a plague starting in the valley.

It was evening and Cassandra and Taleon were reading together but separately. Cassandra put down her book and looked at Taleon, who looked deeply involved in the pages of his book.

"Why are so many people ill, Taleon?"

He didn't raise his head. "Poor food in the valley makes the people weak and when they are weak, people get sick. It's surprising that this hasn't happened earlier. Your father has tried for many years to make sure the valley has enough food, but this spring and summer have been one of the worst. Hopefully that will all be over soon."

"Do you think we are in any danger?"

Taleon shrugged. "Don't know; not likely, but then again there is no knowing."

"Why has my father never attempted an attack before this?"

"Aren't these questions you should be asking your father?"

"I would, but he isn't here."

Taleon smiled to himself and put down his book. "True." Then his gaze grew serious. "He would not endanger you, his only heir to the throne. Archibald has killed your mother, destroyed his cities, and let you live."

"Why, I don't understand."

"Torture."

Cassandra shook her head. "He is so cruel."

"You say that now."

"Now that I know, I see things in such a different light. It's like I was blind my whole life, and now that I see, I am shocked at what is all around me. How can a man do such things? Turn against his own brother, murder my mother—an innocent woman, kill, blind, beat, hurt so many people without a heart." Tears formed in her eyes and she looked away.

"Your father had to protect you the best he could. You were the only heir left."

Cassandra turned abruptly to him. "The only heir left?"

"You had a brother. He died while you were still an infant."

"I had a brother."

Taleon nodded.

"What was his name?"

"Arthur."

"Arthur," she murmured under her breath. "How did he die? Was he also slain by my uncle?" She shuddered at the thought.

"It was an accident; your uncle was out of the country on diplomatic business when it happened. He was riding a horse. I don't know what happened; I just know that he died. Your father has never spoken of it to me."

"Do you know if you bear any resemblance to him?"

"To who?"

"My brother?"

"I wouldn't know; I never saw him and if I had. I probably wouldn't remember it. With such losses, he couldn't bear to lose you. The torture of knowing you were being raised by his mortal enemy was a severe affliction, but he bore it. You were still living, and heir to the throne."

"I don't understand that. Why did my uncle never marry and have children, an heir of his own? You would think that is what he would want, to get rid of my father completely."

"Who can understand a man that has overthrown his brother, taken the crown, and done the deeds he has performed? Tell me."

"You are right; it makes no sense whatsoever."

"Such men are dangerous."

Just then there was a knock at the door.

"Come in," invited Taleon.

A young man entered. "Taleon, a message for you."

Standing, he took it to the far window to read it.

"Is everything all right, Taleon?" asked Cassandra, resisting the desire to go and look over his shoulder at the missive.

"It's fine. Your father has requested my presence immediately."

"What for?"

"Doesn't say."

"How long will you be gone?"

"Why do you want to know?"

Cassandra looked at him blankly for a moment. "Well, with you and Pappa gone, this place will seem rather lonely and unprotected."

"Lord Keenan will still be here, and there are Edith and Brendan to keep you company; then there are the refugees, your sewing class, and books to keep you busy. I probably won't be gone more than three days at the very most, so you needn't worry."

"And if something goes dreadfully wrong in the meantime?"

"Keenan can take care of it. You are far from second in command yet, you know. Now, if you will excuse me I have to get ready to go. This is urgent."

Cassandra looked after him, a pensive mood seizing her. She walked to the window, glancing down into the valley rifting between her and the mountains beyond. This side of the castle was impenetrable unless you wanted to climb up a straight cliff. She turned back to her book, but the page seemed uninteresting and bland.

I had a brother whose name was Arthur. A brother—me, Cassandra, who thought herself an only child. How strange is that? She gazed into the fire wondering. *What would he have been like? Would we have gotten along?*

A smile crossed her face. She had always wanted an older brother, and now she had one, but she had never known him. Cassandra sighed. Restlessness came upon her, and, putting on her cloak, she slipped into the hall. Taleon was in the courtyard, readying his steed.

Uncomfortably, Cassandra wiggled her toes in her slippers. She didn't like the thought of him leaving, and she wanted to say goodbye to him. How was she, a princess, supposed to do that? He was just Taleon. Or was he? Oh, she didn't know anymore.

What compelled her to walk down the inner staircase into the courtyard Cassandra never quite knew. She slowly approached, trying to think of something to say—anything that would make sense and not make her look like a sentimental fool, who really didn't mean anything sentimental at all.

Unexpectedly, Taleon glanced in her direction and nodded for her to come over in a friendly way.

She came, still unsure of what she was going to say.

"Do you have a message for me to bring to your father?"

"Tell him I say hello and send my love." She could have bit her tongue out for telling that last part to him. How exactly would Taleon tell that to her father? She blushed at the thought. It sounded awkward to her.

Taleon didn't seem to mind at all. In fact, he smiled. "With pleasure, Cassandra." He tightened a strap and secured the buckle before turning to her. "Take care, and don't get yourself into any trouble while I am gone."

Cassandra nodded. "I won't, Taleon."

He smiled and stroked away a stray strand of hair the wind had blown into her face.

Cassandra wondered why her heart jumped. It had never done that before.

"I'll see you in a few days," he said, swinging into the saddle, and off he rode.

Cassandra wasn't sure if she should stay and watch him go or disappear into a corner. She decided upon the latter, slipped away to her room, and locked the door.

The following two days were uneventful and as normal as they could be without Taleon. It was on the third that an unexpected blow fell.

Cassandra had just finished her sewing lesson when there were urgent shouts in the courtyard.

"Girls, stay here. I am going to see what is going on."

Hurriedly Cassandra went to the railing that overlooked the courtyard. Men were brought in on carts and laid on the cobblestones. Some had limbs at queer angles and all were bloody and bruised.

Cassandra hurried back to her room, "There has been some kind of accident. Stay in here or someplace out of the way."

Leaving her room, Cassandra hurried down into the courtyard, where women and men were already gathering with necessary supplies to help the wounded. Cassandra helped where she could, but spent most of her time gathering water for the women to wash out wounds and wipe away blood. As fast as she could fill buckets, more were needed as carts continued to roll in with more injured men.

The men's faces and bodies were smeared with dirt. There had been an accident at the mine.

As no new injured men appeared, Cassandra began to help those around her as she could. Her skills were not great, but she could help ease the pain and bind the wounds.

The last cart came rumbling, carrying in only a few men. The doctor went to see what he could do for them. And Cassandra went back to filling buckets. Unexpectedly the doctor came and stood beside her.

"I need your help."

"My help?"

"I need someone who isn't stained by the blood of others. That would be you. Now come with me."

She followed him to a room set aside for the doctor's use.

The injured man looked like he had fought and suffered through a battlefield. His wounds, to Cassandra were horrific. However, it was his left leg that she could not stand the sight of.

In a moment Edith appeared.

"Good, I will need you both. Edith, hold his hand and distract him as you can. You help me."

"What are we going to do, doctor?"

"His leg is crushed. There is nothing I can do to save it. However, I can save his life."

Cassandra's stomach lurched. Closing her eyes, she steeled herself for what was to come.

The ordeal was longer and bloodier than Cassandra cared to know. When it was at last finished, Cassandra found herself helping to bind and mend his other wounds.

The task was soon complete and the doctor left him in Edith's care with detailed instructions of how to care for him until he returned. Cassandra left the room at the doctor's side.

The whole world seemed to sway and be sickening around her. Uncomfortable sensations surrounded her; memories clung closely to her, flashing before her eye with horrifying vividness. Who was this standing before her, speaking her name?

She blinked once, twice. The fog around her brain cleared.

"What happened, Doctor?" Taleon asked, his clothes dusty from travel. There still had been no rain in the valley.

"There was a collapse at the mine. She just helped me with a necessary but unfortunate amputation."

"Cassandra helped you?" Taleon looked at her, surprised. *No wonder she looks so dazed.*

"Yes, it was quite a messy ordeal, but she was a great help. You see when I…" and he began going into great details of how the surgery had gone.

Taleon watched Cassandra slowly, slowly grow more and more pale.

Suddenly she excused herself, covering her mouth with a hurried step.

She could not stand to relive it at all. Cassandra rushed to a far castle window where she could be guaranteed privacy. She wanted no one to disturb her, no memories to be readily at hand, no sounds that could send her twisted butterfly filled stomach into worse knots than it already was. She leaned out over the low edge of the window, trying to breathe in the fresh air and concentrate on anything but what had gone on in that little close room. Pictures flashed before her eyes and the contents of her stomach turned inside out. Her stomach spasmed and she lost everything over the edge of the cliff.

A gentle hand touched her waist. Instantly she knew who it was and cringed. She wanted to flee but couldn't. *What is Taleon doing here!*

After several moments passed and nothing more came, Cassandra pushed away from the ledge, still queasy and lightheaded. She turned away from Taleon, but he caught her shoulder and turned her around.

"How are you feeling?"

"Fine?" she answered weakly, closing her eyes against another nauseating rise. Her limbs trembled beneath her. Hesitantly Cassandra leaned against the window, pressing her clammy palms against the cool stone and trying to calm her nerves which felt as if they had been stretched to the point of breaking.

"Are you sure you don't have any touch of the fever?"

She nodded. "I am fine. It was just that room…"

"You have some of the symptoms…" As he touched her forehead with his hand, she shied away with a blush.

"Well, there is some color," he said with a smile.

If the floor would only open up and eat me I would be eternally grateful.

"No sign of a fever," he said with a satisfied sigh.

"Like I said…it was that room."

"I wanted to check. We can't be too careful, you know."

Cassandra nodded. Unexpectedly her stomach spasmed again and she lunged for the window as it rose in her throat. Her clammy hands slipped on the low ledge, sending her headlong out of the window.

Taleon had quickly slipped his arm around her waist as she had moved towards the window and now was holding and pulling her back. Once her feet hit solid ground, she sank to her knees.

Taleon sat on his heels beside her and looked into her eyes. Blue, like her father's, they had pools of tears in them. They were tired, filled with fear and pain. A sympathetic smile twitched at his mouth. He pushed a stray strand of hair away from her face.

Wearily she leaned her head against the castle walls. Shutting her eyes, a tear slipped down her cheek.

"Are you going to be all right?" he asked in a whisper.

Cassandra didn't reply. She was still trying to gather herself into one piece. Her heart was pounding like a drum in her chest.

Taleon sat down beside her. Slipping an arm tenderly around her waist, he pulled her close. Without hesitation, Cassandra buried her face in his shoulder, trying to hold back the sobs that rose from her heart, but they came anyway.

Taleon let her cry. After a short while, the tears subsided save for the occasional gasping breath that rasped at her throat.

Slowly she pulled away from him and looked up into Taleon's face. "How do you do it?"

Taleon cocked his head to one side.

"Be so strong. You take on everything. How do you do it?"

"One step at a time," he said with a soft smile.

"But how did you become so strong?"

He shrugged off her question.

"Taleon. Will you help me? Help me become strong."

Her blue eyes were so helpless, pleading, needy. At that moment she needed it more than anything.

"I will try, if that is what you want."

Cassandra only nodded her head. She laid her head against the windowsill. She was so tired. She glanced up at Taleon.

"How many men?"

He gave her a puzzled look.

"The mine."

"Twenty-five."

"That is awful. Any dead?"

"Not yet."

"Will there be?"

"Probably, but there is always hope."

Cassandra nodded. "How is my father?"

"Well. He will be back soon and he sends you his love."

Cassandra smiled and looked off into the distance. The world had stopped spinning around in her mind. Now it felt black. Darkness slowly crept upon her, fading out the world.

Chapter 21

Before Cassandra even opened her eyes, she was aware that her body ached. Her mind searched for the reason; then it dawned upon her. The mine. Had that happened just hours ago or forever ago?

Taleon let out a slow sigh of relief.

Turning, Cassandra opened her eyes. Taleon was sitting beside her, searching her face with a relieved smile.

She tried to sit up.

"Stay," he said gently, laying his hand on her shoulder. "You need your rest."

"What happened?"

"You fainted, I think you'll be all right now."

"Everything just went black."

"I am sure of it."

There was a hand on Taleon's shoulder. Cassandra's gaze shifted. It was Lord Keenan.

"Come, Taleon, let's leave her to the women and to get some rest."

Turning her head, Cassandra could see three women standing and waiting at the door for them to leave.

"I'll see you later," Taleon said with a sideways smile.

Cassandra nodded, too tired to speak.

Once the door was closed, the women took over with great care, changing her blood stained gown for a clean nightshift; they pulled the curtains and sent her back to bed. Though Cassandra protested, one woman would stay with her just in case her health was in danger.

Two days passed and Cassandra was not permitted to leave her bed despite her restlessness. It felt strange to be once again waited on hand and foot—to be given almost everything she asked for and to be doted on as a general rule. She missed Taleon's company, though her sick room was no place for him.

It was late afternoon and Edith and Brendan were with Cassandra. Edith sat in a rocking chair knitting, while Brendan and Cassandra amused one another with various games and peek-a-boo with the bed sheets.

Brendan was hiding and refusing to emerge from under the coverlet when Cassandra unexpectedly turned to Edith. "Will he be all right?"

"Brendan?

"The man who…" She couldn't bring herself to finish the sentence as the memory of it all made her shiver.

"He will be," said Edith in a calm voice, "He knew as soon as he was trapped it he would lose his leg. He is grateful that it wasn't his arm."

"Why?"

"He is a carpenter by trade. He needs his hands for his work."

Cassandra nodded numbly, still trying to grasp all that had gone on days before. She tugged at the sheet still held tightly over Brendan's head. He screamed in protest and Cassandra sagged back against the pillow.

"You know, for a while I thought you were going to pass out. You kept changing from white to green and back again."

"Don't remind me," Cassandra said with a shake of her head, the very mention of it turning her stomach in somersaults.

A time of silence passed between them.

"How do you know all of this anyway?"

Edith smiled, "I have been his nurse. The doctor has been so busy with the other injured men, I took the responsibilities of his care; and he needs someone to talk to and things to talk about. So we talk about our lives."

Cassandra looked curiously at Edith, wondering if she had shared her own life tragedy with him.

Edith met her eyes. "What are you looking at me like that for?"

"Nothing, I was just wondering if…" she decided she would rather not finish that sentence, and reaching forward, she snatched the blanket off of Brendan's head. He laughed and disappeared behind it again. Cassandra tugged playfully, but to no avail. She tickled Brendan's feet. He kicked and squealed before pulling them behind his shroud.

Edith was looking at her. "Wondering if?" she asked.

"It's nothing really."

"You are wondering if I told him my story?"

Cassandra blushed. *It is sort of a personal question.*

"I told him last night. He was in such pain. I didn't know what else to do. He tried to bear it silently, but I couldn't just sit there and let him suffer, so I held his hand and the way he held it so tight...I wanted to sing to him to put him to sleep, but you don't exactly sing to a grown man the way you would sing to Brendan, and of course a made-up story wouldn't do, so I told him mine. It was the only thing I could think of. Now I wish I could have thought of something else."

"Is that why you are in here today?"

"Mind your own affairs and I shall manage mine," said Edith rather shortly.

Soon Cassandra noticed the work slip from Edith's hand and into her lap as she rocked back and forth contemplatively. Her mind was wandering in deep thought.

Cassandra tried to make up for her fault by playing with Brendan, who was still set on being an explorer underneath and behind blankets. *Oh, I wish I hadn't said anything. I made a perfect mess out of it now.*

Just then there was an authoritative knock at the door.

"Who is it?" asked Edith, breaking away from her reverie.

"King Aric. May I come in?"

"Yes, please come in."

The door creaked open and King Aric appeared.

"Hello Pappa."

Just at that moment, Brendan chose to emerge from the blankets and exclaim, "Eek a boo."

King Aric and Cassandra laughed.

With a smile, Edith swept Brendan from the blankets despite his squalling protest and exited the room.

In a moment, Cassandra found herself in her father's arms.

"How are you?"

"Much better now that you are home. How long can you stay? Will it be long this time?"

"As long as possible."

Cassandra let out a contented sigh and looked up into her father's face, studying it with affection.

"Taleon says they have been guarding you like a dragon. He hasn't had a chance to even see you."

Cassandra laughed. "They have been spoiling and babying me. I am growing quite restless."

"They are taking the best care of the future. The only future heir and hope of Chambria."

She wanted to ask him about Arthur, the brother she never knew. But she didn't feel the timing was right for such a question.

"Come, I shall release you from your prison. Get dressed and you and I shall take a walk if you like."

"Oh yes, please."

In a few minutes they were walking the castle wall, and he was pointing out various things that she had never noticed before. They stopped when they came to the east wall and looked down on Chambria.

"It's beautiful, isn't it?" Cassandra said.

"That it is."

"How long before we are there?"

"In Chambria?"

Cassandra nodded.

"There is no knowing. Most are saying by Christmas. Although that is what they say about every war, and it usually takes more time than that."

"So you are not going to predict anything?"

"No, I am not. It is over when it is over and not before. I have more important things to worry about than when it will be over."

"Has the mine been a setback?"

King Aric nodded. "That is where all of our gold for our money comes from. Until we can get back to work, we will have to watch how we spend. We are on the verge of war. Wars eats money. We'll be good for a few months yet, but the question is: will the mine even be safe? Will the men be in greater danger? I can't put people in a situation like that. It's not worth it."

Cassandra leaned upon her father's arm with a sigh.

There was a long pause.

"I love you, Pappa."

King Aric looked down into his daughter's eyes that were raised trustingly to his. "I love you, Cassie."

She clung to him closer, her heart beating with a wild and strange fear. Destiny was at hand, but what was the course it would take, where would it lead them, and who would be the champion?

Chapter 22

The summer was passing quickly. Work in the mine had resumed and King Aric returned to the valley. Cassandra's duties were always tied to Taleon's and she found the responsibilities changing frequently to wherever there was a need. Slowly Cassandra found herself growing to admire this man whom her father had left in charge. There seemed to be nothing that he could not do.

Taleon and Cassandra were to entertain a group of children; whose mothers were tending the ill from the valley. Even Archibald's army had become ill, losing men in large numbers, causing them to retreat back to Chambria's capitol city. The plague, was not affecting the mountain people, making their unaffected army a strong presence in the valley below. The war might be over sooner then they dared to hope.

As Taleon and Cassandra were preparing their morning plans, Taleon had been summoned into the council chamber, for a grave discussion that wasn't for Cassandra's ears. She was still left out of some of the deliberations that happened in that room. There were secrets that not even her ears could hear.

The heat of the day was making the children she was in charge of restless. Cassandra knew of a place not far from the castle where a thicket of berry shrubs grew, and less than a stone's throw away was a shallow stream in which the children could amuse themselves and cool off their fidgety spirits.

Armed with a basket on one arm and Brendan in the other, Cassandra set off with a dozen children all singing a merry old holiday song.

As always is the case with children, they ate more than they picked—all except Cassandra, whose mind was too employed with keeping an eye on all of them rather than eating, so slowly her basket filled. In an hour's time the baskets were abandoned and the stream was considered the best amusement.

Cassandra, with Brendan in her arms, joined them in the stream. Their fun was of short duration, for Brendan was accidentally splashed in the face and they retired a little way up from the river to watch the children.

Her damp skirt hung close to her, like a cooling mantle from the heat of the day. Brendan, also slightly damp, was perched in her lap, still talking his half-gibberish–half-understandable–full-length conversation all to himself. Cassandra joined in the "conversation" and showered his face with kisses. She could tell that he was growing weary. His eyes were drooping shut and Brendan's head came to rest on her shoulder as she held him close.

In a little while, small Sarah Benet came up from the stream, her mouth puckering from a pout and sadness in her green eyes.

"What is the matter, darling?"

"They won't let me play with them. They say I am too small."

"Come here," she said, reaching out with her free arm to bring Sarah to her side. Cassandra comforted Sarah and wiped her tears away, then began to make conversation with her.

The council meeting was productive. They would be ready when King Aric came back from the valley. Walking down the twisting path to where he had been told Cassandra was with the children, Taleon tried to clear his mind from business. Cassandra's mind was full of questions, and if she suspected his mind was elsewhere, she would have a hard time not guessing. Suddenly he noted how hot the day was as sweat began to rise on his skin. Quickening his pace, he entered the shade. Shrieks of delight met his ears. He smiled. They were playing in the stream. It would be easy to find them.

Taleon watched, concealed from everyone's eyes. Cassandra showered Brendan's face with kisses until he laughed and she laughed with him, rocking him back and forth in her arms. He laid his small head on her shoulder and closed his eyes. A small girl with fuzzy yellow braids came up to her with a small pout on her red lips.

"What is the matter, darling?" she asked.

Taleon couldn't help but smile at that dear and familiar address that a princess was using with a peasant child.

"They won't let me play with them. They say I am too small." She burst into tears.

Cassandra reached out with her free arm and brought the little weeper to her side. He couldn't hear the words she was whispering in her ear, but in a few minutes, the girl was nestled comfortably by her side and they were talking in confidential tones.

He could tell by the way Brendan had relaxed on her shoulder that he was asleep and heavy. Cassandra was growing increasingly uncomfortable with an arm around each, but would not move for the sake of either child. He noticed how she was scanning the area more often and speaking less often with the little chatty thing who had begun to talk nonstop by her side. Something else was making her uncomfortable. He scanned the area. There was nothing, but the wood had become uncomfortably quiet, all except for the sound of the children's play.

Unexpectedly she was on her feet. "Children! Children, come on; it's almost time to eat; we need to be heading back to the castle."

Brendan stirred at the sound of her voice and she covered his ear with her newly freed hand.

Slowly the children began to drag their feet towards her.

Taleon moved forward to help her. He caught a quick motion out of the corner of his eye. Turning, he saw a horseman galloping towards Cassandra. Leaning low in the saddle, he hung to the left. His arm lowered in a hook-like fashion, barreling towards them.

"Cassandra, get down!"

Turning, she saw Taleon, then the horseman. She dropped to her knees. Grabbing the little girl with the braids, she ducked low.

The horseman pulled his horse to a stop.

"Alexandra! Come with me."

She glanced over her shoulder. "No!"

"Come on; we don't have much time." Leaning down, he grabbed her hair and, with a wrench, started pulling her to her feet.

Cassandra screamed in pain. The grasp was loosened and Taleon had his arm around her shoulders. "Don't look back. Take the children and go to the castle, I will be there in a moment."

"Taleon..." she said turning to him.

"I said go." It was firm and indisputable. "Send Keenan to me."

Resisting the desire to look back, Cassandra gathered Brendan in her arms, taking the quivering little girl's hands. She started towards the castle. Soon the other children were clustered around her; they were all wide-eyed with surprise and shock. Tears shimmered in a few faces; some quivered in fear.

"Come on, children; the worst of it is over. Let's get home as fast as we can."

As soon as they were in the castle, many of the children dispersed to their families. Others hovered close, too afraid to let go. Getting an older boy's attention, she asked him to fetch Keenan for her. Going down on her knees, she allowed the children to cluster very close to her—drying tears, saying comforting words.

In a moment Keenan appeared. "Your highness? The lad said it was urgent."

"Taleon wants you. He is out in the forest by the stream where we were playing."

"There is blood on your dress," he said, touching her right shoulder.

She glanced behind her. "There was an accident. We were attacked. It all happened so fast; I don't know what went on. Do you think Taleon is all right?"

"Did Taleon send you for help?"

"He just said to get you."

"Then he is fine. You should go get changed." He snapped his fingers to get the attention of some attendants. "Take care of these children." Then, grabbing a ready steed, he urged it out of the gates, down the path, and into the wood where Taleon waited.

Cassandra found herself responsible only for dear little Brendan who, surprisingly, had fallen back asleep.

"You little dear, can sleep through anything, can't you?" she murmured in his ear. Taking him to Edith's room, she entered. The room had been partitioned so Edith could wait on the man with the amputated leg, without inconvenience so he could get the rest and quiet that he needed.

Edith was sitting on his cot when Cassandra entered.

Still in a blur of excitement, Cassandra noticed nothing unusual—that his arm was around her waist or how close they seemed.

"Cassandra!" said Edith, standing on her feet, her face flushing a bright red.

"Shhh, Brendan is sleeping."

"You can put him in his cradle," she said with a cold gesture towards that particular object.

Cassandra did so and suddenly Edith was by her side.

"Are you all right, Cassandra? There is blood on your dress."

"I am fine. There was an incident in the forest, but all the children are fine. Now, if you will excuse me, I should go."

"Are you sure you are all right?" Edith asked, grasping her shoulders.

Cassandra looked into her eyes.

"I am not sure, but I need to go change before I scare anyone else. Thank you, Edith."

Cassandra left with a nod and hurried to her room. Changing, she went to the window, folding her arms and hugging herself. Something had gone dreadfully wrong that afternoon, but what? Cassandra did not doubt that Taleon had severely wounded, if not killed, the horseman who had tried to steal her away. What was going on in the valley?

Chapter 23

Taleon pulled himself to his feet and stepped away from the man's body when he heard hooves approaching. The man had been killed instantly by his sword. It had been a clean thrust. He wished there had been some other way to take care of the situation, but with so much at risk—Cassandra, the children, maybe even himself—it was the safest tactic, unfortunately.

"What is the matter, Taleon?" then Keenan saw the body.

"He was trying to take Cassandra."

"Any idea who he is?"

"It looks like one of Archibald's men. The only thing is, how did he breakthrough our ring of security? The mountain is surrounded with scouts. How did we miss this?"

"I'll have the scouts report and see what is going on. If we have a spy in our midst, we are in trouble."

Taleon nodded his head. "He is getting desperate, isn't he?"

"Very desperate. There is no saying when it will be over, but sooner is better than later, and I have a feeling that it will be so."

Taleon smiled at the thought. Chambria free at last! "Keenan, I was wondering."

"Yes?"

"Should Cassandra learn how to use a weapon?"

Keenan's brow wrinkled in thought.

"She was completely helpless; if I hadn't been here, there would have been nothing to prevent her being taken."

"Teach her, then. Equip her with sword and dagger. There is no better teacher than you."

"Are you sure, my lord?"

"Quite sure. You have her trust, and with your skills, she will learn well enough how to handle a sword. I pray to God she will never have to use it. However, it is best she knows how just in case something

155

should happen. Teach her, Taleon, and teach her well. Now go up to the castle and send three men to me. We need to bury the body properly. Then go to Cassandra and tell her what plans have been made."

Taleon nodded and slowly turned away.

"Take my horse, I will walk back with the men."

Taleon mounted and galloped back to the castle. With quickness, he sent three men to aid Lord Keenan and asked for Cassandra's whereabouts.

He knocked on her door and waited for her answer.

"Come in," she answered, a slight trembling in her voice.

She was standing at the window gazing out, her arms crossed, hugging herself tightly as if to comfort away her fear. There was no turn to recognize him or see who had entered the door. She was frightened and confused. Coming up behind her, he slipped his arms around her. She turned to face him, her head resting against him.

"What happened, Taleon?" she asked.

"A man tried to kidnap you."

"I know that," she answered, slightly annoyed. "But was he...?" She didn't finish her sentence.

"He's dead, Cassandra."

There was silence.

"Are you all right?" she asked, looking up into his face. "Did he hurt you?"

"No, he didn't lay a finger on me. And you?" he asked, stroking her still loose hair.

She tried to laugh, but it failed. "It's all still there, I think." Cassandra said, running one of her own hands over her hair. There was a lump in her throat and she glanced down. Her voice was husky when she spoke. "Thank you for being there...for saving me. If he had returned me to the valley, I don't know what I would have done." She shuddered at the thought and stepped away from him. Cassandra walked the length of the room before she turned to face him.

"What is going on, Taleon?"

Taleon walked to one of the chairs before the fireplace and motioned for her to take a seat. Cassandra did so, her eyes raised, full of questions, to his.

"Cassandra, the man who attacked you was one of Archibald's men."

"I know. I recognized him from the valley. He came to see my uncle often."

"He did?"

Cassandra nodded. "I don't know why, but he did."

Taleon nodded. "Anything about him in particular you can remember?"

"If you search his horse, you should find a roll of paper and maybe a pouch. He always handed my uncle a pouch and my uncle handed him a paper. That is all I ever saw pass between them."

"He is probably a bounty hunter."

Cassandra nodded in agreement.

"A while ago you asked me to help you be stronger." He looked at her questioningly. Would she be ready for what he said? "Keenan and I were talking and we think, just in case something would happen, you should know how to defend yourself. If I hadn't been there today...."

Cassandra stood up with a shiver and turned to her window.

"Would you rather not learn how to use a sword and dagger?"

She turned to face him. "I'd like that. I can't stand the thought of what would have happened if you hadn't been there today. It would have been the end of everything. This war needs to end. They need help in the valley. I want to help them so badly, but my hands are tied in so many ways."

"What do you mean, Cassandra?"

"I am not strong. I am not everything I should be. I look into that valley and I see needs—needs that I cannot meet. How can I ever be a queen? I want to help them so badly. What do I do, Taleon?"

Taleon rose from his chair and put his hand on her shoulders. "Be who you are. Cassandra, you have already come miles from where you were when you came here."

"Have I? There are so few things that I can actually do and it seems like I know so little about anything that goes on around here."

"The reason you know so little is just in case of something like what happened today. Cassandra, if they would take you, if your uncle would question you, if he would..."

"Torture me. He wouldn't stop until I told him everything and the less I know the better."

"How did you get to be so sensible?" he asked with a laugh.

Cassandra shot him a glare that was a bit miffed.

"Cassandra, I only meant it in jest."

"I know but..." She let out a long sigh and pulled away from him.

"Would you like to select a weapon?"

"Today?"

"There is no time better than the present."

"Give me a few minutes to prepare and I'll meet you in the armory."

"I'll be waiting for you." He left the room and leaned against the wall across from her room. He was going to wait right there for her.

Chapter 24

Cassandra watched the door close before sighing with relief, a flush of embarrassment climbing into her cheeks. She had relied too heavily on Taleon.

But what else am I to do when I am so nervous? What if there is a time when no one is there for you to lean on and it is just you?

Cassandra tried to put her nerves away as she brushed through her hair. She appreciated Taleon, but his nearness always made her feel queer.

Plaiting it, she went to her door. She would have the walk to the armory to soothe whatever ruffled feathers were left in her spirit. To her dismay, when she opened the door, Taleon was waiting for her.

"Taleon, I thought we were going to meet in the armory."

"I thought we could just walk there together and I could explain things to you along the way."

As they walked, he launched into a deep one-sided discussion on weapons and what made which ones best.

Cassandra tried to wrap her brain around everything he was saying, but felt as if she was failing miserably. Arriving at the armory, Taleon took her to the long wall of swords.

With wondering eyes, she gazed at them and walked the full length before selecting one.

Taleon smiled at her choice. "That is an excellent sword."

With care, Cassandra swung it.

"Very good," he said, withdrawing his sword, "Now when you hold your sword..." He showed her how to hold it and some basic maneuvers.

"Are you ready?"

"Ready for what?"

"A duel."

"Taleon, I barely know how to hold his sword, much less be able to fight and defend myself. It takes years to learn how to use a sword properly."

"Well, we don't have years. So I suggest you start now. Now, for practice we don't use the real blades until I know you can swing it without killing me by accident," he said, taking up a wooden sword and tossing it to her.

Cassandra caught it by the blade.

Taleon's tongue clicked in disapproval. "Never take a sword by the blade or you'll get cut."

"But it is only a wooden one."

"Bad habit in the making. Toss it back."

Rolling her eyes, Cassandra threw it back.

"Ready?"

Cassandra nodded, and Taleon tossed it. This time she managed to grab it by the handle, though it was a bad catch.

"Much better. Now are you ready?"

"I hope so."

"Sword up. You can't let it just hang on the ground when you are getting ready to fight someone. You'll get killed that way." He made a direct lunge for her.

"Ah!" Cassandra screamed and stepped back from the wooden blade that could have nearly thrust her through.

"Careful!" she admonished.

"Sword up," Taleon repeated.

Reluctantly Cassandra held the sword in a ready position.

"You may attack first."

"I don't think so. I'll be killed!"

Taleon threw back his head and laughed before becoming serious once again. "No, I really mean it. You strike the first blow."

It was concise and hard. Taleon struck back and verbally coached her step by step until he was in a corner, his sword rendered useless.

She smiled at her victory.

"Very good, but one thing you must watch for. A right handed swordsman is trapped but a left-handed-swordsman..." The attack was sudden and Cassandra found herself giving back ground faster than she had gained it. Her sword was flying through the air and she had stumbled to her knees. The point of the wooden sword was at her throat.

Taleon's face looked cynical. "Do I give a maiden quarter?" His eyes swept her face with a look of a hard man, then he dropped the sword by her side. "I cannot kill such a pretty face." Turning, he walked away.

Cassandra didn't wait a second. Taking her sword, she lunged at him from her knees, prodding him harshly in his back.

"Ouch!" With a spin, he turned, swept the sword aside and began a fresh onslaught.

Moments later, she was pinned in a corner, her sword horizontal, struggling for dear life as Taleon's blade tried to descend on her.

Cassandra stamped on his toe.

"Hey! Stop that."

Still he didn't give ground.

Cassandra kicked his shin.

"You aren't playing fair!" Taleon complained as he stepped back, losing some of his leverage.

Cassandra thought she saw a possible way to freedom and made a mad dash. She turned to see him hot on her heels and with a scream, she fled from the armory, up a flight of steps, and through a hallway into her room. Slamming the door, she turned the key in the lock just as Taleon came heavily against it.

"Cassandra!" Taleon scolded through the door.

She dropped to the floor laughing and panting.

"Well, well, what is my little daughter up to?"

"Pappa!" and she flew to her feet coming to his side. "When did you get here?"

"Only a little while ago. Now what is going on?"

"Taleon is supposed to be giving me sword fighting lessons, but I am not sure that it is going well. He says I cheat."

King Aric laughed. "Fetch me your sword and I will fight him for you."

Cassandra took her sword and handed it to her father.

"Now stand behind me and I shall teach this lad a lesson or two." Leaning forward, he unlocked the door and Taleon lunged in.

Cassandra watched in wonderment as they danced around the room, the wooden swords making a solid crack-like sound when they met. In a few minutes, however, King Aric drove Taleon to his knees and successfully "killed" him.

Cassandra approached and King Aric put his arm around her.

"There, how is that?"

"Much better, Pappa, but he really looks quite dead," she giggled under her breath.

"You think so?"

Cassandra nodded and slipped to her knees beside him, trying not to laugh. "Are sure you aren't dead Taleon?"

He sprang to life, grabbing her shoulders with a shake and a loud roar.

Cassandra screamed and sprang to her feet, almost darting behind her father, but hesitating.

He sat up. "You cheated."

"I do not cheat, sir."

"I can see the two of you get along capitally while I am away."

Cassandra blushed. "We usually get along better than this, Pappa."

"So I see," he said, offering Taleon his hand to get up. "To a well fought opponent," he said with a nod as Taleon stood and dusted himself off.

"So what have the two of you been doing?" he asked, taking a seat by the fireplace. Taleon took the other chair as King Aric pulled Cassandra onto his knee.

Cassandra seemed to sober. "Taleon saved my life this morning."

Taleon's mouth twitched as he thought of a remark that would have stung slightly but held it back.

"I have heard about that. I want to hear from both of you what happened."

The story was short as possible from both sides.

King Aric nodded when their story was finished.

"Well, it couldn't have been handled any better if I had been here myself. Now for these sword-fighting lessons of Cassandra's. I will join both of you until I have to leave. We will make sure she doesn't 'cheat' anymore," he said with a smile.

"Oh Pappa."

He kissed her cheek and pulled her close. "Now Taleon and I must go. I have some business to attend to."

"Can't I come with you?" Cassandra asked.

Taleon became tense.

The king was thoughtful for a moment before he spoke. "Not today, Cassandra; maybe later," he said, rising and helping her to do so.

Cassandra watched him leave with Taleon. Jealousy puckered up in her heart. Curling up in the chair he had just vacated, she rested her head against the back. Closing her eyes, she breathed in deeply. There was a lingering scent of her father—one she wanted to remember always.

Chapter 25

Cassandra was sitting by the fire thinking. She had spent dinner with the council, her Pappa, and Taleon. Now she had been sent away, as they had business to discuss and once again she was to be excluded. She had been taken into their council chamber once before; why be denied it now? Cassandra pushed back the grudge that was creeping up in her heart.

There was a soft knock on the door.

"Come in," Cassandra answered casually.

"Cassandra?"

"Oh, hello, Edith; how are you?"

"Well, very well indeed; can I disturb you?"

"Please do. I have nothing better to do at the moment."

"Well I—I wanted to tell you about what you saw this afternoon."

Cassandra struggled through her brain searching for what Edith could possibly be referring to.

"The reason I was sitting so close to Blake this afternoon was that he proposed and I had just accepted."

Cassandra's jaw dropped and she let out a squeal of joy, rushing to embrace her friend. "Oh Edith, I am so happy for you."

"I am happy too."

"Oh, I am so sorry I disturbed you. That was awful of me to come barging in like that. Forgive me?"

"You are quite forgiven."

"When will you be married?"

"As soon as Blake is on his feet again and well enough to move into the next valley. It will be very soon. There is already a place where he knows he can get work and I am ready to move on with my life. My husband has been dead for over a year now and I would like Brendan to grow up with a man in his life. His father will never be forgotten,

Brendan will keep him alive, for he is his father's mirror image in every way. I am happy and ready to start a new life, Cassandra."

Cassandra found herself wiping away tears. "I am so happy for you, Edith."

"So am I, Cassandra. To be honest I think I am floating on air, but I must go. Brendan is almost ready for bed. Good night, Cassandra."

"Good night, Edith."

Cassandra watched her go, wondering what it was like to be in love. Love to her had never really existed before. She had said she loved her father King Archibald, but knowing the way her Pappa loves her and the way she loves him, she knew that she had only feared King Archibald. There had never been any real love between them.

The love that Edith was talking about was an entirely different kind of love—one that she had never even considered possible in her own experience. Since her earliest days, such fanciful thoughts of falling in love had been crushed. She, Cassandra, was a princess born under obligation to marry for wealth and power and to produce an heir to the throne of Chambria. If love followed she would be incredibly blessed, but that was not to be hoped for.

Cassandra traced her thoughts back to what she had believed earlier—that bearing her first child would kill her. Certainly the weak thing she had believed herself to be in the valley would have died, but did she need to be fearful of that now? There was still so much unsettled. But the thought of cradling her own child, like Brendan, in her arms warmed and delighted her heart. Her own child—heir to his mother and grandfather's throne, a noble little boy. Images floated through her mind. She was walking through the halls of Chambria's castle, cradling the infant in her arms, singing to him a soothing lullaby. Her father appeared to dote over "his little prince," as he would be called.

But who would the baby's father be? Would he be the prince in the painting? Cassandra shivered at the thought and shoved him from her nind. Was she still engaged to marry him— she shuddered. No, she would never marry him ever, that was certain.

Unexpectedly a tall, blond-headed figure with serious but mirthful blue-green eyes that stood before her in fine garments. It was Taleon. She blushed and tossed away the entire daydream with a hot feeling of embarrassment. Marriage and children could wait a good long while. She was a princess with duties and obligations. A nation needed her help; they were her first objective. Whatever happened after that would be...after that.

Grabbing her cloak, she climbed to the castle walls and looked down on Chambria—a faraway city glimmering in the dusk. Beyond it, the valley widened and vanished in the far horizon. Cassandra could not help her sigh.

"Why the long sigh, your highness?"

Cassandra whirled around. It was Lord Keenan.

"Good evening, my lord. I was just admiring the valley."

"That doesn't explain the unhappiness of your sigh."

The corner of Cassandra's mouth twisted and she leaned into the breeze that swept back her hair and kept her eyes dry from tears. "I was just thinking of how much the people are in need, my lord. There is so little I feel that I do to help them. Up here I am safe from harm..." The words died on her lips. That sentence was no longer true. "I am comfortable, my lord, and they suffer hardships that I could never endure. What right do I have to be happy when they are not?"

The silence was long before Keenan spoke. "The people are full of hope, Cassandra. You are their hope and joy. Do not despair. The kingdom shall not come to weigh fully on your shoulders yet. Be grateful for what time you have to be free."

"How much longer will they suffer, my lord?"

"Not much, your highness. Hope is near at hand."

Chapter 26

The next few days shed light on how King Archibald's bounty hunter had snuck his way up the mountain, killing the one watchman who had attempted to send a warning signal. The bounty hunter was skilled. Cassandra and Taleon had gotten off easy.

It was late one evening when her father came to her door. "Cassandra, there is a meeting at the council table tonight. I wish you to be there."

"Are you sure, Pappa?"

"I am quite sure. Lord Keenan has requested your presence. He thinks you should know what is going on in the valley, and the council has agreed."

"Then I am more than willing to come," she said, rising to her feet.

Cassandra entered on her father's arm. There was nervous tension in the room—one that quivered the air, almost loud enough to make it sing. Quietly she entered the alcove and took her seat. Taleon leaned against the wall, too deep in thought to really notice her.

"Well, men, we received word today that our spy closest to Archibald was caught and killed. We need eyes and ears in the palace, close to Archibald, but who can take his place? Who is trustworthy enough? Who won't be suspected?"

The men tossed names around, but none seemed to suit the purpose. They were either too well-known by the enemy or too essential to their own campaign to be let go.

"The question, my king, is this, do we even need eyes and ears? Can we not just charge and take the city by force? We will surprise him by taking the north wall; what more can we wish for?"

King Aric took a deep breath. "It will be just like last time if we do, and that is not something I am willing to repeat. We lost too many lives on that day—woman, children and men. There is not one of us

169

who wasn't touched by that slaughter. We need to know what he intends to do to Chambria and its people when we make our advance. I want to know what it is and how many lives are at stake."

"Without the shedding of blood there is no freedom."

"But the price must still be counted. Is there anyone in his household who might be able to gather that information without creating a stir?"

"There is a soldier. However, he only carries messages, though he has done some work for us. But there is risk of him being discovered, as he was close friends with our last spy."

"No, it would seal his death warrant and we wouldn't discover his plans. We need someone he won't suspect."

Cassandra felt numb, as if she wasn't really herself but rather someone else who stood up and spoke.

"Send me." Her voice trembled as she said the words.

The men turned to her, a look of shock crossing their faces.

"I could go into the valley dressed as a peasant. I could say that I exchanged my dress with a poor girl newly arrived here, that I bribed her to take my place and I slipped away into the night, and was far down the mountain before the break of dawn." Cassandra tried to focus. The world seemed to be spinning around in her head, her mouth was dry, and her fingers were icily cold. She was surprised at how easy the plan came together before she had even thought. It was if it wasn't really her at all.

"Do you think you could fool him into believing it, child?" asked an elderly noble of the table.

"Yes, I do," she answered without hesitation, even though everything seemed to shake about her.

"Your majesty, she is perfect. She is well acquainted with the castle and Archibald; the information would be readily available to her."

Cassandra only had eyes for her Pappa. He was gazing at her with a deep affection and intensity she wanted to understand. She could feel it touching her heart, but she wanted to hear him speak.

"My lords, please give me a few minutes with my daughter."

Quickly the men vacated the room, leaving her standing and waiting, with him seated, a thousand expressions covering his face. Neither really noticed that Taleon had stayed in the room.

For a long time neither spoke. The silence grew to an unbearable height, but yet they did not speak.

Slowly King Aric broke the silence in a voice hovering just above a whisper. "Cassandra, do you wish to return to the valley?"

She shook her head, then, rushing to his side, knelt beside his chair, hiding her face against his knee. He lifted her face to meet his gaze. "I do not wish to leave, Pappa. I don't want to leave you or the people. I love it here. It came to my mind and I could not be silent. There is nothing I would hate more than to return to the valley without you as its king."

"Do you know beyond a shadow of a doubt that you could fool him and deliver us messages containing the necessary information?"

For a long moment Cassandra thought, searching her mind and heart. She looked up into her Pappa's face, meeting his steady loving gaze. "Yes, Pappa. I know I can."

"Oh Cassandra." And King Aric began to weep. Standing, he walked away and faced a far wall. Slowly, hesitantly, Cassandra followed him.

"Pappa, are you angry with me?" Tears were falling unchecked down her cheeks.

"No, no, no, Cassandra," and turning around he held her so close she could barely breathe. "I am torn. You are my daughter. I love you more than my heart can bear. I do not wish to let you go, but—there is something strange about all of this, I feel as if I must let you go, but I do not know why. Oh Cassandra."

"Pappa, don't let me go then. I will stay here by your side. Pappa, Pappa!" She clung to him, her heart feeling shattered. She could not hold to him tight enough.

Slowly King Aric relaxed his grip on her and wiped away both of their tears.

"Cassandra, my beautiful Cassandra." He pressed a long kiss to her forehead, one that seemed to implant his love upon her forever. "I cannot decide whether you should go or stay. I will leave that for the council to decide."

She clung to him tighter. "Are you sure, Pappa?"

"I was surprised by their reaction. If they want you to go, Cassandra, then you must go."

"Pappa, I…"

"Hush." Releasing his daughter from his clasp, he went to call the council. Cassandra had a sudden urge to run after him—to cling to his arm and never let go. But she stood where he had left her, watching his every move. By this suggestion she had practically broken his heart, and hers too.

In a few minutes, the lords were sitting around the table.

"Who will take Cassandra's suggestion into consideration?"

Cassandra found a wave of shock and fear pour through her as many of them nodded yes.

"We will not take a vote tonight. I would like you all to consider it deeply. If there are questions you would like to ask Cassandra, please feel free to do so, either tonight or tomorrow. Any questions at the moment?" Cassandra noted how lifeless her Pappa's voice seemed.

There was a long silence.

"Very well. We adjourn until tomorrow evening."

With a numb heart, Cassandra watched the men slowly disperse, leaving them once again alone.

"What shall we do, Pappa?"

"Pray, and that with all our hearts, that the best choice be made." Taking her hands in his, he knelt on the hard, cold stone floor. Sinking to her knees, she bowed her head, her heart crying for the best choice.

In complete silence, she listened to her father's prayer: heartfelt, fervent, trusting. He did not ask for an answer one way or the other, but for peace no matter how it fell.

Cassandra felt the presence of another person. Opening her eyes, she glanced up to see Taleon kneeling beside her father.

When her father's amen came, Cassandra opened her mouth, but found the words would not come, though tears came in their stead. In a moment she was pulled into her father's arms and a firm hand slipped into her own. She did not have to blink back the tears to know it was Taleon. She looked at him. His head was bowed, but his grip was strong, as if imparting the strength she needed. Closing her eyes, the words came, burning with her heart's craving. Just as she had uttered her amen, a lord entered and requested the king.

"Taleon, make sure Cassandra gets back to her room safely," he said, looking down into her face and wiping away the dampness on her cheeks, then, rising, he left.

"With pleasure, sire," said Taleon, not stirring. He watched King Aric leave before he spoke. "Are you trying to break your father's heart?" Then he turned to her with a piercing gaze. "Because you are doing a pretty good job of it."

Cassandra looked at him, baffled. "Why would I do that?"

He was silent, but his gaze was anything but quiet. Reaching over, he wiped a lone tear away. "You've cried for more petty reasons than this. How do I know you are not acting?"

Cassandra's jaw dropped at the force of the suggestion. "Do you honestly think I would betray my Pappa?"

"You betrayed your uncle. What is to prevent you from doing the same once you reach the valley? What is to prevent you from going back to being the little weakling that came up here?"

"Love and truth. I now have both in a way I have never experienced in my whole life and I will do whatever it takes to feel it again. Neither of those do I find in my uncle."

Taleon didn't say anything.

"I know I cannot convince you, Taleon. There is nothing I can say or do that will make you believe me." She looked into his eyes, feeling hopeless.

Taleon had her hand and was pulling Cassandra close so he could look directly into her eyes. "Give me your word."

"My word?"

"Swear on your father's name that you will not betray us."

"On my father's name? Taleon, why I could never..."

His fingers touched her lips. "Swear," he barely whispered.

Cassandra's heart beat wildly. To swear on her beloved Pappa's name seemed to break some sort of code of honor. If she were to break it, she would be shaming her Pappa's name, but she did not plan on bringing dishonor and shame to him. His name also brought some sort of standard—a measuring stick for her own conduct. The gravity of the whole situation stunned her while her emotions pulled her apart.

"Taleon, I swear to never bring dishonor or shame upon my Pappa's name. And by my Pappa, King Aric the rightful ruler and King of Chambria, I swear to never betray my Pappa, you, or the kingdom of Chambria. I will take death more lightly than break what I swear to you."

Taleon was on his feet and assisted Cassandra to her feet.

"Your uncle is an excellent swordsman. I think you need another lesson should you ever need it."

"But the council..."

"You need to be ready for whatever comes. Now come, Cassandra. You need to be ready."

Chapter 27

The next day, Cassandra spent most of her day in the armory with Taleon, just to keep her mind from what fate lay ahead of her. As evening was gathering, a lad appeared in the doorway.

"You are both wanted in the council chambers," he piped before disappearing.

Cassandra looked at Taleon uneasily.

He didn't reply, even with his eyes, putting down his wooden sword and walked through the door.

For a moment, Cassandra hesitated before following him. She was sweating from the exertion. Her hair was a mess and she was altogether in a disgruntled state. They couldn't be kept waiting, though. So sweeping back her hair and tucking the loose strands back into the loosened weave of her braid, she ran after Taleon.

When she reached his side, he remained silent. Suddenly there was nothing more in the world that she wanted than to hear him speak to her. But in a moment, they were at the council chamber, and he was sweeping the doors open for her.

With a quiver in her heart, she entered. All of the men rose to greet Cassandra. Her father was smiling and beckoning her to his side. She retreated to him with joy, slipping her hand into his. As long as she was by his side, all would be well.

"First of all, before the men ask you questions, we would like to give you a temporary seat at the table."

Cassandra looked up at her father surprised, then glanced around the table. The only empty chair was completely on the other side of the table from him. She would have to stand on her own two feet. There would be no comforting presence, no hand to cling to beneath the table if she was nervous. It was all her.

Taleon stood waiting behind the chair.

"Now, go take your seat, my darling."

Masking her fear with a smile of confidence, she walked around the table and was ready to take her seat when her father took his.

Taleon pushed in the chair for her; then mutely walked into the alcove to watch. He found himself battling resentment. She was sitting at the council table, something he had never been allowed to do. They had asked for his advice and questioned him, but never offered him a chair. And now she!

His throat constricted, making it impossible to swallow.

He had been overlooked time and time again, and now she, she...

Taleon could not even bring himself to say her name in his mind.

Under a critical eye, he watched as they pressed and plied her with questions.

With care and quick thought, she rose to the occasion, scaling their queries and concerns with relative ease. Yes, she had a plan.

How long has she had a plan, does she really intend to use it? Can I really trust her? Is everything she has done in Raven Castle just a façade to lure us into safety?

Taleon wondered. He couldn't help it. For nearly three hours they questioned her, probing her innermost thoughts and ideas, countering, quizzing, trying to trip her up in her own words, but she did not fumble. Either she was much better than he had thought, or this was genuine. She would be true to the last.

When the questions were all over, the men looked around, thinking.

Then King Aric spoke. "Cassandra, we have some more things to discuss. Please retire to your room."

"Yes, Pappa," she said, rising.

The men rose as well.

She glanced around the table before lowering her eyes and offering them a royal bow. "I am your servant. Do as you see fit, my lords." In a moment she had turned and left the room.

Something pulled at his heart. What, he did not know, but it pulled him to go after her. But he was determined to stay and hear what was to come.

The door closed. Her footsteps faded away before anyone spoke, and it was not the king.

"Shall we put it to a vote, my fellows?"

The answer was unanimous. They had made up their minds.

King Aric spoke. "I cannot vote on something my heart is so deeply tangled in."

The men nodded.

"All in favor rise. Opposed, remain seated."

Every man stood save King Aric. Slowly, oh so slowly, he rose to his feet. Taleon's heart twisted in his chest.

"I stand with you, my men. If you see fit to send her, then it should be so."

The men took their seats. There were still other matters to discuss.

King Aric motioned Taleon to his side.

"Go to Cassandra. Tell her I shall be with her shortly."

"And if she should ask?"

"Tell her."

With a nod of understanding, Taleon left.

How will she react? How much should I tell her? Will she want to know that the choice to send her was unanimous?

Hesitantly he knocked on the door.

"Come in," the answer was soft and relaxed—entirely what he had not expected Cassandra to be.

Slowly he opened the door. Cassandra was leaning out the window, her expression peaceful.

"There are promises beyond those hills, aren't there? A people waiting to come home." Cassandra turned around and faced him with a smile. "Is my Pappa happy with their decision?"

"Why do you want to know if he is happy?"

"If he is happy, then I am happy. I only want to do what my Pappa wants, nothing more. I am glad to be staying here for a while longer yet—until my Pappa's standard flies all over Chambria. Then all will be well with the world."

"How do you know that you are staying here?"

Cassandra looked at him happily. "Pappa told me last night he would come himself to tell me if I was to go, and you are here, so I am staying."

"Cassandra." Taleon's voice was grave.

She looked at him, paling.

"You are going."

Shock flew through Cassandra's body. She sank to the floor, covering her face in her hands.

"No, Taleon, it cannot be. It cannot." She raised her head and looked at him, tears streaming down her face. "If I go, I will break my father's heart. I can't do that."

Something propelled him across the room and to his knees before her.

"Cassandra." *Where was his voice? Why was it suddenly gone? What should he say to her? God, please help.*

He began again, taking her damp hand into his. "Cassandra, they believe it will save the people. They are sending you. It was unanimous, Cassandra, not a single vote against you. They want you to go. They believe you can do it."

There was a long silence in the room.

"Do you believe I can do it, Taleon?"

Why on earth do you have to ask such a question of me?

"Cassandra, I am not the one whom you should be asking that."

"Then of whom should I enquire to receive your opinion?"

The words stung.

"Cassandra," he said reprovingly.

"I am sorry, Taleon." Her hands squeezed his, then loosened, asking for release.

He held on.

"Why does my opinion matter? You have the approval of a dozen other men."

"You are a better man for the job than I could ever be, Taleon. I..." the words died on her lips.

"You spoke up before I had a chance to volunteer."

"I wish you would have silenced me."

"How could I? It all came out before I had the faintest clue you were going to say anything."

"It came out before I even thought, really. Now what am I going to do?" The question was rhetorical. She pulled away and stood up, hiding her face in her hands. "I must do this." Her shoulders straightened. "I will do this. My uncle shall never see the destruction about to fall on his head. This war will be over and my father shall sit on the throne."

"And you after him," Taleon murmured.

Cassandra turned to him. "Let's hope so."

There was a long silence.

"Will they wish to see me yet again tonight?"

"Your father will, but they still had more business to talk over."

"I won't be able to mention this to anyone, will I? They must all believe that I have betrayed them." She bit her lip, keeping back the tears that shone in the corner of her eyes. "The poor people. How will my Pappa bear it?"

Taleon stood and came to her side placing one hand on her shoulder. "He will bear it as he has for the last thirteen years of your life."

Cassandra pulled away. "But he shouldn't have to."

"But he will. He loves you. He loves the people, and you will work as a team to destroy Archibald: one on the inside, one on the outside. It will all be over before you know it."

"Be there for him. Be there like you have been for the last...forever. You mean an awful lot to him, you know."

"You mean more."

"Taleon." Cassandra's words died on her lips. Reluctantly she turned to face him. "I am his daughter and I always will be, but that doesn't make you any less important to him than me. To be very honest, I am jealous of you at times. You understand my Pappa in a way that I crave. You know him inside and out; I am practically a stranger to him and his ways. All I have is my blood connection. You have something deeper, something I want but will never have. I might have parts of it, but you have something I can never attain. Watching you sword fight the other day, my father defending me and you leading the charge—you have something special, Taleon, and just because I am his daughter doesn't mean you don't have a special place in his heart. You are his son, Taleon."

Taleon shook his head. "I am not his son, Cassandra, and I never will be. Now good night." Walking to the door, he closed it firmly and walked to the top of the castle. He needed to clear his head. Cassandra understood him better than he thought possible. She knew what he was suffering from in some small way, but still....there was so much more.

Chapter 28

Cassandra sank down in the chair and closed her eyes.

Why is it so important that I have Taleon's approval? Why can't the council see him? Was everything I said to Taleon a complete loss? Oh God, preserve me and do with me as thou seest fit. Why do I feel such a cloud of doom and death about me? Why? Oh please help.

It was in praying that Cassandra fell asleep in her chair.

The hand that gently stroked back her hair woke her. Opening her eyes, she saw King Aric hovering over her.

"Pappa!" she exclaimed. Sitting upright, she wrapped her arms around his neck.

He gathered her in his arms and held her close.

Cassandra hid her face against his chest, nestling herself under his chin, thus hiding her face from him.

"Cassandra, what do you think of the choice we have made?"

There was a long silence.

"I don't know what to think, Pappa. I didn't think they would actually send me—that I would return to the valley before you were once again secure as its king."

"Neither did I, but it has happened and we must face whatever is to come."

Cassandra nodded, sinking as close as she could to him. King Aric held her tight.

"Oh Pappa, don't ever let me go."

He held her closer than ever. "I can't do that, my darling. You have been called away to a duty and I know you perform it strong, and steadfast."

"I will, Pappa, for you, for the people. I will not fail them."

He pressed a kiss to her forehead.

"I love you, Pappa."

"I love you, Cassandra."

They stayed like that until Cassandra fell asleep on his shoulder and he tucked her gently into bed.

When Cassandra woke up the next morning, life felt strangely empty but so full. There was so much going on, so much that was going to happen, a life unknown. Reluctantly she rolled out of bed, braided her hair, and straightened out her rather wrinkled attire. She sagged into the chair by the window. All she could see were green mountains and valleys. It was not satisfactory. Cassandra left her room and climbed to the top of the castle.

There below her was Chambria. The light had yet to creep over the mountains and dawn on the valley. The city lay in a shadow, cold and uninviting. The valley was trapped in darkness while the sun was shining fully on Raven Castle—shining on the steel colored stone in all of its glory. Cassandra knew from experience that the sunlight shone dazzlingly bright on Raven Castle, making it glisten in the morning's awakening.

A shiver ran through her spine. What would her life be like once she returned to the valley? She hated the thought. She could not stop shivering, but stood there staring at the valley, her teeth jarring against one another in her head.

In a few minutes she knew she wasn't alone. Taleon was standing behind her.

"Good morning, Taleon."

"Morning," was his brief reply.

He was waiting for her to turn around. She did so.

In his hand was a leather sheath with the sword she had chosen resting in it.

"It's time you knew how to use this one properly."

"But Taleon, I don't think I am ready."

He stepped forward and slipped the belt around her waist, tightening it gently so it hung ready at her left side.

"You'll never be ready if you don't practice and prepare. We are running out of time."

Cassandra's hand rested gently on the sheath. The leather was soft and exquisitely tooled. "It's beautiful. I have never seen anything like it before. Who made it?"

Taleon shrugged. "Our country has never seen a crisis like this before. On guard," he said, withdrawing his own sword.

"Not up here, Taleon."

"What better place is there?"

She looked at him for a brief moment before withdrawing it. Slowly she held it in a ready position.

Taleon and Cassandra nodded at one another, signaling that they were ready, and the dance of the swords began.

To her surprise, the sword felt natural in her hand as she swung, blocked, and lunged. The combat was anything but mortal. It was a challenge of skills, strength, and cunning that flew back and forth along the castle walk. To her surprise and fear, Taleon jumped up on the castle wall. Climbing to the upper part, he kept her in a merry dance. She glanced his sword out of his hand and onto the castle walkway. Her own skill surprised her for a moment, and Taleon ran along the top of the wall, leaping across the battlement gaps with great bounds. Cassandra realized she was missing an advantage and ran to get his sword.

Taleon was there first. With a cat-like leap he tumbled from the wall, his hand finding his sword. Instantly he raised it in time to catch a blow from Cassandra. Once again the swords flashed back, then forth, up and down and over side to side. Taleon flicked Cassandra's sword from her hand. Catching it, he lunged at her. She stepped to avoid it. He swung in for what would be a killer move—when she stepped close to him, took the dagger from his belt, and held it to his throat, at the same time both blades crossed hers.

For a moment neither moved. Both were panting from the excursion. It was a perfect draw. Taleon dropped his blades and Cassandra turned and offered him his dagger. He slid her sword back into its sheath before taking the dagger and putting it back in his belt, then sheathed his sword.

"That was well done, Cassandra."

"I have had an excellent teacher who keeps me on my toes playing the left and right handed swordsman."

Taleon smiled briefly. "I am glad that hasn't irritated you too much."

"How could you possibly irritate me too much?"

Taleon looked curiously at her. Wasn't she always annoyed with him? She honestly meant it.

"You annoy me once in a while, but you teach me more than I could ever expect to learn under different tutelage."

Taleon smiled with some gratification. Someone was really seeing him. He wasn't just Taleon. He was...Taleon.

A cool wind swept up from the valley. Cassandra turned to face it. Her expression became grave. The wind played with her hair. "In less than a fortnight I shall be there again at my uncle's side acting like a blind fool."

"Is that how you describe your work for your father?"

"No, it is the way I describe myself before I came up here. There are no ignorant fools in Raven Castle. Unless of course you consider me one; well then..."

Taleon broke into the middle of her sentence. "You are no fool, Cassandra."

"Do you remember who you are talking to?" laughed Cassandra lightly.

"Yes, and you are no longer blind. All will be well, Cassandra. This will all come right. Trust me."

"I already do."

Taleon smiled. "I have work to do."

"Can I help?"

He paused and looked at her. "All right."

After spending nearly an hour with Taleon and having him disappear, Cassandra went to visit Edith.

"Come in!" came the happy voice from inside the room.

Cassandra entered and was very surprised to find Blake not only standing in the room but taking steps across it, with a wooden rod where his leg came to an end.

"See, I told you I could walk quite well, Edith, and all by myself."

"Oh Blake!" and she impulsively threw her arms around his neck, but it did not set the man off balance as Cassandra was sure it would. He stood his ground steadily.

Brendan let out a squeal of joy and clapped his hands.

Cassandra scooped him up in her arms. "Isn't he doing well, Brendan?"

Brendan warbled off a long dialogue that proved to be a monologue, for no one could understand exactly what he was saying.

"Is that quite so?" asked Cassandra when he had finished.

But Brendan was too enthralled with looking at the way his hands were neatly folded together to answer.

Cassandra now looked at Edith. Blake had slipped his arm around Edith's waist, and she was looking trustingly into his eyes. Cassandra couldn't miss the look of pure, trusting love. He bent and whispered in her ear and she nodded.

"Cassandra, do you know where your father is?"

"I am not sure where he is exactly, but I know I could find him."

"Is someone looking for me?" asked King Aric, stepping through the door, his hand coming to rest gently on Cassandra's shoulder. Cassandra slipped closer to her father.

Edith and Blake bowed before him. Brendan looked up into his face with wide-eyed reverence, sighing something under his breath.

"Come, my friends, there is no need for ceremony here. Did someone have a request to make?"

"Yes, your majesty. This beautiful lady has agreed to be my wife. Would it be possible to wed here in Raven Castle?"

"Most certainly. When would you like to marry?"

"There is a group leaving for the Belterra in less than a fortnight and we would like to be in their party."

The king nodded in understanding. "Would the day before their departure be soon enough, or would you like it sooner?"

Edith smiled squeezing Blake's hand, and he answered for them, "That would be perfect."

"Excellent. Now if you don't mind, I have come to claim my daughter."

"Not at all."

As Cassandra put Brendan down, he whined and clung tightly to her.

"I have to go, Brendan."

He buried his small head into her shoulder.

She could not help kissing the small forehead that rested so closely to her and squeezing him tight. He was a memory she must take to the valley—the feel of him in her arms. She was going to risk it all to make the world safer for little girls and boys like him, and maybe someday her own children.

Edith stepped forward and took Brendan from her arms and he let out a squeal of unhappy defeat.

Cassandra followed her father, who did not say a word. They walked down to the stables where two horses were waiting.

"Do you know how to ride?"

"I have never been on a horse's back save for when Willamsen brought me up here."

"You rode long before that, but you don't remember. You had a very small pony and rode him quite well."

"I did?" Cassandra asked with a smile.

"Yes. You did. I used to walk beside you to make sure you wouldn't fall off, but you never were in any kind of danger. But come, let's see if you remember anything from those rides," he said, lifting her onto the saddle. In a moment she was settled comfortably, sitting side saddle.

"Something in you must remember, for that is perfect."

King Aric mounted and together they rode out of the gate into the forest. For a long time they went on in silence. Just being together was wonderful but difficult. There was so much to say and so little time to say it, but how did one go about putting into words?

After they were a goodly distance from the castle, King Aric dismounted and helped Cassandra to her feet.

He offered her the crook of his arm and she threaded her arm through his and leaned close.

At first they walked together neither saying a word, then King Aric spoke. "Cassandra, do you have any hopes or dreams?"

She looked up at him puzzled. "Pappa?"

He turned her to face him directly. "What are the hopes that burn in your heart? What do you desire most in life, Cassandra?"

"No one has ever asked me. I really don't know, Pappa."

"If you are to be a ruler, you must have a vision, dreams, hopes, plans, not only for your people but for yourself as well. What is it that you want for yourself, Cassandra?"

For a moment Cassandra thought, then raised her face to his. "I want my Pappa upon the throne of Chambria. To see the valley restored, the people coming home, the drought to come to an end. A full harvest and a happy people."

"Anything else, Cassandra?"

For a long time she thought. "I want to be better than I am now."

King Aric bent and kissed his daughter's cheek and they continued to walk arm in arm.

"What are your hopes, Pappa?"

"Many of the things you wished for and a few more. To have a happy daughter who is kept safe. Oh Cassandra, I have failed you in the way you should be brought up."

"Pappa, no, you haven't. I have grown more here in the short months that I have been here than in my entire life in the valley."

"That is what I mean. You have been cheated of the upbringing that you ought to have had. If something should happen to me and you are left alone to rule Chambria..."

"Don't say that, Pappa. Please don't."

King Aric was surprised by the tight grip on his arm, the pleading in her face.

"Don't let anything happen to you, Pappa. I couldn't bear it."

King Aric smiled. "I pray nothing will go wrong, but no promises."

Cassandra nodded and bit her lip.

It was near evening before they returned to the castle. Taleon was waiting to greet them. He helped Cassandra down from her saddle.

"There is a meal prepared for you in your chambers, sire."

"Thank you. Taleon, will you do the honor of joining us?"

"Sire, I couldn't."

"Taleon please," asked Cassandra, her grip on his sleeve gently tightening.

He looked down at Cassandra, whom he was practically still holding in his arms even though she was down from the saddle. He dropped his hands to his side.

"If you both so wish it."

"We do," answered the king.

The meal was almost silent, both Cassandra and the king being in a reflective mood and Taleon in the disposition to cooperate.

When the meal was over and the dishes cleared away, the king made an unexpected request for them to duel.

"I am afraid I saw only part of your performance this morning. Keenan told me it was quite a rare sight to behold."

"I am not sure if it is one we can repeat, sire," said Taleon.

"I just want to see you two duel, that is all."

Cassandra rose from her chair and Taleon did the same. They drew their blades, pulled them upright before them, and nodded, dropping them into ready positions.

The swords danced brilliantly in the light of the fire and candle as they battled as if for their lives.

It was once again a draw. Both had killing positions and had they been battling in earnest, both would have died. A thrust by either would end it all.

They slid their blades back into the sheaths and turned to the king, who had remained silent through the entire performance.

Slowly he stood, and walking over to them rested a hand on each of their shoulders.

"You have both done very, very well." He pulled them closer to himself. They moved to embrace him, a head resting on either shoulder.

Cassandra looked up at her father's face and caught a glimpse of Taleon looking at her. She looked at her Pappa. His face was lifted up, his eyes, closed, his lips were moving in silent prayer. She lowered her head and closed her eyes storing away her own prayer in her heart.

Taleon's hand touched hers, and she opened her eyes, looking in his direction. His blue-green eyes met Cassandra's. They were studying her face and seemingly filled with questions as if trying to see into her soul.

Cassandra closed her eyes and bowed her head.

Taleon did the same.

In a moment, the king's grip released, and squeezing Taleon's shoulder, he dismissed him. Cassandra he held in a long hug and kissed her forehead.

"Good night, my daughter."

"Good night, Pappa."

And she too was dismissed.

Closing the door to her father's chambers, Cassandra turned around to find Taleon waiting for her, his arms and ankles crossed.

Silently she moved down the hall towards her chambers. Taleon followed.

"What is it that you want, Taleon?" she asked in a soft voice.

"Why have you changed?"

"What? I have not changed a bit."

"Yes, you have. Something about you is different. Can't you feel it?"

"Taleon, I…"

"Take a moment to think before you answer."

For a long moment Cassandra thought. "I don't understand what you mean."

"Don't you?" he asked, stepping closer.

"No."

"You have changed since you came up here, but you have changed again. What made you second your father's motion for me to come to dinner tonight?"

Then it struck her. But had she really changed? "I keep thinking that I have the world straight, and then something comes along and makes it go all topsy-turvy again, and I don't know what to think of it. When it finally settles into place, I realize that I was wrong to start with and now it's straight until something else comes.

"Taleon, it sent me spinning when I found out I was going back to the valley. It was as if my eyes were opened. I thought I could see before, but now I realize how blind I was, and probably still am."

"You told me you were jealous of me and your father. Where has that envious girl gone?"

"I have been selfish. I thought that because he was my pappa, I could have and be everything to him. But I can't, Taleon. He needs us—both of us, Taleon; and with me going back to the valley, he will need you more than ever. I have been selfish and blind. I wanted everything that you had and was willing to do anything to get it. The world is so much bigger than my selfish needs, Taleon. He needs you."

Cassandra wasn't quite sure how Taleon had come to stand so close that his arms were around her waist, or why tears where sliding down her cheek, but it was so, and she leaned against him slipping her arms about his neck.

"Thank you Cassandra," he whispered, then, releasing her, he stepped away, one hand lifting her face to look into his. "Good night."

"Good night, Taleon."

And with that they both walked their separate ways.

Chapter 29

The week passed quickly. In two days more, Edith would be married, and in three, Cassandra would be in the valley.

It was late in the morning. Cassandra had just finished her sewing class when there was a knock on the door.

"Come in!" Cassandra called.

Edith entered. "Cassandra. I have a favor to ask of you. Can I place Brendan in your care during the ceremony, you are the only one I can trust to keep him quiet and happy."

"Oh Edith, I would be delighted."

"Good, it is settled then."

"Yes."

Edith turned to leave when Cassandra's voice halted her. "Edith."

"Yes."

Cassandra held her tongue. She wanted to tell her the whole story of what was about to happen. She could hardly bear the thought of Edith thinking ill of her—thinking that she betrayed her and her story by returning to her uncle.

"What is it, Cassandra?"

"I—I don't know. Promise me, Edith, you won't believe everything you hear?"

Edith looked at her scrutinizingly. "What do you mean by that?"

"You are my friend, Edith, and I will never betray you."

Edith's brow wrinkled and she came closer, looking Cassandra in the eye. Cassandra met her gaze boldly.

"You can't tell me, can you?"

"I will always be your friend."

"I believe it, Cassandra."

"Then will you do me the honor of accepting this gift?" Cassandra held out a thin string of white, gold, and red thread—the colors of Chambria's flag, with pearls spaced evenly around it.

"I will, and it would be an honor."

"Thank you, Edith."

With that, Edith left and Cassandra turned to her sewing basket and pulling out a piece neatly folded at the very bottom. It was a red and white field with a golden lion—her father's standard. She still had to finish it. Her fingers ran across the edge, then to the lion that was only partly attached. Taking up her needle, she threaded it with gold. With the finest stitches she had ever done in her life, Cassandra sewed until it was nearly done. At the last stitch she hesitated. Finishing it would feel wonderful but frightening. She would be leaving this standard soon and going to the valley. Boldly she did the last stitch, concealed the knot, and gathered the whole flag into her arms, burying her face in its folds.

She wanted to hold onto it as long as possible. Her heart was here in Raven Castle.

"Cassandra?" It was Taleon's voice very near

Startled, she sat upright to see him standing before her.

"You didn't knock."

"I did. You didn't hear me and the door was open partway so I came in. Pardon me?"

"It's all right."

"Finish it?"

Cassandra nodded and released it, letting it unfold from her hands. Taleon caught an edge and held it as he walked backwards, stretching the flag out between them.

"It's beautiful, Cassandra."

Cassandra only smiled and looked at the standard.

"I'll make sure it is first thing that is brought over the wall."

"Over the wall?"

"Once we know everything is in place, we'll be bringing a full blown assault over the north wall."

"But the north wall is impossible to mount over, the woods are so dark. The marsh is so thick, it has never been done."

Taleon smiled. "For by Thee I have run through a troop, and by my God we will leap over that north wall."

"How?"

He smiled and laid his finger over his lips. "It's a secret."

"You'd better keep it that way."

"Oh, I will. Come, your father wants to see you and I think it would be best if he received this from your hand."

Together they folded it and Cassandra tied a white ribbon around it.

"There."

Taleon smiled.

When Cassandra presented the flag she had sewn mostly by herself, King Aric's eyes filled with tears.

"Cassandra. This shall mean so very much to me. Now, I wanted to see you about a few details for your journey. There has been a long discussion about how you should arrive in the valley, and at last it has been agreed upon. Do you think you can manage a horse bareback?"

"Bareback?"

"Yes."

"I have never tried it."

"Well, we can amend that. Before people rise in the morning, Taleon will be taking you out and down most of the mountain. From there, it won't be too hard find your way. I wanted to take you, but the risk is just too great."

"Of course, Pappa."

"Once we know Archibald's plan, we will lay siege. If possible, we will try to get you out first, but the likelihood of that is slim. Finding you will be one of the prime objectives when we reach Chambria. While you are there, find a way to escape or hide once we start to take the city. Understand?"

"Yes, Pappa."

"I am telling you all this now so you will remember it, so in the morning you aren't so nervous you might forget it."

"Thank you, Pappa."

"I love you, Cassandra."

Cassandra flung her arms around her father's neck. "I love you. Your standard will always fly in my heart no matter where I am."

Time passed quickly, and before they knew it, the day of Edith's wedding arrived. The day dawned bright with promise. In the early afternoon, Blake and Edith wed, Cassandra watched with joy as she held Brendan in her arms.

Feasting and dancing followed, and Cassandra found herself swept into a group of girls who were not engaged to dance.

"They are a handsome couple, are they not?" whispered one girl to another.

"I can't wait for my wedding day."

"Did you hear that Ellie and Horace are engaged?"

"No!"

"Yes, it is quite true."

"You know what young man I saw talking to your father the other day?"

"Who?"

"Raymond."

"Raymond! Are you sure?"

"Quite. They talked for a long time."

"I hope so, and I hope it was about me."

Amused, Cassandra listened to all of their hopes and dreams of marriage, husbands, homes, and babies. She was quite surprised when one girl turned to her and asked her a question.

"Do you know who your intended is, Cassandra?"

Cassandra looked at the girls, baffled. "I don't know."

"You and your father haven't talked about it?"

"No, we haven't at all. We have been too busy."

"Is there someone you would like to marry?"

Cassandra blushed and shook her head.

"There must be some striking young man who has caught your eye, or do you intend to wed a stranger? I would rather marry for love than anything, but what about you?"

"I do not know. I was told that I would marry well as a child and that love would have nothing to do with it. That I understood, but my Pappa is so different from my uncle I do not know."

"But is there anyone you like?"

Cassandra's mind whirled and then her eyes fell on a suitable but mischievous answer. "Yes, but I am afraid our marriage could never be. It is just too impossible, though I am quite in love with him."

The girls leaned forward with excitement. "Who?" they asked beneath their breath.

"I really shouldn't tell you," Cassandra said with a modest downward gaze.

"Oh, tell! We won't betray it to a single soul, we promise."

Yes and it will be in the next country by tomorrow morning if I was serious... "Well, are you sure?"

"Oh, quite; not a one shall hear his name from our lips."

"Well, all right. His name is..." Cassandra let them hang dramatically on her pause before shyly raising her eyes to meet theirs. "Brendan."

"Brendan!" the girls exclaimed in disgust at being thwarted. "He is just a baby."

Cassandra giggled. "Yes, I know, but I have quite lost my heart to him." She glanced over the crowd to see Edith glowing with her new happiness, Brendan sound asleep between them. They adored him. How she would miss them both. They were right; it was time they moved on, both of them. Soon the kingdom would be ready for their return and they would move back into Chambria, but until then they needed to build a home of their own.

The girls changed the subject, but Cassandra dove deeply into her own thoughts.

Taleon caught her eyes. He was among the dancers with a young lady, a very young lady. The small girl barely reached his waist, but she was dancing with the best of them.

Cassandra watched and waited far into the evening. No one asked her to dance. She was dressed as one of the common people, but she was not common. It wasn't that her feet itched to dance or that she really longed to, but her heart felt a little miffed that no one would ask her.

Quietly slipping away, Cassandra climbed to the top of the tower and watched the festivities from above. Unexpectedly she found her father coming to her side.

"What are you thinking about, Cassandra?"

"Hopes and dreams, I guess. Who will I marry when you are on the throne?"

"Why do you ask?"

"Am I still engaged to the second prince of Shalsburg?"

"No, he is happily married to a duchess of his own country. Otherwise I would not risk sending you down there. You are too precious to marry just anyone."

"Who would you wish me to wed?"

"He is a man of wisdom and honor and truth, one who will stand by you and be a strength and assist you in ruling the country."

"Who is he?" asked Cassandra, mentally thinking how like Taleon it sounded.

"He shall be a man of your choosing, Cassandra, and as long as he holds all of those character qualities, I shall be a satisfied father."

"But what of connections, title, riches, land, and wealth?"

"If you wish to marry a man who has all of that and what I mentioned, I shall more than happily bless your union. But there is no need to worry about how our country will do when I come back onto the throne. I have agreements with the countries surrounding us, none need to be strengthened by a marital tie. Cassandra, you are free to marry whomever you please, be he peasant or prince, as long as he passes my approval. Come, we should not exclude ourselves so from our people." He offered her his arm and she took it, leaning her head against his strong, battle wise arm.

Upon setting foot downstairs, Cassandra was besieged by a group of small needy orphan children to amuse them, and so she did. As the hour grew late, she found more than one small head pillowed against her lap while she told them a story. Resting her back against the castle wall, listening to the music, and watching the dancing, she slowly found her eyes drooping shut.

Cassandra awoke when a small head was lifted from her lap. She started slightly.

"Shh," came a soft voice. It was Taleon. "Stay still; let me get these little ones in their beds. I'll be back in a minute."

Cassandra looked around her. The children that had fallen asleep beside her were the orphans—the ones with no one to call their own.

It took Taleon a few trips to relieve Cassandra of all the small slumberers. That left her alone in the dark and cold to think, to realize where she would be before the next break of day, and it frightened her.

As Taleon carefully cradled the second-to-last one in his arms, Cassandra followed his example by taking the last small sleeping girl. The importance of what she was about to do struck her in the heart. For them—all of them, and the children that they would have—she was doing it so they would have a future.

Tucking the last two little ones in their beds, Taleon closed the door.

Cassandra had to say something to distract herself, "You are good with the children."

"You're not so bad yourself," Taleon whispered as they started walking.

"Do you have brothers and sisters?" she asked as the question occurred to her.

Taleon smiled, but it wasn't one that reached his eyes. "Not that I remember at least. I was on the streets ever since I can remember. It's all I ever knew until I made the mistake of stealing from one of Archibald's soldiers. He had a dozen hot raisin rolls. I didn't think the man would miss one. He turned around just as I grabbed it and pulled out his sword and I knew I was done for. The soldier was going to run me through for laying my dirty fingers on his rolls.

"Just as I expected it to be all over with, someone pushed me aside. It was your father and a group of his flash fighters. He fought with the man, mounted his own horse, picked me up off the street, and rode off with me. I didn't know what to think. It was sort of like a dream—when your hero comes to save the day. Just because he was my hero didn't mean I won immediate favor in his eyes. My thieving ways weren't looked kindly upon by your father, but he straightened me out."

"I would have never guessed."

"Guessed?"

"You always seemed so...I thought you were the son of a noble."

Taleon's mouth twinged with a smile. "Your father is the closest thing I have ever had to father."

"You are his son, aren't you?"

"In his heart, you will always be first."

"Even if I don't deserve it?" Her voice was nervous as her thoughts traced back to a few minutes earlier.

"I didn't say that."

"But I can't help thinking it. I am so clueless sometimes."

Taleon turned and unexpectedly placed his fingers under Cassandra's chin, so he could look into her eyes.

A lump rose in her throat and butterflies whirled around in her stomach. "I am afraid I will fail him, Taleon."

"Never be afraid of failing, Cassandra. Just make sure you are strong enough to pick yourself back up. He wants you to do your best. That is all he asks. That is all anyone asks."

"But if I fail him, I won't be able to look him or anyone else in the eye ever."

"Then don't fail."

"Taleon, I am not like you. I can't just—"

He laid his finger on her lips. "Not a word of it. Your father doesn't love you because you are like me. He loves you because you are you. Nothing in the world will change that. Don't look at failure, because then you will fail. Just do your best."

"And if my best isn't enough?"

"There will be no regrets."

Cassandra leaned against him. He was so strong in so many ways.

"You know, there is one girl I didn't get a chance to dance with tonight."

"Who?"

There was a smile in Taleon's voice. "You. Should we amend that now?"

Cassandra looked up into his face. "There is no music."

"I don't need music to dance. All I need is a willing partner."

"Well, this partner is willing, but she would like to propose something else."

"What is that?"

"We save the first dance for the victory of my father—a dance in the great hall with marble pillars and a polished floor and music."

"Agreed. Good night, Cassandra; I will see you in a little while."

"Good night, Taleon."

It was her father's gentle touch and tender words.

"Cassandra. Cassandra."

She forced her weary eyes to open.

"Hello Pappa," she whispered. Butterflies tangled her stomach in knots. A cold rush of fears and nerves washed over her. Tears started to come and she wanted to roll into a small ball and disappear, but she couldn't.

I am needed. I need to do this. My Pappa will be on the throne before winter, before harvest comes. He will be king of all Chambria. Be brave and stow your fears away. All will be well. Just believe.

Her father's arms were around her, holding her close, so close she couldn't breathe—but she didn't want to breathe. All she wanted was that feeling to last forever, to hear his noble heart beating always beneath his chainmail, to feel his strong arms surrounding her, to feel safe always.

A moment later, he slowly released her.

"Come Cassandra, the day awaits."

Chapter 30

It was still dark. Not even hints of daybreak shone on the horizon. Rising, Cassandra quickly changed into the peasant gown that had been provided for her from a new arrival from the valley. It was a bit snug, but it gave the impression that she wanted to give her uncle. Cassandra then slipped on a pair of shoddy peasant shoes. Over it all, she put on her thick, rich, warm cloak to keep away the cold morning air.

Glancing around the room, Cassandra wondered how long before she would return to Raven Castle. If she ever would. Opening the door, she found her father waiting. She slipped her cold hand into his large warm one and held tightly. They walked into the courtyard where Taleon was waiting with Keenan.

As they reached the horses, Cassandra dropped to her knees. "Can you send me out with a blessing, Pappa?"

King Aric rested her hands on her head. He prayed a blessing over his daughter, then pulled her to her feet. Pulling her into a long-lasting embrace, he then lifted Cassandra up into the saddle.

Taleon had already mounted. The gate was open.

"I love you, Cassandra. Be careful," he whispered huskily.

"I will be. I love you, Pappa."

And with that they rode through the gate.

A lump rose in her throat. Tears blurred her vision. She wanted to break down and cry, but no, she had a mission to accomplish.

It seemed forever that they rode in silence, swiftly descending the mountain. Coming within sight of a road, Taleon pulled up his horse. Cassandra followed his example.

"That road will lead you to the capitol," Taleon said with a nod.

Cassandra took in a deep breath, and let it out slowly.

Taleon dismounted and assisted Cassandra down from her horse. Taking off the saddle, he brushed down the horse to remove the signs of the saddle, then turned to Cassandra.

"I guess that is everything then," he said, a lump rising in hi throat.

"Thank you, Taleon."

For a long moment neither said a thing but gazed down the roac where for them, for everyone, lay the fate of Chambria. Her whole life depended upon her next move.

"One suggestion," said Taleon, turning back to her. "Let your hair down. Let the wind and ride tangle it. You will be more authentically distressed."

Cassandra smiled, undid the ribbon from her hair and shook her dark head until it ached and her hair flew about.

"That's better, but I suppose I should be sending you on your way."

"I suppose. The sooner I leave, the sooner I will return."

"That is the general idea. Come on now. I will give you a hand up."

Cassandra walked over to her horse and took a handful of mane in her hands, waiting for Taleon's assistance.

Gently he put his hands on her waist and started lifting her onto the horse. A moment later her feet were back on the ground and she was spun around to face him.

"Promise me you'll be safe, Cassie."

"I will, Taleon."

"Do you remember what I made you swear?"

"Yes, I do. I will not betray you ever."

"Cassandra, I don't know why I have this feeling, but I cannot deny it. I release you from your pledge. I take it all back. You may tell your uncle whatever you wish."

"I will not betray you or anyone else, Taleon, much less my Pappa."

"But you may have to."

"No." Cassandra said firmly. "I never will."

"Listen to me, Cassie. Nothing is ever as simple as it seems. You are going into a lion's den. Use whatever weapon falls into your hands.

Whether it be words or a sword, use it wisely and with great care, for there is no knowing when it may turn to bite you."

For a moment Cassandra did not reply. "I will, Taleon."

"Good, because I—I..."

His grip became tighter and Cassandra found she was holding her breath—for what she did not know, but she was.

"Cassie," the tone in his voice, the look in his eye, spoke what his words would not.

What am I thinking; she is a princess. **The** *princess.*

"Taleon, I..."

"Shh, don't speak," he said, laying a finger on her lips. "You must be going." He pulled her closer for only a moment, then lifted her onto the horse. Cassandra's hand caught his as he released her. He raised it to his lips, tenderly kissing it. He released her hand.

"Until we meet again, Taleon?" she asked, dying to say more, but the words would not come to her.

"Until we meet again, your highness."

The word struck her with a pang. *Highness.* He had not called her that since the day he had called her a pain. The words flashed through her mind.

"You aren't a princess. You are a pain, and until you start acting like a princess, I will not give you the honor of that address. You will have to earn it from me."

Had she earned his respect? Had she earned more? The way his eyes burned, touching her own heart, she could not doubt it. The words should delight her, not give her a sudden aching pang deep in her heart.

"Please call me Cassie," she whispered. When he said her name like that, something wonderful happened in her heart and she wanted to carry the feeling with her.

His eyes met hers, almost defiant but tender. "Goodbye Alexandra. Godspeed," he said, slapping the rump of her horse, sending it flying down the path and onto the road.

Chapter 31

Cassandra immediately turned her thoughts to steering her horse. As the horse's hooves touched the road, she glanced over her shoulder and into the woods.

Taleon was on his horse watching her go.

She longed to stay looking back, but her horse was still going at a breakneck speed. She turned forward, towards Chambria and the fate that awaited her.

Within the hour, she reached the city walls. The gates were closed. She drew her foaming horse to a halt and looked up as two guards peered over the top.

"Who goes there and what be your business?"

"Hurry! Open the gates. Don't you recognize me? Any moment we might be set upon by bandits from Raven Castle; hurry!"

"Who are you?"

"Princess Alexandra! Now open the gate! Hurry." There was a groan of chains being put into use and creak of wood as the metal gate rose and the wooden doors opened. Cassandra galloped in. She wasted no time with the guards but galloped towards the castle through the city streets. She passed unharmed through the quiet city, whose silence seemed to rumble with discontent. In only a matter of minutes, she was at the castle, only to receive the same trouble she had at the gate. They would not let her enter even after she had identified herself.

"Get my father!"

The guards growled and turned away.

People started to gather around, and Cassandra began to grow anxious. If the gathering mob were prepared to start a riot and she was the object of their anger, she had no chance of survival. Anxiously she looked up at the castle walls.

Did she dare cry out for their attention again? The crowd was growing tight around her, leaning in and curious. She did not dare speak a word. But then someone shouted.

"That's the princess, all right. Shabby worthless thing, should have stayed where she belonged."

Cassandra turned her attention to the wall. "I demand to see King Archibald," she shouted, feeling as if she had just sealed her doom to the mob. They pulled closer. Silent whisperings passed from one mouth to another like a babbling brook.

Cassandra found her face in the horse's mane as something struck her in the back. Looking over her shoulder, she saw a large partly decayed head of cabbage had struck her. A pebble struck the horse, causing it to prance sideways with a slight rear. Cassandra held on. If she bolted, it would mean life or death for her.

At last a head appeared over the top of the parapet for such a short moment that Cassandra could not be sure who it had been.

A rock flew by Cassandra's nose. Panic swelled within her. She tried to hold the horse steady as it danced beneath her, nearly unseating her off of its slippery back.

The crowd pressed in. She looked at their faces. Thin, worn, haunted and tired, weariness, hunger, fear and hate lurked in all of them. If something didn't happen soon, there was no knowing what her own fate would be. It was death by mob, or life if only someone would just open those gates.

A metallic groan came from the chains, and the hinges of the wooden doors moaned. The crowd surged forward, almost desperate enough to try anything that would rid them of the Imposter. Cassandra pressed her horse further forward. A troop of heavily armed soldiers were waiting just inside the gates. Kicking the horse's sides with her heels, she burst forward only to find herself sliding off of her horse's back. Someone had grabbed her dress.

Cassandra hit the cobblestones with a jarring thud that tingled up her spine.

"Get her!"

"Down with Archibald the Imposter!"

"Long live king Aric!"

A loud cheer erupted after that utterance and Cassandra's silent prayer joined their cry. But she had to take care for her life. They were upon her; her hands and feet hurt. The soldiers were surging forward, but would it be soon enough?

A strong arm grabbed her, pulling her up from the ground, over his shoulder they entered into the safety of the castle. Carrying her through the courtyard and corridors. A few minutes later he was setting her down on the soft bed in her former chambers.

"Your father said to keep an eye out for you. I didn't think it would require this."

Cassandra's brow wrinkled. She had never seen this man before and he talked so familiarly to her.

He glanced over his shoulder, then, turning to her, whispered. "Long live King Aric."

Cassandra understood and smiled, "Amen to that."

Going to the washstand, he poured water on a cloth and touched it gently to her forehead, which felt as if an egg was hatching. "Their aim is getting better," he said, his face screwing up in disgust.

"Wicked people," he said out loud, then whispered. "Trust no one." He raised his voice again to a normal tone. "Can't they see what King Archibald is doing to help them?" then dropping it to a whisper, "Tell me anything that needs to get out and I'll make sure it does."

A moment later they weren't alone. King Archibald burst into the room.

"Alexandra? Alexandra!"

"Father!" She choked on the word but just as well for at the same time tears trickled quickly down her cheeks.

Sitting down, he clutched her to his chest.

Emotional pain tore through her and she burst into sobs.

A moment later he had released her from his grasp and laid her back on the bed.

"Shh, now. Stop your crying. You are quite well." he said, wiping the tears away with his cold hand. It felt anything but gentle. He hated tears. Cassandra felt smothered.

"I know you were frightened, but you have nothing to fear now. I am here to take care of you."

She longed for her Pappa to throw her arms around his neck, to hear his heart beat beneath his chainmail and tunic, to feel protected and safe.

A moment later Judith came in.

"Judith, give her something light to eat, attend to her wounds, and put her to bed. Alexandra, tomorrow I want to hear everything that went on. You are weak and need your rest."

You want me to go to bed? It is still the middle of the morning.

Judith fussed a great deal over her. After a bath, ointment and bandages on anything even resembling a scratch, and a meal of hot broth. Cassandra was put to bed.

Cassandra was emotionally weary and shaken. Was it really only that morning she had left Raven Castle? Closing her eyes, she fell asleep at last, but as night came she opened her eyes and looked around. She was alone; that was a relief, and she began to put her thoughts together once again.

Her door opened, and from well-executed practice, she closed her eyes and breathed deeply and slowly as if she was asleep.

"See, she returned," said King Archibald, in a low voice.

Cassandra battled the chill that ran up her spine and took a deep breath to fight down the butterflies that suddenly took flight in her stomach.

"He'll be back for her. I will fight him—crush him, and after that you *will* marry me."

"I will never marry you," whispered a soft voice, a voice Cassandra had thought gone forever. Shock jolted through her. She wanted to sit up and open her eyes. Instead, she just took a deep breath and sighed.

"Shhh, you will wake her."

"I will not be silent. I have been silent too long. You have locked me away in hope that you will destroy my husband and his country. You have had thirteen years; don't you think you have done enough damage?"

"Not until he is destroyed."

"You cannot destroy him."

"I will, and then you can have no further objections."

"Keep your hands off of me."

"I always loved that about you, Serena."

"And I hated that about you."

"Come, now that you have seen her; it is time to go."

"I want to speak to her."

"She is sleeping."

"Give me another minute with her? Please."

There was no reply, but in a moment, Cassandra felt her bed depress quite near her. A hand ran gently over her hair.

"Why didn't you stay with your father, Cassandra? You were safe with him."

"She is safer now," answered King Archibald.

"Safe from what?"

"Becoming you or Aric. Come, you've had enough time with her."

A soft kiss touched her brow.

"Good night, Cassandra, and may God protect you from your uncle Archibald."

"I said quiet!" Archibald spat between his teeth, rage roaring within his words.

There was gasp of pain. "Let me go, Archibald."

"Never."

There was a sound of scuffling, then a scream. Cassandra shot up in bed.

"What is going on?" she asked after a moment in a loud scared voice.

Archibald swore under his breath, but Cassandra caught the words just the same.

"Guards! Guards!" he shouted.

In a moment the room seemed to be flooded with men.

"Take this woman where she belongs! She is mad."

"Cassandra, don't believe a word that he says." Then her words were cut off as a hand clapped over her mouth.

"Father, who was that?" Cassandra asked in a panicked voice.

"Nothing you need to worry about."

"How come people call me Cassandra? It scares me."

"I am sure it does, poor child," he said, coming and putting his hand on her shoulder. He sat down on her bed.

"What did they tell you on the mountain? In Raven Castle."

"They called you all kinds of names and said all sorts of lies about you. None of them are true, are they?"

"No, just desperate people. What did you think of my brother?"

"Is he really your brother?" Cassandra asked, wide-eyed.

"Yes, Alexandra, he is, though I am ashamed to admit it."

Cassandra let the shiver that had been hiding at the back of her spine travel up to her shoulders; she shook at the end with a tremble.

"I don't think he is very nice. He tried to convince me that he is my father."

"Do you think that is true?"

"I don't see how it could be. You and I look so much alike."

He kissed her cheek. Cassandra wanted to cringe away but resisted the urge and laid her head on his shoulder for a moment.

"You are a smart girl. My girl. How did you come to escape?"

"I bribed a girl with a new dress and all of the pearls I had in my hair the day they took me captive. We looked rather alike, and when she came in with my dinner tray, we traded clothes. She owned a horse, so in the morning I took him out of the stables, saying I was on urgent business, and came riding down here. But I had to do it before daybreak so no one would recognize and stop me."

"How very clever of you."

"It took me forever to think of it."

"I am sure it did."

"What did that woman want?" asked Cassandra.

"Nothing you need to worry yourself about. Now go to sleep; I will protect you."

"Good night, Father."

"Good night, Alexandra."

Cassandra waited for him to leave before she turned and buried her face in her pillow. "I love you, Pappa. I love you; good night," and a few tears hid themselves in the soft pillow.

Her heart was beating wildly. She had heard and seen her mother. She wasn't dead. Her mother wasn't dead. Her mind reeled. Thirteen years. For thirteen years that fact had been kept a secret to everyone. Where was she hidden in the castle and why did no one know? Why did no one speak of it? Why had she not tried to escape? What was really going on? Should she tell her Pappa? She was here to reveal Archibald's plans to her father and help sabotage them. Would this complicate things?

Her mind seemed to whirl. There were too many things to think of. She was in over her head. Way over.

Chapter 32

Cassandra never knew how she fell asleep, deep into dreamland.

The recurring dream had never been so vivid. Her father, her mother— they felt so real. They were real. Cassandra awoke with a start. The gravity of it all took away her breath.

"Alexandra, are you all right?" asked Judith, who was hovering over her.

"I am fine," she said.

"You can't fool me, Alexandra," said the woman, sitting beside her and taking her face into her hands.

"It was really nothing."

"It was something. Now tell me, Alexandra."

Cassandra's heart rebelled. But she must obey. She mustn't seem to have changed too much.

She looked down, disappointed "I had *the* dream again."

"*The* dream," Judith asked.

Cassandra nodded.

"You know it is all a fantastic fantasy on your part, don't you?"

"I know, but why does it keep coming back? Why does it haunt me? Tell me, Judith," she said, with a pout growing on her lips.

"There is no knowing, child. But come; let me get you ready. Your father is eager to see you."

Cassandra found it incredibly difficult to stay still and do exactly as she was told. Her brief stay in independence had spoiled her, but she could not complain—not out loud at least. Her mind ran questions through it instead.

Was it really my mamma I saw last night? Could it really be possible that I saw her? It must be true, but how have they kept her hidden all of these years. How can I find her? Is she still alive or did uncle...father?

She sprang the question on Judith as it popped into her mind. "How did my mother die?"

Judith stopped dead and glanced at her.

"What, my dear?"

"How did my mother die?" she repeated the question.

"I don't think that is something that should be talked about. It isn't delicate."

"Was it like the woman who tried to kill me last night?" she proceeded unchecked.

"Alexandra, your mother, she died a most painful death. You know she died protecting you from the horrid rebels."

Cassandra let a shiver run up her spine. "I know, but how? Was it a sword or dagger? Was it single man or many?"

"Why do you want to know?"

"I am just wondering if they won't try to kill me like they killed her. I want to be on the lookout just in case— I am afraid they will come after me again."

"Oh, you poor thing, Alexandra, the things you must have suffered up there."

Cassandra let her eyes fill with sad tears.

"Well, I don't think you will have to worry. She was killed by a sword. She didn't suffer long. It was a very quick death."

Cassandra took in a deep breath and sighed. Judith's reluctance to answer the question made the belief that her mother was still alive grow strong within her.

"There, you are all ready. Your father will be waiting for you."

They left her apartments and headed for her father's. He greeted her with a smile. That was it; nothing more.

"Come sit by me, Alexandra," he said, not rising from his chair.

Cassandra came to his side and sat down, looking at him expectantly.

He took her face in his hands, gazing deep into her eyes.

She wondered what he was looking for in them.

A smile quirked at the edge of his mouth. "Yes, you are quite well, my little daughter, aren't you?"

"Yes, Father, now that I am here with you," she said, looking sweet and innocent.

"If you don't mind sitting here all day, I have some work to get done that shall not take me out of my chambers, but I cannot bear to have you out of my sight for one moment."

"I don't mind."

"Good. Judith has already brought in your workbasket, as you can see, and this couch has blankets so you can rest well while I work. Will that do for you?"

"Very nicely."

"Good."

The morning whiled away into afternoon and Cassandra found herself easily annoyed by reminders to take it easy and take a nap now and do this and that and the other thing. To think that she had blindly obeyed, heeded every order given to her by them, was distressing.

In the middle of the afternoon, she was told to lie down for a nap.

There was a knock at the door. Archibald answered it.

"I have the plans you requested, your majesty."

"Good. Bring them in here and lay them on that table, but be quiet. Alexandra is sleeping." A moment later she knew that Archibald's shadow was hovering over her, seeing if she slumbered yet.

Cassandra contrived to breathe deeply. He left with a sigh of satisfaction.

"Now, tell me what you have found out."

"My scouts have searched, but I haven't found a single man— though we did have another run in with a group of their flash fighters. All of the forces have been brought into the city except one."

"They'll just have to fend for themselves. How are our stores holding up?"

"Well enough, your majesty. We should be able to get through the winter well enough."

"And the citizens?"

217

"They won't make it. The city will be a ghost town come spring. They're half-starved as it is. Our forces hold no risk of being overpowered by them."

"Glad to hear it. Imagine what my brother will feel when the city he loves so much is laid to waste with no one left alive but his enemies."

"If he loves it so much, why doesn't he come rescue it?"

"Oh, he will. I am counting on that. I always told him his daughter would be the first victim, and that has been a slight deterring factor for him, but now that she is on my side," he laughed with a twisted sense of joy. "And when he finds out I still have his wife, I shall kill him. To know his beloved wife has waited for him for thirteen years behind these walls—that will be torture for him that his spirit cannot bear.

But as to our strategy. I was wondering: who should we kill first? The men seem like a good idea since they could cause problems, but it would just tear my brother's heartstrings to know that it was the women and children that went first."

"Why not do it a family at a time. They give us trouble; they are dead; simple as that."

"Excellent. We'll need to have a strong presence in the city and we have to ensure that we have no mobs on our hands. The soldiers must keep them subdued. Let the peoples supplies slowly dwindle and ration their portions sparingly."

"Of course, your majesty."

"Good; well, I guess that is it for now. Let me know if there are any changes."

"Yes, your majesty."

Cassandra heard his footsteps fade. A moment later she felt her uncle's cold shadow hovering over her. He leaned down and stroked a stray hair from her brow.

He whispered her name.

Slowly she opened her eyes and turned to look at him.

"Have a good rest?" he asked.

She nodded, pretending to be still sleepy.

He took a seat by her, and slowly Cassandra sat up and taking her needlework.

"Alexandra, do you remember your mother?"

Cassandra looked up at him rather blankly, unsure what to make of this question.

"A little," she stuttered out.

"I wish you could have known her. She was an amazing woman."

"How did she die?" Cassandra asked.

"Defending you. I thought you knew that."

"I know that, Father, but how did she die as in who killed her?" she whispered delicately.

He sighed. "It was the Rebel Aric who finished her off. He...strangled her to death trying to silence her screams. He was trying to take you away from me."

Cassandra shivered. Not in her whole life could she see her dear Pappa strangling anyone but the man that sat before her. He was capable of anything. She knew that now as she had watched and heard his plans for the coming winter.

"Then you came and saved me," she whispered.

"Yes, I did, and how you screamed for your mother. I should have killed Aric when I had the chance, but I had to save you. By the time you were safe, he was gone, to be a menace to society ever since." He was sitting beside her and putting his arms around her. "I am so glad you came back to me, Alexandra," he said, pressing a kiss to her forehead.

She leaned against him and forced the words to come out very naturally. "I love you, Father."

"I love you, too," he said quietly.

Cassandra could barely breathe.

"Why don't you tell your father all about this dream and see if we can't unravel the mysteries about it."

Cassandra found her mouth dry. She closed her eyes, took a silent deep breath, murmured a prayer in her heart, and began.

"Oh, you poor child. I wish I had known about this long ago. I could have dissolved it for you."

"Really?"

"Yes, oh Alexandra, yes. You see, I didn't want you to know this but...well. Long ago I had to go to war, just after you had been born, in fact. I was gone for nearly two years, and in that time my brother took over the throne and tried to make you and your mother conform to his ways. That is why you remember him, Alexandra. He tried to be your father, but it is I who truly am." He pressed a kiss to her forehead. "There, you see?"

"But why do I keep having it?"

"I think it is your mother trying to keep herself in your heart. It is the only memory you have of her. It is the only way of keeping the two of you close."

He put his arms close to her and she let him, though on the inside she felt as if he was trying to suffocate her to death.

How long they stayed like that Cassandra didn't know; she was just trying to breathe. There was so much to tell her Pappa. How much should she tell him? The people, her mother? What? How long before they could raid the valley? Closing her eyes as she rested against her uncle's shoulder, she prayed, prayed that it would be soon.

Chapter ??

Being in the valley things seemed to blur her mind and heart. Things that had seemed so crystal clear now smudged and blended into one another. Everything she had ever known was challenged in Raven Castle, and now that she was back in the valley, everything she knew about Raven Castle was slurred. She had to spend time away from people, which was easily done, just to clear her head and think straight against all the lies Uncle Archibald and Judith were hurling at her constantly. It seemed as if they knew the way she thought.

She wondered if she hadn't already betrayed herself and they were just toying with her, like a cat waiting for the right moment to kill the mouse, or were they waiting for bigger prey? A raven, perhaps. She had passed on all that she had heard secretly to the soldier in a note, and now she had to wait.

Cassandra was staring out her window. Two weeks had passed since her return. Things were taking shape. She knew that the army would be in the valley hiding in the north woods soon. How they were going to scale that north wall she had no idea. But if they had an idea, it had better be a good one.

It was evening as she sat in her bedroom alone, her work sitting idle on her lap.

A hand was on her shoulder. Cassandra jumped with a gasp.

"Shh, it's me." It was the soldier.

"Oh," and Cassandra sagged back into her seat. "Did you get my message to them?"

"Yes, your father has the information now."

"Anything new?"

"None today. Everything is continuing forward. How are you holding up?"

"Good, I think. Sometimes I can't help but fear that they have discovered my secret, but at other times I know they haven't, but I am always on my toes. Waiting, listening—it's driving me insane."

He laughed softly. "It's hard to lead a double life. You never know who you can trust."

"I wonder about my mother though." He had been the one person she had entrusted the secret to under the promise that he would not reveal it to her father unless necessary. She needed to tell someone or burst. "I wonder how she has lived for thirteen years trapped by him. I just wish I could see her and talk to her."

"I am sure," said the soldier with a nod.

"Do you know where she is hidden?"

"No, but I think I could find out."

"You do?"

"Everybody has secrets, you know, and I think I might have the right one up my sleeve."

"You won't risk anything."

"You needn't worry. I'll be very careful."

Two days later, the soldier bumped into her. She found a note left in her hand.

We are here, Cassie.

That was all that it read. She smiled and slipped the little piece of hope into the fire. All would be well, and that soon. The freedom of the people was near at hand, waiting for a signal to come over the wall.

That night, she found another slip of paper beneath her pillow.

I have something to show you. It concerns your mother. Stay awake; I will come for you.

Your servant

She smiled, hope rising in her heart. *My mother, if I can only see her.* Now how was she supposed to get rid of the paper? She couldn't lay it on the fire; she could be spotted by Judith, and she dared not try to conceal it until morning.

There was only one option. Cassandra shoved the small piece of paper in her mouth and started to chew. She wanted to gag. It tasted awful, but she dared not make a noise. She swallowed it and felt worse. Her stomach growled in discomfort. For several minutes she lay there trying not to make a noise. Unexpectedly, a hand was resting on her shoulder and another on her mouth.

Cassandra turned over. It was the soldier with a finger over his lips. He nodded towards the door. Silently Cassandra slipped out of bed and followed.

Once outside her bedroom door, the soldier slipped a cloak around Cassandra's shoulders.

"I found your mother. You need to go see her."

"You did?" asked Cassandra in disbelief.

"Yes. Now listen to my instructions very carefully. You are going to go to the end of the corridor near your father's apartments and press the large grey stone. It's worn with time and usage. You should spot it easily. A small passage will open, and down that corridor is where you will find your mother. Hurry back. I'll stay here to deter Judith with something if she finds you missing."

"I'll be quick," said Cassandra before slipping out of her suite and down the hallway. She kept her head down to be inconspicuous as possible.

In a few minutes, Cassandra was standing very near her uncle's apartments. She looked for the gray rock and gently touched a large worn looking stone. It moved beneath her hand. Breathlessly she pushed harder and a passageway appeared silently to her right. Cassandra slipped in, closing the door behind her. Her heartbeat soared as the darkness surrounded her.

She stepped forward, her hand feeling her way in the dark.

A light appeared in the hallways before her, Cassandra held her breath. Who was at the end of the hallway? If it was her uncle, she was as good as dead.

The figure of a woman appeared—a woman with black wavy locks just like herself.

223

"Hello?" the woman whispered into the dark.

Cassandra could not restrain herself. She flew down the corridor and stopped inches from the woman. Her mother.

"Cassie?" she asked in disbelief, putting down her candle and pulling back the hood.

"Mamma."

Both women broke into tears and embraced. Cassie could have let that embrace go on forever, but in a moment she found herself free.

"What are you doing here?" she asked, "How did you find me? Where is your...Archibald?"

"A friend helped me find it."

"A friend?"

"Yes. We are quite safe."

"Cassie, how did you know? Why are you here?"

"I know everything, mother. I came back to the valley to be a spy. We needed to know his plan of action and now that we have it, Pappa is moving in. He will attack soon."

Serena sank down into a chair a look of disbelief and shock. "He is attacking soon?"

Cassandra smiled and knelt beside her mother. "All will be well," she said, slipping her hands into her mother's. "We'll be a family again, all of us."

"How do you know everything?"

"I was more than captured by Raven Castle; it stole my heart and I saw the truth for the first time in my life."

"Oh, Cassie let me look at you. You have grown up so beautifully." She buried her face in her daughter's hair, letting tears fall freely. "Oh, Cassie, my beautiful Cassie."

In a few minutes she had recovered herself. "You have your father's blue eyes, you know. How is your father?"

"Doing well, and I know he will be doing even better when we are both safe in his care. Mamma, let's leave. We can hide until Pappa comes. I know of a good place"

"You know the way out of here?"

Cassandra looked at her blankly, then, with a feeling of dread, she realized she had no instructions on how to escape this room.

"I don't know either, but it can't be too hard since he told me how to get in here."

"Who?" Her mother's question was cold and stiff.

"A soldier who works for Pappa."

"He told you how to get in here?"

"Yes."

She covered her face in her hands.

"What is it, Mamma? What is the matter?"

"He works for me. That is the matter," said a voice from the darkness.

Cassandra's heart froze in her chest.

Archibald stepped into the small circle of light, a sinister grin on his face.

Chapter 34

Cassandra rose to her feet, anger boiling in her heart.

"How dare you," she spat out. Her eyes sunk daggers into him.

"My, how you look like your mother when you are angry, and I can see my brother's righteous anger-sparkling in your eyes," he said, moving forward and catching her chin to look her directly in the face.

Cassandra batted his hand aside. She had never stood taller or straighter in her life.

Archibald chuckled under his breath. "You aren't the daughter I raised you to be."

"I am the daughter my father raised me to be."

Their eyes dueled in anger. Cassandra found herself pushed aside by her mother as something came sweeping out of the darkness. As she felt something catch at the side of her face, hard and painful, she fell to the floor. The world was spinning and different colored lights were flashing and dancing before her.

"There was no need for that, Archibald." She felt her mother stepping over her, protecting her.

"Really? Thirteen years with me, and she throws it all away after three months with her father. I think that was called for."

Blinking, Cassandra made the world focus. He held a club in his hand. No wonder nothing would hold still. She pulled herself slowly to her feet.

"He has the truth and she knows it," said her mother.

The club swung; Serena ducked; it missed.

"Did you catch your little bird?" asked a voice coming in from the dark. A moment later the soldier appeared.

"How could you," snarled Cassandra beneath her breath.

He looked at her, his eyes betraying pain. "I am sorry. I had no choice. It was betray you or let my family pay the price for helping your father. I couldn't pay it."

"Yes. Now for your favor, I am releasing your family. They'll be waiting for you in the courtyard. Take them and go. You are henceforth banished from this kingdom."

"Thank you, your majesty." The soldier bowed and turned away.

A moment later Archibald moved, his dagger flashing in his hand, stabbing the soldier in the back between his plates of armor. The young man gasped and dropped to his knees.

Archibald smiled and withdrew the blade. "Yes, go join your family in their grave. It's already been dug."

"But..." the young man spluttered, death written on his face.

Cassandra wanted to turn away, to close her eyes, but it was too late. The soldier slipped from this life into the next with a shudder.

Archibald laughed and, turning away, he wiped the bloody dagger before placing it in its sheath.

"Well, Alexandra, your game is up. You play my game now or you all die."

"Never," she whispered in defiance.

"Guards, seize them and bring Alexandra to my chambers. I hate dead bodies."

Before she had time for a second thought Cassandra found herself seized. They dragged her through the hall way and into Archibald's apartments, forcing her into a chair they bound her hands firmly behind. Archibald circled like a wolf coming in for the kill.

Circling, Archibald slowly drew ever closer.

It was driving Cassandra crazy. At last she found her tongue and voice.

"Why did you do it? Why?"

"You don't understand, do you?" he asked, looking at her as if she were an imbecile. *I wasn't born yesterday.*

"No, I don't."

"Your father was never fit to be king. When we were lads, he was better than me at a lot of things. As we grew older, that began to change. I worked and trained until I could beat anyone that challenged me. I wanted to prove that I was just as fit to be king as my brother.

What made him fit to rule beside his birthright? Tell me. What makes him fit to be king?" he yelled at her.

Cassandra waited a moment before answering him. "He is wise."

"Really; do you think leaving the people to my care all of these years has been wise?"

Cassandra swallowed the lump in her throat. "He did it for many reasons."

"Don't I know it. A lot of excuses if you ask me. There is nothing—*nothing,* I say, that makes your father more fit to be king than his birthright. The very act of being born first gives them everything; the title, the lands, the money, the adoration, and the woman they love, regardless of anyone else's affections or interests. It's all about them. Simply because they are born first, not for their abilities."

"It is not all about them," Cassandra shouted back.

"Oh, yes it is. I loved your mother long before your father ever took notice of her. Long before, and you know what it got me? A broken heart. No one cared that I loved her. Aric loved her and she loved Aric for his title and his title alone. Eventually, she managed to fall in love with him, but what else would endear a girl to marry Aric other than his title?"

"A lot." whispered Cassandra, mentally comparing the two men. They were completely different.

"Like what?" asked Archibald with a grind to his teeth and narrowing his eyes with hatred.

For a moment Cassandra forgot her own name, the look was so hateful. Then she found her voice. "He loves the people, and takes care of them. He cares about their wellbeing far more than you do. All you care about is power and being feared. No one loves you except yourself. You don't care a thing about what happens to Chambria."

"Oh, yes I do. I want to destroy my brother, and when I succeed. I will be happy. It took me years to create an army—an army of forgotten and looked over younger sons. We amassed our troubles and misfortunes together. We swore we would take down those who lorded over us as betters. We would prove to them that we were just as strong,

229

powerful, clever, and deserving as they. I waited seven years to get my revenge. Then the day came that I met a dissatisfied nobleman from another country and pulled him into our scheme. We plotted against our crowns and laid in wait, starting a war between our two countries. By the time they figured out that they hadn't started a war with one another but we had started it for them, they had been at it for three months. When he came back to confront me and straighten everything out, we attacked.

"Your father laid siege to us for weeks, but we were ready for them beyond their imaginations. Only half my forces were on the wall the other half lay outside behind them, waiting to ambush when the chance arose. We would have crushed them utterly, but I gave him terms of surrender after a particular bloody encounter and he refused them. I had my troops drawn up and would have killed them if one of your father's scouts hadn't discovered my men. That night they ran away to Raven Castle, like the cowards they are, and only there will he reign as king. Where is your father, Cassandra?"

"I don't know," she said. He was somewhere in the woods to the north, but other than that she knew not where.

"Oh, you do know. You just won't tell me, will you? Well, let's see if we can't loosen your tongue just a little bit?" He drew closer. Slowly pulling out a long dagger, he put the pointed edge against her throat. It pricked painfully. He moved the blade directly against her neck. It sent a painful shiver through her body. The blade was sharp, it would only take one moment to cause her pain. He moved the blade and pressed it against her temple sliding it down her cheek, but still he did not cut. He pressed the blade against her heart, then whirled it away.

"No, I will not harm Alexandra. You are not afraid for yourself, but for someone else you might be. You don't understand; I did this all for you. Why do you think your brother is dead?"

Shock sang through her body. "You killed my brother?"

"Yes, I did. I was out of town when it happened, but I am the one who arranged it. I thought, of all people, you would understand, Alexandra. I did this for us, and you don't even say thank you."

"There is nothing to thank you for. You ruined my life."

"Now that you've turned against me, I haven't begun to ruin it yet, just wait Alexandra," he said, leaning closer and closer to her. He shouted, making Cassandra flinch in surprise. "Men, bring her in!"

A moment later the door burst open and two men dragged in her mother. Cassandra's heart somersaulted in her chest, then began to pound loudly in her ears. They pushed her to her knees before Cassandra, bound and gagged.

Archibald smiled. "I will give you a choice, Alexandra. Your mother, or your father. I promise I will only kill one. Who will it be?"

Another wave of shock staggered through her, fraying her tightly wound nerves.

"You won't keep your promise," she whispered.

"Who says I won't?" he said offhandedly.

"If you kill my mother, you'll still kill my father."

"That is a fact, but you can save your mother, and once your father is dead, I can marry her and we can all be a happy family, Alexandra. So what is it? Tell me where your father is hiding and I can end all of this suffering. I know he is in the valley. Where is he?" He pulled out his knife and ran it along her mother's neck.

"I am not going to tell you," shivered Cassandra.

"You are not?" he asked directly.

"No," she whispered, trying to find the courage she needed.

Her mother lay on the floor trying not to writhe in pain. Cassandra moved to help, but she was still bound to the chair. It was cutting off her circulation. Her fingers curled and uncurled, wanting to lay her hands on Archibald's throat. He pulled her mother upright.

"Where is your father?" he asked again.

Cassandra's eyes dropped. She would not answer.

"Your soldier boy said something about them being to the north. I don't believe him, but you, Alexandra. You could save your mother all this pain..."

There was a long pause. A heavy blow fell, sending her mother forward to Cassandra's very feet.

Archibald pulled Serena to a kneeling position by her hair. Cassandra couldn't help cringing.

His dagger twirled eagerly in his hand as he circled her mother. Taking a handful of hair, he cut it off. He then struck her to the floor.

"Please stop it." Cassandra was fighting back the tears that swelled in her eyes.

"I will stop it, Alexandra, when you tell me where your father is," he said, pulling Serena back up by her hair.

Cassandra was silent.

He turned to her his eye piercing. "Will you tell me, or no?"

Again she was silent.

"You are not helping her by your silence, Alexandra; you are only prolonging whatever pain I choose to give her." The dagger slipped back into its sheath.

The question was repeated over and over with the same result. Every answer was like plunging a dagger into her own heart, but she could bear the pain.

Serena's face began to swell from the blows. Bruises were appearing on her bare arms; swaths of dark hair were scattered on the floor.

It only made it worse because it hurt someone else—one of the dearest persons in the world to her—and she could do nothing about it.

It was nearing an hour of agony when Archibald straightened.

"I am not going to break her like this. Seeing pain isn't enough for you is it. None of this damage is permanent." Taking out his dagger, he thrust it into the fire's coals.

After several minutes of silence he pulled it out of the fire and smiled. The blade was beginning to glow. "Just a few minutes longer."

He came back to where they were waiting and pulled Serena to her feet and gazed into her eyes. Archibald removed her gag. "It's a real pity, my pretty love," he whispered, "I'll give you one last chance. Marry me now and I won't have to do this horrible thing to you or your daughter."

"Never," she answered.

"I don't see why you love him still. He has left you here to die in my care; dear, give in."

"I will always love Aric."

Rage soared through him and he struck her down and pulled her back to her feet.

"Look at your daughter and memorize her well. It will be the last time you ever see her again in your life."

Striding across the room, he pulled his dagger from the heart of the white and gold coals. The blade glowed in the darkness of the room. Daylight had yet to appear.

"On her knees and hold her fast. No, don't bother putting her gag in. I want Alexandra to remember her mother's screams that she could have prevented. Hold her eye open."

With horror Cassandra watched as the blade slowly began to fall.

"No! Don't do it," Cassandra screamed.

It continued downward.

"*Stop! **Stop!!!**"* she screamed, her voice piercing the room with desperation.

It was about to touch her mother's brown eyes, blinding her forever.

She screamed. There was nothing else she could do.

Before taking her sight, he whirled around, holding the glowing knife a fraction of an inch from Cassandra's throat. The heat burned even from there.

How can mother bear it in silence?

"You are making more fuss than your mother; now, be quiet!" and he turned around.

Again the torturous descent began.

Cassandra couldn't stand by and just watch it happen. "I'll tell you. **Stop!** *Please!* I'll tell you if you just stop!"

The dagger clattered to the floor and he turned to face her. He tilted the chair back, back, back.

"You will tell me where your father is?"

"In exchange for my mother's release," she whispered, barely believing that she was uttering the treacherous words. *He would kill us both if I don't tell him. I am sorry, Pappa, but I can't help it. I can't let him take both of us—not after everything that you have gone through.*

"Done," he said, releasing his hold, the chair dropped to the cold stone floor.

The drop jarred her whole body. She couldn't repress the cry of pain from landing on her arms tied behind the chair back. With a kick, she was turned on her side.

"Cut her ropes."

Once free, Cassandra staggered to her feet. She wanted to go to her mother, to tell her a thousand things—but no, Archibald stood between them.

"We will go to whichever gate you choose and free your mother. From there you will tell me exactly what you know. Where would you like your mother liberated?"

"The north gate."

"Men, take Serena and make her ready. Alexandra, you are coming with me."

He bound her hands and led her to the castle walk. In a short while they were standing at the North Gate.

"You know that the north wall is impregnable," he said aloud.

Cassandra looked up at him, surprised.

"Don't look so shocked, child; it doesn't become you. Of course he told me everything. Your betrayal was the proof I needed, and now I have it."

"I know," she answered softly, going back to the north wall question.

"Does your father remember that?"

"He does."

"No one has come over the north wall and conquered. So where is your father really hiding?"

Cassandra shook her head. "We agreed that information would be given at my mother's release, not before."

He hackled a chuckle.

Cassandra turned and watched the city, waiting for her mother to arrive. In a few minutes, they paused below the gate. She and Archibald peered over the castle wall.

It was her mother's swollen face that looked up. Archibald nodded her through the gate.

Together they watched as she rode away, when Serena had reached bowshot's distance, she halted with a backwards look.

"There you have it, my pretty," he said, his hands encircling her neck, like he was getting ready to choke the life out of her. "Your mother is safe. Now tell me where your father is."

"He is hiding in the forest on the north end."

"I see." His hand rubbed tighter. "Anything else I ought to know?"

You are choking me? But that is too obvious. "He will conquer you."

Archibald threw back his head and laughed heartily. "Oh, Alexandra, you amuse me," and he kissed her cheek.

"Stop that," she said, trying to push down the tears so she could watch her mother disappear safely and not let the feeling of utter abandonment overwhelm her.

"I am your uncle, you know, Alexandra," he said, drawing her into an embrace.

She remained stiff.

"Come, Alexandra," he said, remaining lighthearted. "I am only letting her go because I know I will get her back again. There is nothing that you can do to prevent that. I will conquer your father and then I *will* have your mother. See how it all works out in the end. Maybe you should have let me kill her. However, now that you have betrayed my trust and everything else you love, I cannot allow you to live."

"I know."

"Good. So how shall we arrange for your death, my pretty little girl? Shall I do it right now and just have it over with?" he said, tightening his already tense grip on her neck. His hands were strong, stronger than she wanted to know. "Would you like to boil in oil? Hang? Be drawn and quartered? Burned at the stake? Beheaded? Turned on the rack? What?" he said, kissing her cheek again.

Cassandra tried to pull away, only to find a firm grip squeeze her neck.

"Tell me, Alexandra, or you die right here."

"Old age," she whispered.

Archibald laughed, amused. "Well, leave it to me, darling. You were born at sunrise; it's fitting you should leave your life at sunset. You have until tonight to prepare yourself for what I will create just for you. Besides, the dark makes for a more dramatic ordeal."

Dark clouds moved over the sun.

Cassandra curled her hands into tight balls. *Oh God, help me to not be afraid. Please give me strength. Amen.*

Chapter 25

Cassandra stood on the turret ledge. Her hands were shackled before her, the wind whipping her plain white dress and loose hair about her. The scene before her made it hard to breathe. Piles of faggots were placed under a pot of oil. Now they were just waiting for it to boil as they played with the screeching pulley. Archibald was standing before her with a delighted smirk on his face. Her heart was fluttering wildly in her chest. She had a strange calm about her—one she could not explain or understand.

Closing her eyes she tried to hold back the tears that came upon her as she thought her mother and father. Together at last. How they would love, maybe laugh and cry with one another. How happy would her father be? But they did not know the fate that awaited her. She could only hope they didn't. That they wouldn't know until it was all over. She had only lived as a princess for three months, but she would die with the honor and resolution of a queen. The people were waiting for freedom.

Opening her eyes, she turned to look at the mountains. She could barely see Raven Castle through the newly bared branches. Her jaw trembled and she looked away. The sun was nearly set.

She tried to focus on other things. Uncle Archibald had moved the army down to the southern part of the city, the easiest point of attack. She ran his words through her mind.

"Double the guard. I doubt they will give us trouble tonight, but if they do, I want to be warned. And captain, move your army into the southern part of the city. I have good faith that this little wench and the guard were lying to me."

Her thoughts raced to Taleon and his plans. He would be bringing her father's flag over the wall. He would be one of the first over, carrying her father's colors to victory. She smiled at the remembrance of his sword skills and the way he would surprise the men. *Oh, God*

237

keep him safe. Keep them all safe. Let little blood be shed. Protect my Pappa, Taleon, the Council, the people, the fathers, the brothers and sons; we need them safe and at home. Amen.

"Alexandra. The sun is setting; don't you want to see it?"

She looked once again to the mountains. They glowed with red and pink as if they were on fire, ready to burn for the cause. Slowly the sun slipped behind the mountains. The vivid colors in the sky were fading swiftly. In the east, the first stars were daring to glimmer.

The oil was ready.

"It's past sunset, Alexandra. I hope you have a fine journey," said Archibald, checking the chains. "Good night, my pet. Sweet dreams," he said, kissing her cheek for the last time. Leaning forward, he whispered, "And don't forget to scream for me."

A shudder slipped through her as the chains tightened. Cassandra gripped herself for what was to come. She promised herself she would not scream, not yet. She would not. No one would hear her die in agony. She curled her bare toes tightly. She struggled against the desire to fight the tightening chains.

A cold wind swept up from the west feeding the flames. The smoke swirled around her, Cassandra's eyes watered and she shivered in the cold wind despite the heat surrounding her.

She looked up searching for the stars to comfort her. But even they were gone. A thick blanket of clouds covered the heavens. All was dark.

In a moment she was suspended in air, the rudely assembled crane swinging her off the turret ledge and towards the pot of boiling oil. Instinctively she pulled up her knees trying to recoil from the fate almost directly below her.

Archibald was laughing at her. Tears stung her eyes.

This was the end.

Below her there was an outcry of surprise. Swords entered the conversation with a clash. Cassandra tried to look through the veil of smoke surrounding her. Archibald rushed to the edge and let out a vile oath.

"Tie her still; pour that oil onto them; rouse the troops! We're under attack!"

He turned to descend the turret steps and stopped before Cassandra and turned to her, his eyes burning.

"Don't think you and I are done. I'll be back for you. This isn't over yet."

Closing her eyes, she lifted it up the heavens. *All will be well.* In her mind's eye she could see Taleon coming over the wall with her father's colors, the flag in one hand, sword drawn in the other. They would be halfway through the town before anyone realized what had happened. Something damp touched her face. Cassandra opened her eyes.

One damp drop and another; the flames below her seemed to die down—still burning, but the flames were not as strong as they once were. The drops came fast and furious. The battle went on.

The curse on Chambria was broken.

The soldiers were gone and now she was alone, hanging in midair by her arms, they ached; her whole body was seized with the pain.

Her heart pounded with hope. The people of Chambria were being saved. Just maybe she could be too? She called out for help until her voice gave way from the smoke filling her lungs. They could not hear her above the cries of battle.

Swinging her legs, she made slow, steady, and painful progress to the turret edge where she had been standing and rested her bare feet on the slippery rock ledge. At least her arms could rest. Cassandra let herself cry with the rain. It was all over; everything was done.

The night became long, up alone on the turret with the wind and rain. Cassandra fought her bonds but to no avail. She lifted up her voice, but no one could hear her above the cries, the swords, and the pounding rain. No one seemed to know where she was.

Towards the dawn, exhaustion washed over her. Cassandra found despite her shivering and the pain, she could close her eyes. The worst seemed over. She would wait to be free until she was found.

Chapter 36

Her rescue was sudden and unfriendly. A swift slap across her face. Her body tingled with a feverish cold that sank into her core.

"Wake up, Alexandra."

Her blurry eyes didn't need to focus to know that it was Archibald who spoke to her. In a moment her bonds were loosed. She could barely stand, but he dragged her along.

"I have one last play. I will conquer him; I will crush him," he was whispering over and over madly.

Pushing her into a secret tunnel, they traveled she knew not how long. Every step felt like a mile; every joint in her body shivered and quaked from the cold. His warm hand felt like daggers piercing her skin.

Suddenly they were in the light; he pulled her close to him. Placing his sharpened bloody dagger at her neck, he pulled her into the shadows and slunk into the throne room. It was empty. Standing on the stairs. He waited behind the throne, breathing heavily

The doors burst open and in charged King Aric and forty of his men. All wielding red-stained swords.

"Stop right there, Aric, or I'll kill your daughter," Archibald roared.

Aric and his men stopped. Archibald came into full sight, clutching Cassandra closer than his own shadow, the sharp dagger gnawing at her throat. She was a sight, sooty from the smoke; Cassandra was drenched to the skin, her clothes dripping from the rain. Loose strands of her dark hair clung to her face.

"Cassandra!" King Aric cried out, stepping forward.

"Stop right there, or I kill her!"

Aric stopped mid-step.

"You have two options, my dear brother: your daughter or your kingdom. Choose one. You can't have both. Whatever you don't choose is mine for keeps."

"Archibald. Let her go. This is between you and me."

"No. Her or your kingdom? Take your pick."

"She has nothing to do with this fight. Let her go and you and I will battle this out like men."

"Look at your father, Alexandra. Tell him how much you want to live, that you want to grow up. Tell him, tell him." The sharp knife gouged into her neck.

"No," Cassandra whispered, struggling for defiance in her weak state.

The knife slid angrily into her throat, making a small painful cut. She gasped in pain and surprise.

"Make your decision wisely, Aric. What I am doing to her is only the beginning of what is to come if I leave with her."

"Take me in her place."

"Never."

King Aric unfastened a glove from his armor and threw it on the ground before Archibald. "I challenge you. You and I will duel for the kingdom. Let her go."

Archibald sank back. "Who do you think you are, brother? God? No one orders me around. I spit upon you and your honor."

The men lurched forward to avenge their king. Aric held up his hand to hold them back. A small cry of pain issued from Cassandra's lips as the dagger bit deeper, sending a trickle of blood down her neck.

"Her or your kingdom—take your pick, or she dies here and now, and then I shall take your kingdom."

"Archibald. That is not a choice a father should make." He glanced at his men. None of them had a clear shot with a bow or dagger. Archibald held Cassandra too closely.

"No? Well, it is the one I am giving you. Who is more important? Your ravaged kingdom or your priceless daughter?" he said, pinching her fiercely, causing Cassandra to cry out. She bit her lip, regretting her weakness.

Aric stood there, knowing the answer he must give, but dreading the words he must say.

"Cassandra." It was her father's voice, sounding strong and firm.

Cassandra smiled softly at the sound of his voice. It was so reassuring. She knew what was coming. She must prepare her heart; she stored away the sound of his confident voice to give her courage. There was only one choice he could make.

"I know what you have to do, Pappa," Cassandra whispered.

Their eyes met, his affection so strong, so loving and protective, the sign of tears gathering in his strong blue eyes. She longed to run into his safe arms—to have him hold her next his heart, to hear it beat through his chainmail, to know that all would be safe. But that was to never be. Everything as she knew it was coming to an end.

"Choose the kingdom, Pappa; choose the people. I am just one and they are many," she whispered hoarsely, her voice almost refusing to obey her.

"Cassie, I love you with all my heart." The words were so tender. There was a pause before he spoke again his voice strong, bold, decided, and slightly cold. "Archibald. You may have my daughter but not my people. Take her and leave."

"Then I have your word that you will not attempt to pursue or harm me?"

"You have my word, upon my honor which you so detest. I will not stain it."

Archibald snorted in triumph. "Will you provide me with protection? Not everyone will know that you have given me your word, and I would rather not have to kill Alexandra senselessly."

There was a long pause.

"I am your brother, you know." He reminded Aric tactlessly.

"You have no need to remind me. I know full well what you are to me. To make sure my word is kept," Aric turned and looked at his men. His eyes met with a few of the warriors from his council. They nodded and stepped forward.

"They will escort you safely out of the city. Then you are on your own. My men shall not follow you."

The men stepped forward, weapons sheathed, and surrounded them. With a jerk, Archibald pulled Cassandra away with him, keeping the dagger tightly at her throat.

Walking down to the stables, they had to prevent a few attacks on Archibald. Seven steeds were saddled immediately.

Mounting, Archibald moved his foot from the stirrup and nodded for her to mount behind him. Cassandra made a feeble attempt, but she was so weak she made no progress. In frustration, he struck her and she tumbled towards the stable floor.

Keenan caught her in his strong protective arms. Anger flaming in his eyes, his hands clenched and unclenched, fighting the urge to pull out his sword and thrust the Imposter through and through. Were it not for his king's word, he would have struck the man down and sliced him into pieces. Instead, he pulled Cassandra to her feet, holding her until she stopped trembling. The kind arms about her seemed to breathe life into her. How she wished that they could protect her. She longed for Taleon to be there—to see his confident face once more, for him to make her laugh—to say farewell to her mother and be held in her arms. Her father's word rushed over her. "Cassie, I love you with all of my heart." He would be her strength. He would pray for her and she knew it. Tears rose in her eyes, but she willed them away.

"Are you ready, your highness?" asked Keenan tenderly.

"I am," she shuddered.

With an ease that surprised her, he swung her behind Archibald. As his protecting hands left her, a chill slipped through her. *This is my end. When Archibald is finished with me there will be nothing left.*

Archibald crossed her chained arms over his shoulders, drawing her close, creating a shield for his back out of her body.

Ducking the low stable doors, they rode out into the court yard of the castle, across the drawbridge, and into the city's cobblestone streets. One knight led the way, four surrounded them on both sides, and one man brought up the rear guard.

The fighting had ceased. The city was peaceful, trying to pick up the broken pieces of their lives and put them back together. It was still raining, only gently now, like salt-less tears.

Sooner than most wished, they reached the city gates and Archibald broke his steed into a gallop. Bursting past the front guard, he pounded down the road, fleeing.

The men reigned in their horses. "May the Lord God preserve her from him," murmured Lord Keenan.

"Amen," chorused the rest of the men almost silently.

Chapter 37

How long they rode, Cassandra did not know as she dipped in and out of consciousness. His body, cruel as it was, slowly began to warm her chilled and weary bones. He pulled the horse to a stop near a deep ravine. Freeing himself from the chain that held her so closely to him, he dismounted, walked to the edge, and looked fearlessly over.

"The river flows directly to Chambria," he said aloud, striding back to her and pulling her down from the steed.

"What are you going to do?" she asked, trying to get her feet beneath her as he dragged her towards the edge of the ravine.

"That is for me to know and you to obey." He let go of her. "Now turn around and kneel."

"What?" she asked, turning around.

"KNEEL!"

Cassandra carefully lowered herself onto the grassy bank after a backward glance at the steep incline behind her.

"Your father wants you back, you know," he said, withdrawing his sword slowly, slowly, trying to create a dread and fear within her. At last it was free from its sheath.

"First your head," he said, touching her neck with the tip of his sword. "And then I will cut you into pretty little pieces to send down river to your father. I think he will like that, don't you?"

Cassandra didn't respond. It would break his heart, her mamma's, and Taleon's. Why was Taleon's face suddenly the brightest in her mind? Why did her heart feel so empty—so barren?

"Don't you?" he repeated the question, twisting the tip of his sharp sword against her Adam's apple.

"No. I don't think he would like it." Her weary bloodshot eyes for the first time met his.

He clicked his tongue in disapproval. "Such a pity. He won't appreciate my gift, though I am sure he will notice the pains I took with you. Imagine the torture he will go through when they find little pieces of you everywhere. I am sure it will keep him busy for days."

"What will you do after I am dead?" She couldn't help but ask.

"Raise another army. I'm not finished with your father yet, though I am finished with you. Now close your eyes."

Cassandra obeyed. She could feel him drawing back the sword raising it high. He would swing it and then…a shudder passed over her. *God help me please.*

Strength flooded her body. She opened her eyes just as the blade began to descend. Her arms raised up to stop the sword. The blade sparked as it crashed into her chains but did not break them.

Archibald was stunned. This was not what he was expecting.

Cassandra wrapped the chains around the tip of the blade and tried to jerk it out of his hands.

He recovered and pulled the sword away at the same time raising Cassandra to her feet.

Archibald swung a mortal blow. She danced toward the edge of the cliff but did not step over. The blade swept toward her; she deflected it with the chains. Pulling away, he moved to thrust her through dead on. She could not move fast enough. A deep gash sank into her right side. The blade withdrew and she moved towards him. Coming face to face, she snatched the dagger from his belt. He stepped back and swung the sword upward. In a moment it was crashing downward.

Cassandra held up her hands to the sky and stepped away. The sword broke the chains in half. The blade breezed past her face, missing her by a hair's breadth.

He stepped forward to thrust her through. She curved her body, letting the blade pass by her. Thrusting the dagger toward him, she let it fly from her hand.

The dagger sank into his throat. He staggered towards her, trying to gasp for a breath, still swinging his sword at her desperately. Cassandra stepped away. Archibald stumbled, then careened and tumbled over the edge. Numbly she watched. His body made a great splash, but did not reappear. For several minutes she stood, searching for any movement.

"He's gone. Gone." Relief swept over her and the adrenaline started to fade. Cassandra realized how close to the edge of the cliff she was. A weak dizzy feeling swept over her and she stumbled towards safety.

Looking down at herself, she realized that she was wounded. The chains had helped, but they were no shield.

Carefully she approached the skittish black steed. "Shh..." she said, gently laying her hand on his neck. He was sweating white foam from his excursion.

"I need your help." She laid her head against his damp neck as a wave of pain struck her. Cassandra whimpered. Her hands wove into his mane, clutching it for support. The steed stood steadily, his nostrils flaring.

She moved the horse down the gentle slope and stood on the high side. Hopefully this would give her enough of an advantage to mount him without too much trouble.

After much pain and fumbling, she managed to mount the black steed, turning him towards Chambria and urging him forward at a walk, for she could not take the strain of a faster pace. Struggling, she tore lengths from the hem of her dress and bound them around her wounds, pressing her hand against them to stop the bleeding. Her hands slowly grew red and wet with blood. She tore more lengths and pressed them. The bleeding seemed to stop at last, but her head felt so light and dizzy that it was a trial just to see straight, much less keep her eyes open. The pain drove away her power of concentration.

Cassandra was on the ground. How she got there she had no idea, the pain made it impossible to move. She writhed, trying to sit up, but to no avail. Pain pinned her to the ground. Cassandra raised her voice. "Help. Help!" but it didn't get much beyond a whisper.

Quietly she lay there, too tired to fight, to think, to breathe. *God help me please. I can't go on.*

Her eyelids tugged downward and she let them slowly close, too tired to fight.

It was all over. Over.

Over.

Chapter 38

He was hiding in the depths of the forest, a group of a hundred men ready to follow him to life or death.

They were waiting for dark.

Stamping the ground impatiently, he fidgeted. He couldn't wait to get into the city to make sure that all was well.

Glancing back into the forest, he saw the dim silhouette of King Aric waiting on horseback with another two hundred men. He was holding his head high, but he knew that what had happened that morning had disturbed his sire.

She had come riding into camp: Serena, the queen who had been thought dead for thirteen years.

He would never forget that moment, seeing his king struck beyond words when she rode into camp.

They had looked at each other mutely. Then he ran to her, taking her off the horse and into his arms. They held each other crying, crying so hard they sank to their knees. Taleon thought he had never seen a love so deep, so sweet. Both had waited for the other. Their hearts were still one after years of separation.

Sweeping her into his arms, he had carried her into his tent and tended to her wounds with his own hands. They had been left utterly alone. No one dared disturb them. King Aric reappeared in the early afternoon. His emotions were mixed. There was part of him that was overjoyed; another part, heavy.

"We take it tonight. No matter what," he had said very simply. That was all.

No one questioned his words or doubted his motives, but questions enwreathed the camp. Where was Cassandra? What was going on? They were to wait until dark.

251

The word had been passed along in the city to listen for a disturbance along the north wall, then to create a ruckus of commotion and disturbances in the street. Taleon turned back and looked at his men. They were waiting and anxious as he, the drought had made this route of attack possible, the swamp was dried enough for a troop of men to cross. The ladders were ready.

He glanced at the mountains. The light was just fading from them at last. They could move soon.

Twilight fell. The first star showed its face. Taleon moved to the front of his men and motioned them forward until they were out of cover of the forest. "For the King and Country! God save us all. CHARGE!" he had commanded at the top of his lungs, and with a battle cry of a hundred voices, they charged. Sword in one hand and standard in the other, he had been the first to mount the wall, exchanging blow for blow. The city was in an uproar; the sound of battle was everywhere. The wall was taken beneath the colors of King Aric—colors that Cassandra had sewn. As they had called for victory in the name of their king, he couldn't help but utter beneath his breath *Cassandra.*

He led the group that opened the North Gate and let King Aric and his mighty troop gallop into the very heart of Chambria. They would take the city by force.

Taleon looked up at the evening skies. They were still tumbling out a gentle soaking rain. The city had been taken. He glanced toward the castle. The colors of King Aric floated beneath the flag of Chambria. He smiled and headed towards the castle.

The battle had been long. He and his sword had acted as one. Instinct saving his life many a time as he met blade with blade.

He walked, a feeling of weariness creeping upon him, but the joy was too strong in his heart to be beaten down. Taleon sheathed his sword. The closer he got to the castle, the faster his heart beat. He had hopes—hopes to find someone waiting for him.

In all of his misgivings about seeing Cassandra go, he had not doubted once that he would see her again. Even when Queen Serena arrived, something about that gave him hope.

Arriving at the Castle gate, he was greeted by Keenan.

"Good, you are here. I was just about to go looking for you. The King wishes to see you."

Something in Keenan's voice made Taleon stop dead in his tracks.

"What is the matter, Keenan?"

"The king is waiting for you in the princess' chambers."

"What is it, Keenan?" Taleon's heart leaped in fear, pounding in his chest.

"Just go."

Taleon needed no directing. In all the years of planning, he had memorized the castle layout like the lines in the palm of his hand.

He sprinted upstairs and dashed through the hallways, his steps softening when he came to what he knew to be Cassandra's chambers.

Taleon knocked gently, hoping above all else to hear the soft melodic voice of Cassandra bidding him enter.

"Come in, Taleon." It was the king's voice. It was a grave sound, one burdened with disappointment. He hesitated a moment before entering. What awaited him?

"Sire?" he asked, stepping in.

"Taleon, come here."

"What is it, sire? Where is Cassandra?"

King Aric's blue eyes met his. The answer in his eyes.

"No sire, she can't be dead."

"She is not, at least not yet. Archibald has taken her."

"Then let's go after them. I will get a group of men and we will track them down," he said, moving towards the door.

"You cannot go, Taleon. I gave my word that we would not."

"Why!" Taleon asked in disbelief.

"He was going to kill her in my presence or take her and let me hope that he would not slay her."

"You what?" Taleon was incredulous

"I had no choice, Taleon. It was either having him leave with her, or have them both die. I tried everything I could think of, Taleon, but there was no availing."

"Sire. Let me go after her," Taleon urged.

"No. I gave my word."

"But I did not give mine."

"I said none of my men. You are no exception."

"Archibald will kill her!" shouted Taleon, trembling with rage.

Aric had never seen Taleon so vehement before, so full of hate, because he was filled with something that was so the opposite.

He had been watching them. He had seen it in their eyes, their manners towards each other, and he had approved. It was for this reason that he wanted to tell Taleon himself.

"I know," Aric said, laying his hand on Taleon's shoulder. "I know he will kill my daughter. It was that or letting him kill you and all of the other people here. My army, my kingdom, my people. I could not do that to them. He would destroy them and delight in it. I gave her up for you and for everybody else here."

Taleon jerked from the king's hand and turned to walk away. "I am going after her!"

"You do and he'll come back. Taleon, if you have any respect for me, you will remain here and help me keep my word."

Taleon turned to Aric, his king, his nearly adopted father. "How can you give her up?"

"It was her, Taleon or all of them, one for many. The price is very dear, but they will count it worth it, and in time," he halted, "in time, I will call the price painfully dear, but worth the pain. I love Cassandra more than my own life. Sometimes for the greater good, we must sacrifice our hearts, Taleon. Come here, stand by me."

Reluctantly Taleon did so, his heart urging him to run, to find her, to hold her safely in his arms, to tell her... He wished he had spoken, so that she could at least take the knowing of his heart with her to the grave. Every word he had not spoken now haunted him, for he knew now it was more than just a feeling; it was a part of him—a part of him that she would always have.

Aric rested his hand on Taleon's shoulder again.

"Look at the people. They are happy. See the children playing. They would be screaming in terror if I left it to Archibald. The city will laugh and be filled with joy yet."

Even Taleon's grief-stricken eyes could see the joy of the city awakening, blossoming into something greater than it had been.

"There is one more thing I have to ask of you." His hand tightened on Taleon's shoulder.

"Yes, sire?"

King Aric took a large sigh, let it out, and spoke in a whisper. "Will you be my son?"

"Your son?"

"The kingdom needs an heir who is ready to take the throne. You share our vision, Cassandra's and mine."

"How can you ask me now?"

"She saw it coming." He handed him a sheet of paper. "One of the men found this in her room. I think you should read it." He handed it to Taleon.

To my dearest Pappa, Mamma, and Taleon,

The time has come. Uncle Archibald has sealed my death sentence and given me these few hours to prepare. I must. There is no escape for me; I am at peace; you needn't worry for me. But the burden is not with those who are leaving, but with those who must stay. I am afraid I am leaving that sad burden to both of you and my dear Mamma.

The reason you are reading this is because I am gone. I have one request of you; that is, please take Taleon as your heir. I have learned from him so much and I know he will carry on your dream and with you; he will bring the kingdom up from the dust. There is greatness in him. For many years he has been like a son to you. Let him be your heir, since I cannot fulfil those dreams.

There was an impending doom upon this place when I entered and I am afraid I have fulfilled its destiny for me.

I shall rest in peace for I know you shall conquer.

With all my love,
Cassandra.

Taleon broke into tears and the king wrapped his arms about him. Their hearts were breaking.

After several minutes, Taleon composed himself and Aric repeated his question.

"Taleon, will you be my honorable son and heir?"

Then for the first time in his life, he called King Aric the name he had always wanted to call him. "Yes, Father. I will."

Just then Serena entered the room. Her face was swollen from abuse of Archibald and her eyes from crying.

"Have you asked him?" she asked, tears hovering in her eyes.

"Yes." And Aric nodded his head in reply to the second question given only by a look.

Walking up to the young man, she took his face in her gentle hands, pressing her cheek against his. "Welcome home, my son." And her tears mingled with his.

Chapter 39

It was late the next afternoon that a body was discovered floating, snagged in the river. When it was fished out, it was discovered to be that of the late Imposter.

There was a leap of hope in everyone's heart. Search parties for the princess commenced searching the entire length of the river. Save for a few discoveries—the body of the Imposter and the place where they had battled—nothing brought light to Cassandra's fate. It was as if Cassandra had fallen off the surface of the earth. Chambria's princess was nowhere to be found.

As the truth about what the princess had done in returning to the valley spread, the people's affections grew for her and they spread out in the search, but still to no avail.

Princess Cassandra was gone.

The small harvest was brought in and the first winter snows fell with it. Hope and dreams were laid aside and Taleon was crowned the noble prince of Chambria.

For many the day was joyous. For Taleon, it was a death and a dream all bound into one.

He had at last the father and mother he had always craved, but the price was far too high.

Winter settled in long and hard, and slowly the three bonded deeply into a tight family, all bearing the same wound, hiding the same hope, cherishing a love for the dream that had died.

Spring came into the valley and with it came rain to melt the snow even in the heart of the deepest woods.

It was a sunny brisk day in April when Taleon went out to supervise the building of irrigation trenches several miles out of Chambia. As evening approached, he mounted his horse and prepared to leave.

He looked to the east. Not far away from here, the last battle for Chambria had taken place. He had visited it so many times, but he could not help himself. He must see it again. Maybe he would find something he had missed before.

"Are we going home, my prince?"

Taleon looked at Willamsen, his attendant. "I want to see the ravine."

Willamsen nodded. Taleon would never be satisfied until she was found, but how long would they spend there this time?

Legends were beginning to surround the princess—stories, fantasies that all solved her disappearance, but none satisfied him. He would not be content until he saw her face once again. Some people really believed that she had loved her uncle more than her father and had fled by choice with him. Others knew the truth, but still it pained them.

Taleon rode to the ravine and looked over the edge. He had memorized how they had found it a battleground that only left one body, the one that had floated down the river. They had traced hoofprints that turned back towards Chambria, then disappeared into thin air.

"Where did you go, Cassandra?" he murmured into the wind. It swept away his words without deigning a reply.

Something about all of it unsettled his heart still. He knew there was not a day that went by that his father did not look out the window for her, that his mother did not sigh for her. In his heart he knew she was still alive. But where? Where had she gone and why had she not returned? He looked out over the landscape, his heart still aching and burning; he missed her. He had fallen in love with her and now she was gone.

Oh Cassandra.

"She's not here, my prince," whispered Williamsen, who had not dismounted. "And it is growing dark. You will not wish to worry your father."

Taleon turned around. "Thank you, Willamsen."

The man nodded.

Taleon was determined to hunt for her, but Willamsen was right. Today was not the day for it. But would it ever come?

Mounting his horse, they turned back towards Chambria. It was going to be a long ride back. Reaching a large meadow at the edge of the woods, they paused. Chambria was a long way off, but they could see it in the distance, small but beautiful. It was a saved city. A few months' work had done wonders for it and Chambria was being considered once again a successful nation.

To their left came a loud noise of something large barreling through the forest. Both men laid hands on their swords, ready for whatever was going to come.

In the dark shadows of the forest, a slender girl in a coarse dress appeared. Her cheeks were hollowed. Everything about her seemed thin, even the horse she rode; it looked like a noble beast, but lack of care had made him look shabby, though he carried himself with a proud air.

As they came into the meadow, she leaned over his neck and urged him into a gallop. Her black loose locks flew about her, mingling with the mane of the black beast. They rode as one.

Taleon's breath caught in his chest, almost choking his lungs. *Could it be? Could it really truly be?* Taleon barely dared to believe his eyes.

Crouching over the neck of his horse, he spurred him into gallop. They would be easy to catch, a well-fed horse against the black beast.

At the sound of a second pair of hoofbeats, the black beast kicked up his heels and put his head down further, but the rider glanced back.

Chapter 40

A wave of shock washed over Cassandra. There was Taleon riding, riding towards her.

Pulling up on her horse, she pulled for him to stop. He fought the command but obeyed at last.

In a moment Taleon was beside her. Cassandra started to dismount when the strap slipped from beneath her foot.

Taleon caught her in his arms and held her tight. "Cassandra, Cassandra."

Slowly her feet touched the earth. Tears poured down her cheek.

In a few minutes, he pulled away so that he could see her face. "Are you all right?"

"Is he really gone forever?" she managed to choke out.

"Forever."

She closed her eyes and let the burden slip off of her shoulders.

"How did it happen?"

"We fought on the cliffs of the river."

"I know, but how did you survive?"

"He was going to kill me and piece by piece throw me into the river. But these saved me," she said holding up the cuffs still attached to her wrists, the chains broken off.

Taleon gasped as if someone had stabbed him in the chest.

"Cassandra. You killed him with these and a dagger?"

Cassandra lowered her eyes to the ground and nodded.

"The cliffs; are not so far away. Where did you go? Why couldn't I find you anywhere?"

"With these as my only defense..." Cassandra held up her wrists.

Taleon grasped the meaning of her words and held her close again.

"An old woman who lives in the woods like a hermit rescued me. If it wasn't for her...I am not sure that I would still be here. She hid me in her cabin, afraid that if Archibald's soldiers found out, we would be done for. I didn't become conscious until the first snowfall."

"Cassandra." His heart ached in his words.

Tears flowed down her face. "By the time I was well enough to leave, the snow was too deep to ride him, and if I would have broken through a tall drift I might not have been able to get out. As I was getting ready to leave she became very ill and I couldn't leave her after all that she had done for me. It wasn't possible until today, and until this moment I was wondering if it would be possible at all."

Taleon understood what Cassandra meant, holding her in his arms. She felt weak.

For a long time they stood there letting time pass sweetly.

They were reminded that they were in someone else's presence. Willamsen cleared his throat. "I think the king and queen would like to see her as well, if you don't mind, my prince."

Cassandra looked up at him, joy in her eyes. "My prince," she murmured. "So you are crowned?"

"After the first snow," he whispered.

Cassandra smiled. "It's a good thing."

"Come, let's get you home," he said, mounting his horse, then, leaning down, he took her in front of him.

"I have to keep my eye on you," he whispered, putting an arm around her waist. She leaned against him, wrapping her arms around his neck. Willamsen rolled his eyes, shook his head, and smiled.

The ride was strangely silent, the presence of each other being entirely satisfactory. When they appeared in the city, people stopped in the streets to stare, mouths dropped open, eyes bulged, but somewhere someone started to cheer.

"Cas-sand-ra! Cas-sand-ra! Cas-sand-ra!"

People took up the chorus. Chanting it over and over again they gathered around with smiles and cheers.

Cassandra's eyes flooded with tears as she remembered the way they used to gather around her. There were no stones, no rotten vegetables. They were cheering, cheering for her.

Taleon's arms tightened around her and he whispered in her ear. 'That is the welcome home for a heroine."

She let the tears fall and looked at the people with affection. Someone flung a flower into her lap. Cassandra looked up to thank whoever had showered her with such a precious gift. Unexpectedly flowers were pouring from window boxes everywhere. It was too much. She covered her face and cried for joy. Taleon applied spurs to his steed and they rushed into the open castle gates.

Just appearing in an archway were the king and queen with puzzled and hopeful looks on their faces.

They rushed forward and Taleon set Cassandra down.

The three collided into a solid embrace. Slowly Taleon dismounted, watching "his" family. Tears were pouring down their cheeks and were misting over his own.

Their arms opened wide, inviting him in. He joined the circle with Cassandra happily half-smothered in the middle. It seemed like forever that they stood there before their circle finally opened. Looking around them, Cassandra realized that they were surrounded by her father's noble council knights. She caught sight of Keenan and ran to him, flinging her arms around his neck. She had not forgotten his kindness or how much it had meant to her that bleak day. He embraced her. In a moment she stepped back, remembering her dignity.

"Thank you," Cassandra whispered. She tried to say more, but the words wouldn't come.

"It was my honor, your highness," he said, kneeling before her and kissing her hand. Looking up into her face, he said, "I give my solemn promise that my sword shall defend you always and forever to the end of my days. Never shall an enemy lay hands on you again if it is within my power to protect you."

Cassandra was at a loss for words. *Thank you* was such a small word compared to his, but she uttered it with a squeeze of her hand.

"Thank you, Lord Keenan. From the very depths of my heart, thank you."

He rose. "It was my honor, your highness."

Unexpectedly her Pappa gathered her up in his arms and carried her inside. She was home.

Chapter 41

Cassandra had been loosed of her bonds and put to bed.

Three days had passed since Taleon had seen her.

Taleon was restless. He couldn't sleep. Rising, he dressed and went for a walk. There had to be something to do. Time away from her was eating at him horribly.

It was while walking in the east corridor, he saw her leaning against the window, gazing outward.

As he approached, she turned and smiled at him, then gazed back out of the window.

Coming up to her, he said, "You should be sleeping."

"I couldn't. My eyes just won't shut."

Taleon stepped behind Cassandra. She leaned against him and he slipped his arms around her waist.

Unexpectedly tears were on her cheeks.

"What is the matter, Cassandra?" Taleon whispered, gently pressing his cheek to her temple.

"Nothing," Cassandra whispered.

Slowly Taleon turned Cassandra to face him. She hid her face against his doublet.

"Cassie," he said slowly, tipping back her head. "Your father and I have been talking some things over, and we think it would be best for the kingdom to have one heir."

She looked up at him, puzzled. "One heir?"

"Yes," he said with a nod.

"You aren't leaving, Taleon?" she asked, the grip on his doublet tightening with all of her strength. "Tell me you aren't leaving," she said, tears coming into her eyes faster than ever.

"I will never leave you, Cassie, if that is what you wish."

"I want you to stay," she confessed with her whole heart.

"In that case," he paused and lowered his voice to a whisper in her ear. "I love you, Cassie."

Cassandra started to cry harder.

Taleon held her tight until she was calm.

"Oh Taleon," she whispered, "It was the hope of hearing those words that gave me hope through the winter."

The whole meaning of her words struck him in the chest and Taleon's eyes misted over.

She put her arms around his neck and looked trustingly up into his blue-green eyes. "I love you, Taleon."

For a long moment there was silence. Then from somewhere outside someone struck up a sweet sad song on a violin.

"I guess someone else can't sleep," murmured Cassandra.

"And a good thing too," said Taleon, leading her into a soft slow dance.

Cassandra laughed and then sobered, following his lead. "I missed the celebration, didn't I?"

Taleon sighed with the remembrance of his heavy heart. "It wasn't much of a celebration. I was a newly crowned prince and my rightful dance partner was nowhere to be found. In consequence, no one else could fill your place."

Cassandra laid her head against him. "I missed you more than words can say."

Taleon stopped, and, taking her face in his hands, asked. "Do you know you are beautiful?"

Cassandra blushed under his compliment and looked shyly up at him.

He stepped back into the rhythm of the dance again, whispering in her ear, "It's true."

She buried her face against his doublet.

When the music stopped, they drew their dance to a close.

"You need to get some rest now," Taleon said softly. Taking her hand, he kissed it.

"Goodnight, Taleon."

"Until the morning," he whispered with a smile.

ABOUT THE AUTHOR

Jessica Greyson, a homeschool graduate who loves words, first as a hungry reader, and now as a passionate writer. She seeks to write for the glory of God, and be the writer He has called her to be.

You can learn more about her and her books at www.jessicagreyson.com.

ABOUT THE ARTIST

Louie Roybal attended Pensacola Christian College. He majored in Commercial Art and Graphic Design. He has a love for both and desires to produce fine art at a casual rate while working in the graphic design industry.

Louie currently works full time as a graphic designer, and free-lances to selected clients on the side.

You can see more of his work at www.louieroybal.com.

Made in the USA
Charleston, SC
03 February 2016